The Rule of Twelfths
and other stories

For Jill:

Lovely to see you again.
You and Sam helped me more
than you know.

Love

Michael Carey

Also by Michael Carson:

Sucking Sherbet Lemons
Friends and Infidels
Coming Up Roses
Stripping Penguins Bare
Yanking Up The Yo-Yo
Serving Suggestions (short stories)
Demolishing Babel
The Knight of the Flaming Heart
Dying In Style
Hubbies
Previously Loved (an exhibition and catalogue)

The Rule of Twelfths
and other stories

MICHAEL CARSON

HEADLAND

First published in 2008
by
HEADLAND PUBLICATIONS
38 York Avenue, West Kirby,
Wirral, Merseyside. CH48 3JF

A full CIP record for this book is available
from the British Library

ISBN 1 902096 47 6

Printed in Great Britain by
L. Cocker Ltd.,
Unit A9, Erskine Street,
Liverpool L6 1AU

HEADLAND acknowledges the financial
assistance of Arts Council England.

CONTENTS

For Paula and Peter

Others will enter the gates of the ferry and cross from shore to
    shore,
Others will watch the run of the flood-tide,
Others will see the shipping of Manhattan north and west, and
    the heights of Brooklyn to the south and east,
Others will see the islands large and small;
Fifty years hence, others will see them as they cross, the sun half
    an hour high,
A hundred years hence, or ever so many hundred years hence,
    others will see them,
Will enjoy the sunset, the pouring-in of the flood-tide, the falling-
    back to sea of the ebb-tide.

- Walt Whitman from 'Crossing Brooklyn Ferry'

ACKNOWLEDGEMENTS

'West Wirral Story', 'The Devil, The Nun and The Tango Dancer', 'A
Day by the Sea with Mr Shukry', 'Cormac's Cup Final', 'The United
States of Bed and Breakfast', 'Rock Me', 'Even The Mice Know', 'Very
Much Reality', and 'Constant Repetition' first appeared in Afternoon
Story on BBC Radio Four;

'Golden Retriever': *The Bridport Prize Anthology 2007*

'All Over The Place': *Writers-of-the-Year Competition Anthology 2006*

'All Change At St Bridget's': *The Catholic Times*

WEST WIRRAL STORY

'Te adoro Anton...' Mum says.

'Te adoro Maria...' I reply automatically, shifting to fifth.

'You should've changed the needle oftener...'

Mum stops. Forgetting. I can almost hear the crunch as her brain changes gears.

'You know Mr Bernstein based West Side Story on Romeo and Juliet, don't you?'

'Yes.' God, I ought to.

But she hasn't heard me. She is repeating the sea areas on the Shipping Forecast from the radio, watching Wirral pass by flatly. Then she's humming The Jet Song.

Suddenly, she's back. 'If you'd changed the needle oftener I'd still have my West Side Story now. It was the first record your dad bought me to go with the radiogram.' Mum gazes out at the view. She is agitated. 'We nearly there yet?'

'This is Thornton Hough.'

'Is it?'

'You know it is. You always had a soft spot for Thornton Hough. Your Auntie Dot lived here. The one with the moustache who gave me sloppy kisses.'

Mum nods. 'Daft name, Dot, when you come to think of it. It was a crime the way that L.P. deteriorated. It got to the stage where I Feel Pretty was unplayable. If you'd changed the needle...'

'Come on, Mum, you wore it out!' Like she's worn me out. 'A record can only play so many times, you know. It's got a shelf-life like everything else.'

'Three score years and ten. Well, I've knocked that into a bunch of cherries, haven't I? How much farther?'

'It'll be another fifteen minutes I should think, Mum.'

'Fifteen minutes. That's about what you got on an E.P. Have you seen my Porgy and Bess? It had Sidney Poitier on the outside and that Dorothy Dandridge who passed on. I can't get enough of Sidney Poitier. A pity Mr Bernstein couldn't've written something for Sidney.'

'It's probably in the airing-cupboard. With the Christmas-tree.'

'What is? I've kept all your nappies in the airing-cupboard. If you hadn't done what you did, they'd have come in useful.'

Mum seizes her bag, looks at it intently as if it is a strange object that has dropped from the sky on to her lap. She thinks for a moment, then snaps the bag open and delves inside. I can smell rouge, Yardley and old pennies. She takes out a hanky and dabs her nose with it.

'Mum…'

'What now?'

'You don't have to go, you know. We can turn back and tell them you've changed your mind.'

She snaps the bag shut. Then, remembering she's forgotten to put the hanky away - then forgetting that too - she looks at the handkerchief. The sight seems to startle her.

'I said…' I begin, wondering how I'll feel if she's changed her mind.

'I know what you said. How much farther?'

'Another ten minutes.'

'Doesn't time fly?'

There is contentment in her voice. She has found the bag again, opened it, put the hanky in, snapped it shut. She holds it by the top with both hands. Then she strokes it like she used to stroke Solomon. All is right with the world. She smiles out at it serenely.

'Time. Goes like the clappers.'

The time signal for 2 o' clock sounds.

'They never used to make one of the boops longer than the others,' Mum says. 'It used to go boop, boop, boop boop, boop, boop. Life was simple then. You knew where you were. Now it's boop, boop, boop, boop, boop, booooop. I don't call that progress even if you do.'

'The longer boop tells you the exact moment that the clock clicks to the hour.'

'Gee, Officer Krupke!'

I start to reply, but she shushes me. She wants to listen to the news. I am stuck at a Halt sign, waiting for a gap in the traffic. Behind me, a driver keeps rocking his car towards my bumper, pushing me to take risks. I resist him, waiting for a break that does not come.

'Nothing about Mr Bernstein. I won't forget him even if they do,' Mum says as the news gives way to a play, and I nose out on to the Chester Road.

There was a time when I would have argued with her faulty reasoning, nudged her back to sense as we used to nudge the pick-up of West Side Story. But I gave up. Now I wonder if I'd kept at it we might have made it through to the end and not be on this journey now.

'There's no real news these days,' Mum says. 'You probably don't remember how Tony met Maria. You see, Tony was convinced something was coming and he went with Riff to the dance at the gym. Maria went with Anita. The gym was neutral territory - a bit like St. Nick's church hall. Tony was a nice boy. He didn't want the rumble. He was good to his old mum.' She looks round expectantly. 'We nearly there?'

'Five minutes.'

'If only Tony had met Maria and whisked her off straight away. They have all-night vicars in New York, you know.'

I don't reply. I know the road Mum's on.

'They should have married. Like you should've. If you ask me, it was all the serenading on the fire-escape and the dirty bit that did for Tony. He was weak-willed and easily-led. Like someone else I could mention.'

I force myself not to react. I just do not understand how Mum can remember that and forget her address. Still, life's full of mystery. Mystery is the signature tune of life. Overture and duet, soliloquy and reprise. Over and over.

'Anita and Riff should have helped them when they saw how the land lay. Your dad and me...me and your dad...'

'Mum...'

'Are we there?'

'I think I'm lost.'

'It's nice round here. 'I don't know why me and your dad didn't move out to here when we had the chance. Wallasey's gone down the nick since Tony died. New York! New York's a hell of a town! The Bronx is up and... Maria's old flame shot him under the motorway.'

I am a rudderless boat adrift on Mum's meanderings. The needle in her brain skips, can no longer decode. I keep telling myself that this is not her. But is that right? Perhaps this is really her and everything before was merely concealment. She had always doted on Tony, seemed devastated when we broke up and I came back to Wallasey to lick my wounds.

'I know I'm being an imp, but you know what I'd really like?'

'What?'

'An ice-cream at Parkgate.'

'It's out of our way.'

'Shh!' she commands, the ice-cream having melted out of her brain, 'It's the play!'

I gladly give up on conversation and let her listen in. I've told the matron we'll be there by two, yet here we are heading into Chester. I've missed the way somewhere.

Mum is excited by the play and adds her comments to the action. She doesn't like the American girl who has fallen for a Russian Orthodox seminarian and is confiding to the radio audience that she intends to seduce him.

'Hussy!' Mum calls out. 'Leave him alone! He's promised to Maria! You're all Anybodys these days!'

The seminarian prays for strength. 'That's it, dear!' she tells him. 'Fight the good fight! Don't give in to that Yank floozie! Keep the faith!'

I've always loved the way she talks back to the radio and the telly. I'll miss that. In an hour I'll be driving in an empty car to an empty house.

'Not there yet?' she asks during a lull in the proceedings. I let my irritation show. 'I'm not niffy, am I? You must tell me if I'm niffy.'

'No, Mum, you're sweet as a nut.'

'I wasn't yesterday, though.'

'No, but you are today.'

"Sweet as a nut' - that's what Butcher Hawkins said about the turkey, wasn't it?'

We both remember, and laugh. 'At least he had the decency to give us a fresh one.'.

'He gave us his. Said he was going to eat that niffy one. Bet he didn't! Remember the pong? God knows how he had the gall. It was probably his stint as mayor of the County Borough. Made him cocky. His mince went downhill too after his stint as mayor.'

'It went to his head,' I say. 'Did I tell you that I always took a detour behind his shop after that? I just couldn't face him and his grinning butcher-boys.'

'They used to wolf-whistle at you. They provoked you like the Jets provoked Anita.' She cackles and coughs, 'And you liked it!'

'I did not.'

She looks around. 'Where are we?'

'I don't know.' I do.

'You're taking me to The Home, aren't you?'

We've been through this before. 'It's you who wanted to go to The Home. 'Ring the Home!' you said.'

Mum opens her bag and takes out the hanky again. She dabs her eyes. I glance over and miss the turning that may have been the one we want.

'I only wanted to go because I was niffy. But now you're telling me I'm not niffy. 'Sweet as a nut' you said.'

'So would you rather we went back home?' I try to speak in a neutral way, not taking sides. Which side am I on? Wouldn't it be wonderful to park the car and go into the house knowing that I will be alone there?

'Did I ever tell you that I did the dusting to I Want To Be In America? As soon as you were up the road with your satchel out it'd come and on it'd go. Lord, I felt pretty! I...' Her voice trails off.

There's a 'P' for Parking sign at the side of the road. I pull over.

'Look, Mum, do you want to go to The Home or don't you? It's all the same to me.'

'When you talk all hard like that you sound just like you did that time you came home in a mess. Me and your dad couldn't do anything right...I don't know what Tony would have said, I really don't.'

I've had enough. 'Stop it, Mum! You just can't forget it, can you? I had my abortion around the time we put West Side Story out for the bin-men. My Tony was over the hills and far away. Now will you try to forget it like you forget everything else?'

'You shouldn't have, you know. He'd have been company for you now. Womb to tomb. Birth to earth...'

'Yes...well...' I say, going all weepy. She can still make me do that.

'Don't create!' she says. 'Worse things happen at sea!'

I tell her that's as maybe but she's got to make up her mind. We're already late.

'Remember Mr Bernstein's Kaddish Symphony? It's dead cheeky to God. Still I think He deserves it what with one thing and another. Fancy giving me a daughter who can't be bothered to change the needle and ruins my favourite!'

'Mum…'

Now she is weeping. 'There's no room for me. Niffy or not niffy, it's all the same to you. If this was Holland you'd tell me I'd had enough, stick a needle in me, say bye-bye Mum, play that bloody My Way and go off and have a party. Well, My Way's no way to go! No way to go. My Way, indeed! Anyway, I haven't had enough. I want to see what's going to happen. I want to see the end. I want a happy ending.'

I put my arms around her shoulder and squeeze her lightly. I can feel her bones, feel her in my bones. Too much pressure and we'll both break. 'I want you to be happy, Mum. Really I do.'

'One hand, one heart,' she says. 'What I can't forgive is you buying me the film version when the good one broke. They all mimed, you know, AND they missed out the ballet bit for Somewhere.'

'At least I got you another copy…'

'I suppose so. But I loved the old one. Maria was running down the street on the cover in that lovely frock with Tony trying to keep up. There were bins in the street! How I danced! Oh, you'll never know how I danced!'

It's no good; I can't do it. I suspect there will come a time for me to live - and dance - alone. 'Let's go home,' I say. 'I'll ring the matron and tell her we've changed our mind.'

On the way we call in for an ice-cream at Parkgate. Mum sits on the bench with her cornet, looking out across the Dee estuary to Wales. The wind blows thin wisps of hair across her face.

'Could be,' she says, 'who knows? There's something due any day, I will dum-dum... find my way... something good...'

She looks at me, tears in her eyes.

'Te adoro, Maria,' I say.

'Te adoro, Anton,' Mum replies.

THE DEVIL, THE NUN AND THE TANGO DANCER

Comrades: when I first saw Doña Esperanza dancing at the Bordello de Libertad in Buenos Aires, I knew she would be worth watching. She exuded a glorious physicality - the only endowment the rich envy that the poor possess. Her haughty brown face poured disdain on both partner and spectators. Her body kindled fire while that face remained icy, like some austere saint.

Doña Esperanza was little more than a child then, of course. But not long afterwards the people of Buenos Aires began lighting their secular candles at her feet. In no time at all, fame lifted her away from the bordello to a long career as the greatest tango dancer of her generation.

I realise that I have not done justice to Doña Esperanza's art. My excuse it that I cannot describe her genius. And perhaps such detail is not important. This confession of failure, coupled with a request that you send another to replace me here, does not turn on Doña Esperanza's abilities as a dancer, though had it not been for her detachment from her art I don't think she would have come to my attention, or been the object of so much effort over the years.

I know that I have not been without success during my time in Argentina. I have done the state some disservice - and they know it. But Doña Esperanza and all that flowed from her has undone me. I do not understand how... I feel...

But I shall simply tell you what happened, and leave the judgment to you.

When growing fame released Doña Esperanza from the bordello, she brought out with her twin daughters, Anita and Maria - both illegitimate of course - on whom she devoted all the exquisite care her riches made it possible to bestow. Daily she took the two girls to mass, but never did she mention The Tango to either. You see, she was ashamed of her talent, believing that the tango inflamed passions and sent sober virtue out of the window.

Of course, being of a conventional turn of mind myself, I agreed with every fibre of my being. 'Tut! Tut!' I'd tell her, 'Tango dancing may be all you're fit for, but those dear daughters of yours...well - and I'm sure you'll agree with me - you must save them.' So while Doña Esperanza danced, she was also praying that neither daughter would follow in her footsteps, that God would forgive her and spare her bad blood from being passed on to little Anita and Maria.

I noted her prayers, of course. If you shout upstairs you will be heard in the cellars. Naturally, I sought out ways in which Doña Esperanza's devout hopes would come to nought. I was merely following our procedures manual to the letter: planting an obsession in the parent then darting down to the children and setting to work on frustrating the parent. Pretty pedestrian stuff, but it has worked like a charm for aeons.

In this case, however, it was uphill work. Both daughters as they approached womanhood seemed impervious to temptation. Though I kept whispering beguiling tango rhythms in their ears, and even managed to tempt an itinerant orchestra on to the corner outside the family apartment, neither girl seemed to show the least inclination to follow in their mother's spirited footsteps. And half my hopes faded when Anita announced at the tender age of sixteen that she wanted to enter a convent.

Doña Esperanza was delighted of course, seeing Anita's decision as the answer to her prayers. She gave joyful, tearful consent. Anita packed a small suitcase and was led off to the Carmelite Convent, where Mother offered her up to God. She then walked back to her apartment, a noticeable spring in her step.

I can remember my feelings that day as I accompanied Doña Esperanza home. The righteousness coming off her was making me feel very queasy indeed. But I am sure you all know the feeling.

My training stiffened my resolve to somehow defeat Doña Esperanza, to frustrate her every hope.

Doña Esperanza dropped her guard a little once Anita was safely imprisoned behind the grille in the Carmelite convent, reasoning that it would only be a matter of time before Maria heard and obeyed the dull dinner-gong call to respectability.

Around this time the family's nanny passed on to her reward. And Doña Esperanza did not think to replace her. Each work night she would kiss Maria on the head as her daughter poured piously over school books, then leave the house for The Tango, confident that both daughters were safe and sound.

At that time, I was much taken up with affairs at the Casa Rosada. Evita Peron was dancing her masterly tango on the world stage. But I made sure never to go off duty without calling on Maria and whispering 'Tango! Tango!' into her studious ear.

At first my efforts did not seem to be bearing much fruit. Maria sat rapt at her Latin. I kept at it though, tempting the orchestra on the corner into increasing their volume, while I continued my sotto voce assaults.

The first sign of success came when I noticed Maria's feet making pert - and not unerotic - little tango steps under her desk in time to the music from the orchestra on the corner.

'Bravo!' I whispered. 'Duende! Tango! Tango!'

I left Maria to marinate in temptation, remembering to call in on Sister Anita and whisper 'Tango! Tango!' to her through the grille. I did this with little hope I have to say.

Time passed. One evening I arrived at the apartment to find no sign of

Maria. Music wafted through the open windows. I looked out. A couple were dancing the tango in the street. They had attracted a fair crowd.

Unable to resist entering a crowd - at the very least one can set off bouts of bad temper and petty thieving - I flew down to see what was going on.

Maria was dancing with a young caballero. She was dressed in flame red, and insinuated her hard brown thighs around her partner's. An appalling thing to witness, I think you'll agree. It shocked even me.

The crowd was entranced. 'Who is she?' I heard a man ask his open-mouthed companion.

'No one knows. She appears. She dances divinely. She disappears.'

The dance ended. Maria did exactly as her admirers had predicted.

Back in the apartment Maria changed out of the red dress and into her school uniform. In five minutes she was back, hunched over her books.

I looked at Maria and shook my head. Doña Esperanza would have to be informed. That was only right and proper.

When Doña Esperanza learnt what had happened, her horror knew no bounds. She donned a disguise before joining the crowd that evening. Catching Maria in flagrante, she was unable to contain herself. She ripped her daughter away from the handsome caballero, pulled her back to the apartment, where the screams and sobs and pronouncements of Bell, Book and Candle drowned the sound of the orchestra.

It is a common battle that we know well throughout our poor unhappy world. The final breaking of the umbilical cord is never easy. That night it seemed clear to me that Maria would have her way and - even better - Doña Esperanza would not have hers.

I have never been one to intrude on private grief and, feeling I had won Maria, decided to see what magic I could work on Sister Anita.

Back at the grille things seemed pretty hopeless. Sister Anita had developed a reputation for great sanctity. Even though nobody could see her, just to touch the grille behind which she prayed was enough to cure all manner of malaise. Arthritic hands uncurled on contact with the cold steel warmed by the prayers of the devout nun; sense returned to crazed heads; tumours shrivelled like Mardi Gras balloons on Ash Wednesday morn. It was a sight terrible to behold.

Some years later Doña Esperanza died. She had watched Maria rise to the pinnacle of the tango firmament while her own star waned, taking what consolation she could from the fact that Maria had at least been spared her own bordello beginnings. But she died uncertain of her own salvation. She did not despair exactly - that would have been too much to hope for - merely doubted that she would pass muster in The Lord's eyes. After all, He had only answered half her prayers.

Professionally, Maria did not put a foot wrong. Unlike her mother, she gloried in her fame. It was as if all the controls put upon her in those early years had made her grow into the exact opposite of what was intended. All very odd, and oh-so-predictible.

But let us bring this sorry tale to a conclusion before I, like Doña Esperanza, give way to hopelessness.

Without any warning, Sister Anita left the enclosed order. She decided that she had to escape the attention her miracles were bringing and give herself, body and soul, to the needs of the poor of Buenos Aires. She joined The Sisters of the Dispossessed, disappearing into one of the seedier neighbourhoods of the city to minister to the shirtless ones.

I had become embroiled in politics again. A little war over some draughty islands to the east of Argentina - which you have probably forgotten - took up a great deal of my time. And rumours of a holy lady of the slums who cured the sick in great numbers just failed to register. Of course I should have put two and two together, but so legion are those stories in this part of the world that it is easy to overlook one.

It was not until the war had finished - I won if you're interested - that I found time to follow up the rumour. On my way I teamed up with Maria, who was also intrigued by the Holy Lady of the Slums and, along with a large crowd, was making her way through the pot-holed, disagreeable streets where it was said the miracles were taking place.

We arrived at a peeling and malodorous square where a hundred pitiful people knelt around a dry fountain, praying fervently. Maria joined them.

After some minutes, into the square came Sister Anita. The crowds parted for her and the nun gazed at the people with great love. Sister Anita caught sight of Maria kneeling in the dust. Ignoring the others she approached and whispered something into her sister's ear. Maria nodded, then bowed her head in prayer.

Suddenly, the nun began to dance. She danced up to each sick person in turn, lifting them up, leading them around the square for a moment before leaving them, breathless but on their feet, rubbing eyes into which light was flowing, ears into which sound and rhythm were buzzing. Then, having left the crowd as fit as a fart, Sister Anita danced out of the square wearing that same haughty rose-between-the-teeth expression that had so irritated me in her mother. I just watched her go. Completely at a loss.

Meanwhile Maria, oblivious, knelt in the dust with a strange expression on her face.

'What now?' I asked her.

But her gaze went past me straight up to the Opposition. And do you know what she said? 'Rest in peace, Mother! All is well.' Of course, I made myself scarce. I was shaking like a reed. In truth, I have been shaking ever since.

Anita is now a tango dancer - of no small renown - and Maria a nun. And both, though I am loath to admit it, are content. And completely beyond me. A question, Comrades, keeps recurring: 'Is it better to start out as a nun and end up as a tango dancer, or vice versa? Sometimes I have the distinct impression - and when I do I look around to see who is tempting me - that either sister, either way, gets smiled upon. At least that is how it seems to be in this part of the world, where the sun travels across the northern sky and water dances down the drain in a clockwise whirl.

Please, Comrades, take me back to the Northern hemisphere. I'll go anywhere I'm sent. The old world understands me, and I it. Down here, the rhythms are too confusing. I lose my step.

A DAY BY THE SEA
WITH MR SHUKRY

Mr Shukry woke up to the sound of the Arabian Sea. He listened to the waves roaring with laughter and then inhaling across the pebbles to prepare for another guffaw.

'Why must you always laugh at me? It is both ill-bred and misanthropic,' Mr Shukry told the sea in English. He always spoke to himself and inanimate objects in English. That way he practised his craft and stopped the other teachers from coming too close to his closed soul.

With a sigh of 'Ya Allah!' he pulled his heavy head from the pillow, shifting himself to a sitting position. He scratched his ankles. The sand flies had bitten him during the night, as they did most nights. 'You might have granted me respite today. Do I not have enough troubles today without you adding to them, O creations of the incomprehensible God?' Mr Shukry told the long-gone insects.

He listened to the shuffle of flip-flaps over curling linoleum tiles. The dented door of the bathroom banged, setting the thin wall of his room vibrating. Sounds offended his ear, then trickles of water and gargling. It was the Headmaster. The Headmaster would soon call his staff to morning prayer, a green turban wrapped around his head.

'Come on, Mr Shukry. It is better to pray than to sleep,' Mr Shukry told his still-dozing self. With difficulty he got off the low bed and pulled himself into a white dish-dash. He performed his ablutions from an enamel bowl he had come upon discarded in the desert on one of his solitary walks. He thought of the visit of the inspector, and of Zigazig on the Nile Delta where at this moment his family would still be curled in sleep.

'Sleep, my dears,' Mr Shukry told them. 'For you Shukry has ventured across the wide world in order to earn you the little extras that the bounteous

Nile cannot provide for those of her sons who are landless. When Shukry embraced the flame of education, did he not burn his hand? But sleep, my darlings! Only remember your poor father sweating blood for you in oil-rich, education-poor foreign places.'

The gravel voice of the headmaster called him to prayer. Mr Shukry shuffled into his pink flip-flops and joined the line of teachers, their faces towards the rising sun and the blood-red legions of dunes between them and Mecca.

As he bowed, knelt and stood in prayer, he noticed the track that left Tiwi and wound to the hard-top road forty kilometers away. That track would bring the inspector. And Mr Shukry prayed for himself. He prayed that the inspector, an Englishman whose reputation for severity towards Egyptian teachers was legendary throughout the Eastern Region, would look kindly on him. 'For though I am in prison here, a eunuch away from Leila, a slave to a barbarian people…for the sake of my family and my half-built house in Zigazig, I beseech you to grant me a good report from the English inspector.' And he added with passion: 'Remember the sins of the English, my God!'

The inspector of English Language for the Eastern Region was greatly looking forward to his trip to Tiwi and Mr Shukry.

Since his arrival in the country two months before, not a day, not an hour, had passed without the inspector wanting to pick up his suitcase and run away home. The weather, the lack of electricity, the inefficiency, the sense of ever-present threat, the books he delivered and which mysteriously disappeared, the feeling that he was completely without the wherewithal to do a decent job… had bubbled up in his brain, turning what had looked like a challenge in London into a cross of impossible weight.

The English teacher in Mintarib who could not speak, read, or write English, and had succeeded in teaching only, 'Go home, Johnie,' and 'For you, best price,' and 'Death with Infidel,' to his students, had put the inspector into a depression which had lasted weeks. Dull nights alone in guest-houses where camel spiders tried to eat chunks out of his face gave ample opportunity for his negative feelings to combine into a thick soup, inedible, but easy enough to get consumed by.

He felt as he aimed the temperamental Landrover towards Tiwi that he was more than ready for a day by the sea with Mr Shukry.

Mr Shukry had stood out from the start. He was, the inspector recalled, about five foot three in his peep-toe winkle-pickers, had the regulation Egyptian moustache – always in process of growth but never quite indulged to full luxuriance. His eyes were small and twinkling, his hair layered like a grandstand, with the texture of steel wool. He carried his head upright upon a pear-shaped body shaped by beans and rice.

But it was Mr Shukry's energy that had made an indelible initial impression on the inspector. In a lazy place, Mr Shukry bounced, twinkled and flashed.

The Landrover fell off tarmac onto sand. The inspector pushed it into four-wheel drive. It was odd how he could remember Mr Shukry so clearly. They had only met once before, after all. He had just arrived and was giving a training workshop for the teachers at the start of the new school year. The workshop had been held during the month of Ramadhan, the Islamic fast period, and the teachers were either fasting or giving melodramatic impersonations of self-denial. They lounged in their desks and fidgeted as the inspector described up-to-the-minute methods of getting conversations going in class. They yawned, scratched and watched the clock throughout his introduction to phonetics. Some completely gave up the ghost and lay sprawled and snoring as the day neared its end and the inspector tried to raise some enthusiasm with a discussion on the psychology of language-learners.

But not Mr Shukry. He had sat erect at his desk, eyes twinkling. When the inspector asked for ideas, it was Mr Shukry alone who shot up a hand to volunteer answers.

'The main thing I think is that we go near our boys and say the sentence again and again. Only this way can we assure the boys of a good English saying.'

'Very true. Very true,' the inspector had said, cheered.

'And if I may to continue,' continued Mr Shukry, 'I think that we all know from our reading of Pestalozzi and Mr Froebel and Mrs Maria Montessori and the great dead Briton Lord Bertrand Russell, we, because being teachers, must love the boys.'

'Mmmm. Yes. Er. But,' opined the inspector.

'And we because being teacher must open the door and the windows of the classroom and pull in the wind of the world to the small airs of the classroom. Then it is very imperative that we show the winds of the world to the boys and show the boys to the winds of the world and say, 'Here, boys! This is the world's wind! Smell it! Taste it! Feel it!"

'Thank you, Mr Er… That gives us all much food for thought. Thank you.'

'For nothing,' Mr Shukry said, sweating and excited.

From then on the training workshop had become a dialogue between the inspector and Mr Shukry alone. The inspector felt happy, fulfilled and useful. Mr Shukry became a green sprouting branch announcing a kind of spring while all around the sleeping trunks of winter snored on.

Since then experience had made the inspector forget that spring could come. He felt that he was becoming cold and hard. The dying gazelle of his idealism lay panting in the desert. He shouted at teachers. He walked out of schools in a huff. He wrote unflattering memos to the Education Office in the Capital. He also wrote a begging letter to his boss at the Quick School of Languages in Birkenhead asking for his old job back...

Mr Shukry was his last chance.

After prayers the headmaster approached Mr Shukry and said, 'Don't forget, Mr Shukry, my English teacher, today the inspector is coming.'

Mr Shukry stretched a quivering lower lip, and fled back to his room. Every day for the last fortnight the headmaster had warned him about the coming visit and regailed him with tales told by arriving camel trains and coastal dows of the mayhem being wrought throughout the Eastern Region by the new English inspector. And as the headmaster told stories of teachers hounded out of the country for inefficiency, a smile played around his thick, too-red lips, and the rising sun deepened the pious mark on his forehead at the spot where it met the ground in prayer many times each day. Mr Shukry's nightmare of being repatriated tearfully, with his 'Long March' suitcase, and his return to Zigazig and ignomineous unemployment, had been daily fuelled by this. It had driven any kindly memories he might have had of the inspector from his sun-battered brain.

Back in his room he opened the tin wardrobe and removed a bowl of oranges he had been saving for some time. He began polishing the oranges one by one. As he did so, he intoned, 'Here you are, my dear inspector. This is for you.' But then he stopped, thinking, 'Is that right?' He scrambled about for his grammar book, but it did not help.

He tried again. 'Here you are, dear my inspector. This is for you.' Both sounded right. He replaced the oranges in the wardrobe. As he did so, a spoon banging an enamel plate summoned him to breakfast.

Mr Shukry rejected everything except a glass of sweet tea. Through the steam he saw Leila gesturing toward a half-completed house, part-grown children, and never-departing parents. All were dependent on him. He had to stay. It was his only chance. On today rested his whole life.

Mr Shukry shook.

The inspector arrived at last. Mr Shukry gripped his hand and shook it, at the same time pulling him across the threshold of the teachers' house. Then his other hand grabbed a bottle of Mecca Cola and thrust it into the inspector's free hand, closing his fingers around it.

'Nice you see you again!' said the inspector, warmly.

'Thank you, dear my inspector! Now eat orange!'

Mr Shukry could feel his knowledge of English leaving him. He was sweating letters. 'The drink is not frozed…frozen. But what we can do? We are in prison here.'

'Never mind.'

Mr Shukry peeled the orange and the inspector ate it between pulls on the tepid cola. Mr Shukry peeled another one.

'No, really! One's enough.'

'We do not have much…many thing, dear my inspector, but what we have we give to you! Eat, by God!'

The inspector gave in and ate happily. It was a good orange.

Mr Shukry started to peel another orange, which the inspector refused with much enthusiasm. He countered, 'I have books for you, Mr Shukry! Picture dictionaries! And I found a copy of Bertrand Russell's Best in the suk. A bit dog-eared, I'm afraid.'

'First the orange. Second the books.'

'First the books. Second the orange.'

Mr Shukry shrugged, and carefully wrapped the orange in several pieces of Kleenex prior to placing it reverently on the bed. Then he said, 'Tea! Drink tea!'

An hour later the inspector was taken to see one of Mr Shukry's classes.

The school consisted of fifteen tents. Into one of these strode the inspector, followed by Mr Shukry.

The class stood up and Mr Shukry went to the front while the inspector sat hunched in an empty desk. A picture of an insurgent in the act of blowing himself up had been rather well drawn on the top of the desk in blue biro.

The inspector covered this with his note-book.

'Greet dear our inspector, Boys!' commanded Mr Shukry.

'Good morning, Sir! Welcome, Sir!' the boys fired back.

'Sing, Boys!'

And the boys sang:

'I'm H-A-P-P-Y! I'm H-A-P-P-Y!

That means…that means…

I am happy. I am happy. To see you.'

The inspector smiled and squirmed. 'Thank you, Boys… Oh, there's more?' And the boys started on a second verse:

'I'm G-L-A-D! I'm G-L-A-D!

That means…that means…

I am glad! I am glad! To see you.'

'Thank you again.'

'For nothing!'

Then the class began in earnest, and from the very first minute the inspector knew that he was not going to be disappointed. Every boy was included, enfolded in the enthusiasm of Mr Shukry. The same energy the inspector had seen during the workshop was evident in his teaching. Sweat trickled down Mr Shukry's brow as he practised prepositions, moved objects around the room – under, over, in between, on top of, beside other objects. The boys shot up their hands to answer, leaned far forward towards their teachers as if they wanted to touch the round little dynamo at the front of the class.

A smile of contentment which, for once, mirrored a similar feeling at the core of him, grew and flourished on the inspector's face. For the first time since his arrival in the country he felt needed and useful and fulfilled. Here and now, with prepositional sentences whizzing about the room like missiles, his projection of a hoped-for, useful future and its reality came together at last in fine definition and full colour.

Tears came to the inspector's eyes when a timid boy near the opening of the tent confused 'in' and 'on'. The rest of the class began a barely audible jeer which Mr Shukry silenced with a glance prior to clearing up the problem and putting the boy back on the right grammatical tracks. Tiwi and Mr Shukry, the inspector decided there and then, would become the object of his special attention. He would pour books and visual aids into the school. He would extol Mr Shukry's virtues throughout the land. To know while touring the other hopeless schools of the region that Tiwi existed with its wonderful teacher, would keep away the neurotic flies of despair that had been buzzing around him for so long.

The inspector looked forward to writing a glowing report.

'That was a wonderful lesson! I'm very pleased. Very pleased indeed!' said the inspector as he and Mr Shukry walked back to the teachers' house under the sweltering midday sun.

Mr Shukry stopped. 'So you do not wish to send Mr Shukry away?'

'Send you away? The very idea!' replied the inspector, shaking his head.

Mr Shukry kicked at the sand as he walked, pondering the meaning of 'the very idea'. Did it mean, 'That's a good idea' or 'That's a bad idea'? He would have to look it up in one of his books. Still, things looked hopeful, that was true. The inspector seemed satisfied.

But with the English one could never tell. After all, the forefathers of this inspector had built Suez, used it selfishly for a century and then bombed it when Egyptians cried, 'Enough!'. And now, a hundred miles from where they stood people speaking English were tossing tonnes of explosives into the villages of his brother Arabs and…and the rest. The very idea...

Mr Shukry smiled broadly, and his twinkling eyes once again worked their magic on the inspector. 'Come to my cool room, dear my inspector! There are yet many oranges!' said Mr Shukry, hedging his bets.

VICTORIA

On that Monday in January when Philip Morris the multinational conglomerate changed its name, Philip Morris went to meet Victoria at the Wadsworth Atheneum in Hartford, Connecticut.

Philip Morris had not known the multinational was about to kiss itself better with a name change; news did not reach him until the day was almost over. On that day, Victoria would drive down from Northampton, Massachusetts, while he drove up from Bridgeport, Connecticut. Hartford, she said, provided a happy midpoint. But it was all a bit of a jolt to his routine. Philip wondered about checking the oil, tyre pressure, antifreeze on his old car, but decided instead that a quick prayer to St Christopher would be cheaper. This he topped up with worry and dither and a session of shallow meditation which evolved seamlessly into a deep snooze.

When the day dawned, the weather forecast was apocalyptic, and didn't help his serenity one bit. Philip, full of media-induced anxiety, called Victoria. She soon calmed him down, asserting that the weather channels, like children craving attention, had a tendency to overdramatize. Deep down, Philip knew she was right. He would, he assured her, go to any lengths to meet her inside the lobby of the art museum at 10.30. They'd wander the galleries, and recall the times when their sap was singing. He hung up, thinking how Victoria's sap, in marked contrast to his own, still seemed to be.

Bundled up warm, Philip Morris starts driving to Hartford. He listens to Leonard Cohen's first LP on the cassette player. The cassette had been in the player when he bought the vehicle from the disreputable vendor on Barnum Street, and would neither come out, nor turn off. But it would reverse itself endlessly and, Philip thinks, rather cleverly. While humming along, he notes a satisfying logjam of traffic heading for New York. On his side, in marked contrast, the flow is light, the road ahead bright with blue, sunny morning.

He arrives in Hartford at 10:10, finds a parking space easily enough, and even has enough quarters to sign up for the full two hours, though this cleans him out of change.

Philip stamps up the street. The wind is blowing out of Canada. The weatherman had said as much, gesticulating like some wild prophet. The sun is shining immodestly out of that blue sky, but it is very cold indeed.

It is colder than Philip Morris has experienced in some years. Before mounting the steps leading to the the museum entrance, he finds enough warmth in his heart to pity the people waiting on the sidewalk for the M2 bus. Why do they not take shelter in the museum lobby – keeping a weather eye out of course – until a bus happens along? Foolish of them. They'll catch a chill at the very least.

At the top of the steps Philip discovers why. The art museum is shut. It is not shut because he has arrived early. There is no hope that opening will happen at 10.30, or even 11.00. No, this is Monday and a sign says that the Wadsworth Atheneum is closed on Mondays. He looks up and down the street. The sun is still shining. The people at the bus stop shiver and stamp. He is beginning to feel really cold, and his sympathy for them increases. There is no sign of Victoria.

Philip shivers and looks down at himself. He is wearing an elderly navy-blue duffel coat. It has a tartan lining and bone buttons the shape of antler twigs (though they might be plastic and he rather hopes so). These thread through leather loops to close. The coat hood is up over his hat, a polyester Cossack affair in many muted colours that, when he was given it by a friend he is no longer in touch with, he thought he would not be caught dead in. He rather likes the hat these days, even wearing it indoors. He believes the hat helps him think. Philip thinks he needs all the help he can get in the thinking department. He has on winter underwear: polyester long-johns and an old, holed Duofold vest. Over these is a pair of Carpenter's pants in black

31

from Gap, bought at a sale so deep he felt cheap at check-out, and a woollen plaid shirt given to him by another friend, who had grown out of it. He has on thick socks and a pair of leather boots that assert the leather is American, but do not vouchsafe their country of manufacture. Perhaps they had done so on the box, but Philip is not a great box-reader. He has forgotten to bring gloves. He knows exactly where the gloves are: they're sitting companionably on top of the orange crate that serves as a hall table next to his front door, a position that cries out, 'Don't forget me!'

Alas, Philip is still in a state of some uncertainty. No sign of Victoria. No sign of a bus for the freezing people, either. No sign of the museum relenting and opening up. He kicks the base of the sign. Not a hard or vengeful kick – more a tap really. He notices the brown squirrel blood on the toecap of his boot. He had nudged the squirrel out of the road close to his house the previous evening. The wind was teasing its tail, and for a moment the squirrel seemed to be alive. As he looked both ways to see if any cars were coming, he had thought of nursing the squirrel back to rude health with drops of brandy and slithers of nut. But the squirrel was past all that. He thinks of its body stiffening on a bed of dead leaves by Barnum Road.

Then he forgets that too, and looks out for Victoria. No sign. He feels sympathy for the bus queue again, and stands, considering his life. But he can't stand that for long. The unexamined life may not be worth living, but neither is the life subjected to too much examination. The past has passed, and passed him by without a second glance. Philip shivers. He tries to whistle a happy tune, but his lips won't work. He thinks about Victoria.

They had met while teaching English at the Iran-America Society in Isfahan. Their friendship has continued ever since, though the Iran-America Society has not.

And Philip Morris's name? What's in a name? Call someone 'Jason' a few decades ago and the lad would have had a great deal to live up to. Now all the Jasons about town have applied their own wash to the name, banishing the notion that a Jason is likely to want to ditch hamburger-flipping or exhibiting an abiding interest in interest to captain the Argonauts and put out the eye of Cyclops. But being called Philip Morris still rings bells in some quarters, mainly quite glum bells.

Strangely enough, Philip Morris when growing up was not aware he shared his name with a conglomerate. Both his late parents smoked Marlboros, but even then Philip was not a great reader of the fine print on packets. Come to think of it, most of life's fine print has passed him by.

The look of recognition on hearing Philip Morris give his name as Philip Morris only really started when Philip Morris (the conglomerate) got in trouble with the law. Various court cases and subsequent spectacular settlements with the aggrieved relatives of stubbed-out smokers thrust Philip Morris (the conglomerate) onto the world stage, subjecting it to a plethora of unwelcome publicity.

The Philip Morris shivering next to the opening-times sign of the closed museum felt the draught. Strangers hearing his name would say things, no doubt with jocular intent, 'Aren't you ashamed?' or 'How's Marlboro Man?' or, from a raddled bar-tender in a thatched joint at the end of the Dingle Peninsula in County Kerry, 'Your Lights are shite.'

So a sense of unease causes him to shiver when he presents his name across a counter or desk. Also, were he ever to write the one book he sometimes thinks he might have snoozing fitfully inside him, he could not publish under his own name. Still, that is no great problem as he thinks the book, when it rams through his thick skull into thin air in the fullness of time, will be more suited to an author named Tallulah de Mercator.

Philip has a friend in England who was christened Gordon Bennett, though now he is called Gordon Lang. Why Gordon changed his name is due to the fact that in England 'Gordon Bennett' is an expletive. Why this is so is unclear. It is unclear even to those who use the expression on a daily basis...whether looking at the alarm-clock and finding it has stopped, though time has not, or brushing their teeth with Preparation H at the end of a difficult day.

Gordon Bennett was the owner and publisher of the New York Herald in the 1860s. He is chiefly remembered for his drinking and carousing (including an act of urination into the fireplace at the home of his fiancee's parents during the later stages of a grand New York dinner party – the marriage did not take place), and for sending Henry Morton Stanley to find Dr Livingstone in Africa. Perhaps Gordon Bennett looked back from the vantage point of sage old age, feeling that both highpoints might have been better left out of the C.V. But to become an expletive! To send a namesake rushing into the arms of bureaucrats to beg for a name change!

'I blame the parents,' Philip often thinks. He thinks this perhaps more often than is fair for a bachelor. But he does occasionally wish he had asked them, 'Why did you call me Philip?'

Now, of course, it is too late.

There is still no sign of either an M2 bus for the stomping citizens of Hartford, or Victoria. Philip Morris's feet are losing sensation. He decides as a means of survival to walk around the block, a block consisting of the shut art museum. He takes the steps back to the street, turns right, rounds the corner. This side of the block is in shade. The wind hits him.

A truck is backing up to the kerb, lights flashing, further rubbing in its presence with a loud bleep from its rear. Philip Morris reaches the end of the museum, and turns right.

A man is selling coffee from the back of a sandwich van. It is the sort made of aluminium; its surface looks cushioned, as if it might be soft to sit on. A customer is waiting for his coffee, and Philip wonders about buying a cup. He thinks, though, that another cup of coffee will increase the pressure on his bladder, a pressure he has felt since New Haven, and which he had hoped to ease in the bathroom of an open Wadsworth Atheneum. He turns right between buildings and through a little park area at the centre of which is a very large orange sculpture he is not sure he likes. It has echoes of the spiky crown favoured by the Statue of Liberty. Through the park, treading carefully - for the surface is treacherous with old compacted snow - and he is back on the street where he started. The people are still waiting for the M2. They watch him approach.

'Spare fifty cents?' one of the waiting people asks him.

'Er…' Philip says. He fumbles in the chaotic pockets of his duffel coat. He knows there is no change there. All the change has been gobbled up by the greedy parking meter. He finds a note and takes it out. It is a five-dollar bill. This he is is in the middle of handing to the woman before he realises it is not a single. His mind shifts gears speedily. So speedy is his mind that he has time to think how unlike him its speed is. 'I will not miss five dollars. It is definitely not a fifty.' So he does not stumble, take back the note and rummage again. He lets the woman have it and thank him as he walks on. Bashful magnanimity, self-conscious grace, are scrawled all over him.

The truck has now opened its rear door to reveal a number of crates. Some men with carts have appeared through the side entrance of the museum. They stand and watch the driver of the truck, who is lighting a cigarette and does not as yet seem ready to unload. Philip feels a waft of warm air coming from the shut-to-the-public museum. It is not enough to warm him, just warm enough to spark a moment of resentment.

He turns the corner. Now several people are waiting at the coffee queue. Again Philip is tempted, but he is discovering something wonderful: exercise is warming him up! It's one of the few things he knows to be true in life – Definitely True. It has happened time and time again. But it is also one of the things he finds it hard to believe will be true this time. Perhaps all of those experiences that involve a wait and effort are a little like that. This time it will not happen he thinks each time he is cold and cannot get warm, is exercising and cannot get beyond puff and stitch, watching a pot that clearly will never boil and is only there to teach him about eternity.

Then, just as he is about to turn right and give the orange sculpture a second chance to be likeable, he sees the high chimney in the distance. It is belching white smoke into the blue sky. For all the world, it could be a cloud. I am witnessing the birth of clouds. Maybe lots of clouds start like this, belching out of chimneys or volcano vents or getting together in a communal effort from the exhalations of billions of people.

But the smoke is just smoke. So he imagines the smoke cloud rising to meet bona-fide clouds high in the sky. Sparks fly and tears fall. The real honest-to-goodness clouds reject the poor smoke and banish him to outer darkness. 'Be off! Go pollute! It's all you're good for!' The poor smoke! It isn't the smoke's fault he's a smoke.

Maybe it's a children's story I have inside me. Maybe I should write a children's story about a smoke that so wants to be a cloud. Think of all the spirits of things: old mattresses, cigarettes, trees, burning buildings, matchsticks, car exhausts, funeral-home crematoria chimneys. All these smokes contain the spirit of whatever they were in real life... at least that's what you've got to swallow to enjoy the story. They want to be proper clouds and do what clouds do: rain and snow and hail and add mystery to mountains. But no one will accept them.

For his story he'll have to hone in on a few smokes that people can identify with, and take them through quests – no such thing as too many quests - in search of the grail of acceptance. Philip turns toward the M2 queue, forgetting to look out for Victoria, forgetting too that the queue harbours a panhandler.

'Spare a dollar.' It's the same woman as last time. She has also inflated her request from fifty cents. There's such a thing as trying your luck. There's such a thing as spoiling.

Philip is about to respond that he has already been done, but delves in his pocket instead, finds a bill, checks it's a dollar, and hands it over with a smile. Why not? Why not make the panhandler's day? What goes around comes around. I Am A Good Person. No, you're not.

No progress has been made on the unloading. The driver is talking with the museum men. They must be waiting for someone. Philip Morris is dissatisfied about something, though he cannot say what. He isn't cold any more. In fact, some parts are a bit on the too-warm side. There might be a couple of degrees to go in his feet before he could describe himself as comfortable, but elsewhere, even on the exposed face - tip of nose excepted - he is just right. The pressure on his bladder has perhaps let up a mite.

The coffee queue has thinned to one man, and he has bought his coffee. He's talking to the coffee-seller, who is looking across the road at Philip Morris, maybe hoping he can siren him over. But he is too late. Philip has seen the cloud-making chimney and is back in his story, amazed that he could have forgotten such an inspiration. Call yourself someone with perhaps a book inside him! If you were a writer you'd write it down!

But what need to write down such a universal theme? Surely, every time you see the sky you'll be reminded of it. So why, in that case, did I forget it for a whole block? Age? Distraction?

Distraction, he thinks, to spare himself the obvious. He passes the orange Liberty Crown. Familarity is breeding acceptance, even reluctant liking, for the piece. He would like it better if it had not been painted orange. Orange was a mistake. It clashes with the green of the trees. Not that they are green today, but if spared they will be. Also, the buildings are determinedly nineteenth century; they don't approve of orange metal showing off in their vicinity.

There are three smokes: one is the smoke from a tree. He's called 'Tree'. Another is the smoke from a poor child who dies and is cremated. Yes, that's good because all the children will identify with him. Her? And the third smoke is a little girl who dies in an unfortunate accident. And perhaps the boy and the girl are connected in some way, but only find out their connection at the end of the story... Both Children Were Killed By The Tree!

This would set conflict going in the trio of smokes and provide a back-story – mustn't forget the back-story.

Philip turns onto the M2 queue street. The people have all gone. Just like that. An M2 must have snaked along the street when he was on the other side of the Wadsworth Atheneum. It has scooped up the people, carrying them away to God knows where. He stops on the corner where he was twice panhandled. He misses the people. He will never see them again on this side. They will not see how his walk and his wait and his life end. Not that they were particularly interested. Philip hopes that the woman will spend her five - six - dollars wisely. Then he catches himself. Gordon Bennett! What a pompous fool I am! What a fool! He stands for a moment, panting, looking for Victoria.

A man in a suit wearing rimless spectacles is supervising the unloading of the crates. There's art in those boxes. Each case conceals millions of dollars' worth of art. Maybe there's a book in me about a heist of art objects from outside the Wadsworth Atheneum. Of course the book would only be about the heist on the surface. Its deep structure would concern itself with value and values. He says out loud to himself, "Value and Values' by Philip Morris.' No, not snappy enough.

The coffee man has no customers now. Philip smiles at the man, and walks on. Anyway, 'Value and Values' will have to wait until I've got 'The Smokes Who Thought They Were Clouds' fully realised, published, paper-backed and merchandized. It's just made for merchandizing. Mobiles of Boy Smoke and Girl Smoke and Tree Smoke and balloons shaped like clouds, and computer games… shall I let Disney do it? No, I do not think I shall. The trouble is, my follow-up will be a very different book indeed, more of a Persig novel, different but the same. After all, 'The Smokes Who Thought They Were Clouds' will explore the problem of identity and values. How come bona fide clouds get all the positive press? My book will address this vexed issue and seek to tell the smokes' side of things.

He passes the Liberty Crown once again. The colour no longer offends him. Rather, it cheers everything up. Of course, I'll have to get the smokes to have some object for their quest. They can't rain like normal clouds, so what can they do? What? Might a kind old cumulus help them? Perhaps a big old kind old cumulus, a bit like Santa Claus or Walt Whitman, who's seen the world and broadened his mind so that nothing surprises him any more, comes along and becomes the smokes' friend and mentor? When you come to think of it, there must be a lot of mixing between clouds and smokes. Maybe there are alcoholic clouds who behave badly around brewery chimneys; gourmet clouds who like to position themselves above restaurant districts; celebrity clouds who must have the sun rising and setting through them; macho clouds who ascend higher than nature intended; loser clouds who miss every wind on offer and end up in the doldrums, alone, barren and aging, strapped for cash…

He thinks about that. He tries to get himself back on track. It wouldn't be stretching credibility too far to suppose that clouds might have relationships of some description with smokes, would it? Would it?

Not sure.

The truck is half-empty and Philip is half-tempted to ask the driver, who is smoking another cigarette by the ramp, what the artwork is. He decides against this. Mind you, that could be part of the plot. A passer-by asks the art deliveryman about the art, then the art gets stolen and the passer-by becomes a suspect. Would that be a back-story, or a red herring?

Philip reaches the end of the block and, turning right, sees with a sense almost of loss that the coffee wagon has disappeared. Smoke is still escaping from the chimney, but greatly diminished. He searches the sky. There is no sign of the gigantic plume he had seen on previous circuits. He shakes his head. How things pass, change, transmute! Nothing is permanent. He half expects the sculpture to have disappeared too, but there it is: a shard of stillness and faith in a world of shifting allegiances.

A new crop of stamping wrapped-up people stands, waiting for the M2. Where is his panhandler now? His six dollars? Victoria? He looks at his watch. It's 11:10. Where is she? Come to think of it, why didn't she know the museum shut on a Monday? While Hartford is mid-way between Bridgeport and Northampton, Victoria has spent longer in Northampton than I in Bridgeport. It really is too bad. Too bad. But then he remembers that Victoria has a family to think about. He does not. He'd forgotten that. Again. And his bladder is bursting.

Of course there are no public bathrooms anywhere about. That would be much too much to ask. Why does some plucky capitalist not invest in clean and airy privately-run public bathrooms? Something really useful for a change. A thoughtful supply for a predictible demand. Piped Bach and hot towels. The Philip Morris Gourmet Bathroom on Gold and Main. He'd pay a buck, a couple of bucks, for one right now, right this minute!

Philip keeps on walking. The truck that has left billions of dollars' worth of art at the museum has disappeared. Now a white stretch limo sits smug in the truck's place, its driver seated inside with the engine running.

All the events that cheered the walk are deserting his block. Still, there remains the idea for the book that might be inside him. Now let's see. He nods to the Liberty Crown as to an old friend. Let's see. There are these three smokes and they meet a kindly old cloud after receiving the bad news that they're pariahs. Antagonists! I forgot antagonists! Typical. They might include Hurricane Edith, Biting North Wind, etc. The boy and girl smokes do not know that the tree smoke is the very tree that fell on them, thereby causing their trip to the funeral home and thence up the crematorium chimney. The kindly old cloud teaches the smokes all he knows – not much – but eventually he has a brain wave. And the brain wave is…the brain wave is…

Another M2 must have come and hoovered up the people. The road is empty. He turns right and the limo has gone. Everyone is deserting him, leaving him with no Victoria, his time fast ticking away on his parking meter heart, no spare change, no brain wave for his kindly old cloud, and the cruel physical reality prodding him through the icy air.

But Philip Morris, stuck with a name he would not have chosen, a life in Bridgeport that is far from satisfactory, a cold, foggy and insecure future, a full bladder and an empty block, walks on around his route, feeling, in spite of everything, serene. Alive. Whatever next? he thinks. He aims a glowing smile at the orange sculpture, loving its stillness and its daring, and forgiving right readily all its peccadillos.

At last, he comes out of Liberty Crown Park and makes a left. He finds the public library and begs use of the bathroom. An understanding librarian lends him the key. He loves her.

The place smells of bowling alleys and Yankee Candle stores. He takes his time, and the long moment of ineffable relief inspires Philip. Victory! The kindly old cloud takes the smokes to the portals of Cloud College. There, the headmaster, Professor Torrentialus, accepts the smokes. He is shortsighted, doesn't notice the smokes are not eager cloudlets. The smokes are taught how to rain, snow, look beautiful, perform impressions of dragons and bearded men in profile, by the faculty members. (Names: Dr Sisiphus Cyclone; Ms Irma Windchill-Factor; Victoria Contrail-at-Sundown). Then they return to the kingdom of clouds to give and not count the cost, fight and not heed the wound. Or maybe the people in the bus-queue for the M2 were really staking out the museum. They did not get on the bus but disguised as panhandlers and moving-men took the billion-dollar art to a safe house – owned by the man in the limo. The man selling coffee was in on it too. At this moment of bliss, they are miles away unpacking Rubens and Van Gogh and Winslow Homer and Grandma Moses, while the clouds gather overhead, weeping and wailing for a world out of joint. Then all the art catches fire, and the smokes rise to meet the clouds. And the clouds spend a long and happy time - a heaven? - discussing art with the smokes of Turner landscapes and Leonardo cartoons and Portraits of HenryVlll and Thomas

More after Holbein and Constable Cloud Studies...

Full of prospects, relieved of every worry in his world, Philip Morris returns the key to the lovely librarian and gets back to his walk around the Wadsworth Atheneum in the midday freeze. After another half hour, Victoria turns up, penitent. He forgives her - just as she has often forgiven him - and they go to the Mark Twain House, tour and talk about the old times in Iran. 'Remember Ruhullah, The Shaking Minarettes, The Iran Tour Hotel, The British Council Couple, Neil and Larry from the Peace Corps, Joanna and Sally, The Zayandeh Rud, The waiter at The Sheharezade who did Tom Jones impersonations at the drop of a hat, The Call to Prayer in Maidan-e-Shah with pigeons and swifts wheeling about the minarettes, the climb to the Zoroastrean Fire Temple, the view over the valley, Pasolini making 'Arabian Nights' in the Friday Mosque and propositioning an Ayatullah, the Valley of the Assassins, the man washing carrots in an icy stream and offering free samples, the trip to Khonsar on the little Honda, the puppy we adopted and called Barry Lewis - which means 'Good Morning' in Armenian, the little figure you bought in Abadeh of a man holding a flower, the way those three years passed and we didn't quite see, appreciate, get, that Isfahan would be the best?'

In a few hours Philip Morris will arrive back at Bridgeport, wondering what the fluttering paper under his wiper is all about, to hear that Philip Morris has returned his name. It will feel like an omen. He will sit down at his desk and write: 'Isfahan means 'half the world'. Zayandeh Rud, the river that runs through the great city, means 'Giver of Life', though the three smokes who thought they were clouds as they drifted above the fairy-tale mosques, caravanserai and pleasure palaces, did not know that. Not then. The smokes still had so much to learn, so many adventures before them...'

He labours on into the night. In bed he thinks about the day and crowns it with the feeling of liberty that having his own name back is giving him. Why this should be, he is by no means sure. There are probably many other Philip Morrises in the world. Good, bad, indifferent, cantankerous, foolish, kind, miserly, lost, forgetful, lustful, scatterbrained - all a bit like him - and mainly unknown past town, county or state boundaries. His name has come in out of the public cold. For today - and what do we ever have but today? - he is his own man. And his story, despite all evidence to the contrary, might yet come right out of the blue, like a passing cloud or a six-buck samaritan.

Victoria!

CORMAC'S CUP FINAL

Note: In February 1995, a friendly match between England and Ireland at Lansdowne Road in Dublin was stopped after twenty minutes because of the behaviour of English fans. Among other acts of violence, they threw their seats from the stands onto the Irish fans below. A riot in Dublin's city centre followed.

Cormac Heveran of Drumcliff, County Sligo, was walking along the banks of the Drumcliff river at a point about half a dozen goal-kicks above the churchyard where W.B. Yeats is buried.

Cormac was eleven, an age when it should be hard to say that your life is in tatters. But that was how Cormac felt. He cast a cold eye on everything he saw, though everything that eyed him back was merry with May. Larks chased one another up the sky between himself and the table mountain of Ben Bulben. Less ambitious birds chirruped from the fresh-leaf trees. Even the Drumcliff stream on its easy journey of an afternoon from Glencar Lake to the Atlantic seemed pleased with itself for being on the move, delighted that it had the puff to run straight down the centre of green towards its easy goal.

Hoping to fill the nagging void in himself, Cormac had left his house half an hour before. There was nothing to keep him there. The television, always in the old days on and blaring out Saturday soccer was, at the hard insistence of his da, off and unplugged. The dark screen had reflected only Cormac's hunched body and dour face. His two sisters, Lorraine and Lucille, were demurely reading books on the sofa. Ma was sorting the freezer prior to stuffing it with meals for the anticipated blow-in B. and B.ers of summer. Da was letting off steam on the golf-course.

Cormac and his da had exchanged hardly a word on the way back from the England v. Ireland match that February night. The lights from the bus caught broom and fuschia hedges, turning them ghost-grey. By the time they reached Roscommon, rain had set in.

The angry silence in the bus contrasted painfully with the outward journey early in the morning. Then there had been the singing, the chanting and the faith - The Faith! - that Ireland would do for England. That morning the English had been the friendly opponents. There were several English players whose pictures Cormac kept on his wall. But come that night, the English were enemies. Cormac was running back to Drumcliff ahead of the bus, dashing to his room, tearing the pictures into pieces so tiny...tiny ripped to tinier...that no one would know faces had ever been there. Then he threw the shards on to the sidelines of his life.

He knew, as he had known on two or three other occasions in his sage eleven years, that he would never forget that day. The Irish goal, followed by the sounds from the stand above. The first crash of wood nearby as the English fans threw their seats down on strangers. The first scream. But more than that, more than the angry shouts of his father, 'Show some respect, will you?', and the jackals gathering around him, pushing, barging, prodding, cuffing, punching, kicking...he knew that he would never forget the silence that had descended on his da that day.

He'd first noticed it as the Red Cross saw to his da in the tent. No ointment could balm, no kind words from the nurse warm him back to being the old merry Da. Months had passed, but still football was anathema. And the silence of Da's humiliation screamed.

The bus dropped them by the Drumcliff church. In silence father and son walked to their home. Lights were blazing.

Ma was standing in the hallway. 'Did you see, Ma?' Cormac asked.

'I saw,' she said.

He was surrounded by her. She hugged him tighter than she had in years. Would he remember that, too? Hard to tell. He thought he would. Then from Da, 'Bed, Cormac.'

Upstairs, Cormac ripped the pictures of his heroes from the wall. He lay in bed, staring at the patterns of light from the lamp-standard outside, listening to the drone of Ma and Da talking in the room below. Da's voice was angry. Ma was Ma. He could not hear what they were saying. He did not need to. Sweet Jesus, he would never forget it! That day was erasing the cheering, the lines of results, the hobbies and holidays of his heroes, from the hardening disc of his brain. He would kick that day with him down the long field of his life.

Months had passed. Nothing changed. And thus far on the river bank there was still no hope. No sign either of Declan, a sixteen-year-old whose job it was to keep back the briars on the Drumcliff path. And Cormac missed him. Declan could lift him. He was the only one who could. The last straw it was, not finding Declan.

He mooched, and then even mooching became intolerable, and he started running. But that was no good either because as he ran he thought of it, saw his da, and hated the men who had made Da so silent.

Cormac stopped. He saw an overhanging branch and in a trice was up on it, tip-toe above the stream. He held tight to the base of the modest twig that might or might not support his weight. It was a toss-up. He wondered about that as he tested it. He did not very much care if the twig gave way and sent him headlong into the drink. Dicing with, if not death then at least a drenching, might do the trick. There might be some hope there in a coma of cold.

Declan caught him there, appearing from nowhere as was his way. 'Still not allowed your Liverpool strip?' he asked.

Cormac turned, jumped down off the branch on to the path. 'Hi, Declan,' he said.

'I asked you about your Liverpool strip,' Declan said.

'No.'

'You're not the Cormac I know without your Liverpool strip,' Declan said. 'Your da's still sticking to what he said, is he?'

'He is,' Cormac said. 'No football! He's still sore about it.'

'Well, I can understand that,' Declan said. 'I wouldn't like to be biffed by those English maggots, with the cameras of RTE, the English Broadcasting Society and Lord knows who, on me. I'd be sore too. I'm sore for your da meself, so I am.'

'Yes,' Cormac said. 'I'm sore for him, too. It's just that I don't know what to do. There's just no end to it...'

Declan put up his fists and started shadow-boxing with Cormac. It was an act as quick and unpremeditated as the skylark's aria. And, as Cormac dodged and weaved away from Declan's pulled punches, Declan said, 'He'll get over it. He's not the first, your da. I'll tell you something, Cormac. In all the years I went on the football bus across the North, over on the ferry to Stranraer, then down the long old road to Liverpool or Manchester, we had a lot to put up with. We did, Cormac. A lot to make us sore. The searches on the way through the North and the soldiers swearing at us and making the wee ones cry and the bus miss the ferry. Still, you know what I always say, Cormac?'

'I do, Declan.'

'What do I always say?'

And, together, on cue, Cormac and Declan shouted to the ascending larks and the racing waters and the sheep-backed clouds: 'Our boys'll get you! Our boys'll get you! Our boys'll get you!'

They kept the chant up for a minute or two. Cormac felt his misery lifting, headed away from him like a medicine-ball into the belly of an English bully.

They sat back down. 'If I had a gun when they were biffing me da,' Cormac said, 'I'd have let loose. Both barrels. Then, I'd've hit the maggots of their bonces with the business end!'

'That would have made a great show on the 'vision, Cormac.'

'It would've, wouldn't it?' cried Cormac. And he was seeing himself caught by the cameras, avenging his da's hurt.

Around five, Cormac left Declan at the end of the path. He walked home wondering who had won that Saturday's fixtures, knowing that it was forbidden knowledge, like what happened between his legs, like what Ma and Da had got up to to get him...

Lorraine told him the news. Cormac and Da were going to the FA Cup Final in England. Everyone, they'd said on the news, who had been robbed of their match and their pride that February night had been invited, all expenses paid, to go to Wembley to watch. Coaches had been hired all over Ireland. Accommodation was to be provided.

'But tickets are like gold dust!' Cormac said.

'But the English fans think it's only right to give up their tickets. They want to say they're sorry.'

'You're mean, Lorraine!' Cormac said. 'You shouldn't tell lies. You'll go to hell! You will!'

But Cormac had to apologise to Lorraine when the news came on again. It was true. The robbed fans of Ireland were to be compensated.

Cormac and Da sat on comfy seats near the front for the match. The band played the Irish National Anthem, and the capacity crowd, half of them Irish, cheered.

The match was brilliant, but more brilliant were the chants of the English supporters. 'We're sorry! Sorry! Sorry Ireland! We let ourselves down! And then, staccato and endless, 'Enjoy your day! Enjoy your day! Enjoy your da-ay!'

Cormac looked up at his da. 'It's great, isn't it, Da?'

Da nodded. 'Not bad, Son.'

At the end of the match the Queen of England said that she wanted to say a few words before the FA Cup was presented. The crowd quietened down like a field of wheat when the breeze suddenly stops.

'May I take this opportunity,' The Queen said, 'to welcome all the Irish fans today. It give me great pleasure to add my voice to the voices of our English supporters - those who have managed to squeeze in, that is. We're sorry for what happened at the England versus Ireland match at Lansdowne Road last February. It brought shame on our country, and our flag. We knew how you were feeling as you made your way home from that night - your hopes of a joyful evening of sport dashed by thugs who wrapped themselves in the Union Jack. Please make your way to Buckingham Palace, at a time convenient to yourselves, for a slap-up tea. My husband and I shall be leaving shortly to put a welcome on the mat and a kettle on the hob. Tonight, London is yours.'

Applause filled the stadium. As the captain of the winning team held the FA Cup aloft, the din did not increase. It could not have increased.

The winning captain and his team made a lap of honour. The captain stopped directly in front of Cormac and his da. He approached them, holding the great trophy aloft. He seemed to be looking at Cormac. He vaulted the fence - and those nearby shrank back, remembering recent events. But the captain stopped to reassure them, then ran up the gangway and excused himself along the row where Cormac was sitting. He gave Cormac the FA Cup.

Cormac held the cup, saw his startled face in its shine.

'Run a lap with me!' said the captain.

Cormac looked up at his da. 'Shall I, Da?'

'I don't see why not, Cormac.'

Cormac ran around the huge stadium, past the green, past the red, past the cameras that were beaming his triumph and his happiness across the sea...to Dublin and the green lands of Meath, across the Shannon and over

Connacht with its bogs and rocky mountains and deserted farms, to the television of his ma, Lorraine and Lucille in distant Drumcliff. There, Cormac's family saw Cormac running past the Queen, past the gold instruments of the marching band in a blur and a din of delight.

'Sorry about what happened, Sir,' said the captain, returning Cormac to his seat.

Da nodded. Cormac saw the nod - then Da's old smile - reflected in the cup. 'It was a nice gesture you've made,' Da said.

'It was the very least we could do, Sir,' the Captain replied.

THE UNITED STATES OF BED AND BREAKFAST

Though it did not seem so at the time, losing his parliamentary seat was the best thing that ever happened to Oscar Todd.

As he stood on the stage waiting for the result, like a naughty schoolboy for the cane, one of a crowd in a dole queue, a refugee in a line at Immigration, Oscar Todd remarked to the woman next to him (the No Sweets At Check-Out candidate), 'You know, I was never really cut out to be a politician.'

Before the No Sweets At Check-Out candidate could respond (she was chewing a toffee) the returning officer called for order. In no time at all, just by reading a few numbers after each of the candidates' names, he turned Oscar Todd's life upside down.

His wife upped and ran off with the Liberal Democrat party agent from a neighbouring constituency; his grown-up children suddenly grew up and left home and, to top all this, Oscar began receiving letters from a variety of companies on whose boards he had snoozed stating that his services were no longer required.

At first, Oscar reacted a mite negatively to the profound changes fate had forced on his life. He took to imbibing more gin than a wise man ought. Through a glass and a blurred close-up of lemon and cracked ice, he saw his life as a shapeless and tatty garment, holed by compromise, stained by spin. Nevertheless, without a seat, without Member of Parliament after his name, he felt as if the most important and pleasurable bit of him had been cut off. The democratic process had unmanned him.

One morning as he kicked cats out of his way down the High street of Gummer East - his former constituency - on his way to the Off-Licence,

Oscar saw a bike in the window of a Charity Shop, a charity shop of the sort that had sprung up in large numbers throughout the town centre since permission had been given for the great and good Lord Marmesbury to build his out-of-town Hypermarket-'n'-Leisure-'n'-Therapy-'n'-Undo It All complex.

Oscar stared at the bike. It was ancient, with a three-speed Sturmey Archer gear shift that took him back to fundamentals. It had a well-worn leather saddle, a basket on the front, even a strip of leather with a buckle around the front hub to keep the dust off, and was covered with tea-cosies knitted and artfully displayed by Tiny Mann, a concerned lady of the area.

Thinking of what a great sage had said many years before about getting on a bike in order to be all you can be, thinking too that riding a bike might be the making - or the saving - of him, Oscar Todd entered the charity shop and asked the price of the bike.

'It's a ladies' bike,' said Mildred, the volunteer behind the counter.

'What does that mean?'

'It means,' said Mildred, knitting away as if her life - or somebody else's life - depended on it, 'that it doesn't have a crossbar.'

'I've never seen the point of crossbars, to tell you the truth,' said Oscar Todd. 'Might I see it?'

'The point is that if you as a gentleman ride a ladies' bike people will shout sissy at you in the street. There are some round here who could take it - the previous owner of the bike was impervious - but looking at you, I think it would take the wind out of your sails.'

Oscar Todd considered this.

'You look like the sensitive type.' Mildred continued. 'Don't I know you? You weren't the gentleman who helped me out on the Bluebell Appeal outside Woolworths during the great flood of 2001, were you?'

'I used to be the M.P. for this constituency,' Oscar Todd said.

'Good Lord, so you did!' said Mildred. She stopped knitting for a moment, then started again. 'You know, I really felt sorry for you at The Returns. I'd always rather disapproved of you before that. I was in London for the Demo, you see. But at The Returns you looked really vulnerable. I wanted to kiss you better. Still you handled it very well. At least you didn't wet your pants like that skinhead candidate with the angry tattoos in Ringway North.'

'Thank you.'

'I expect you can ride a ladies' bike and bear the slings and arrows of outrageous whatsits. Water off a duck's back to you, I'd say. If you get my drift.' She reached for a bunch of keys and added, 'It'll mean disturbing the tea-cosy display, but seeing it's you.'

Mildred opened the backing to the display window. Light and hubbub entered the musty shop. It was as if a stage curtain had swished open before the audience was quietened; before the house-lights had been turned down. The bike stood out, worn but resplendent, a hefty diva, voice depleted, but thanked for the memories.

Oscar helped Mildred pull the bike into the body of the shop. 'Sit on the saddle,' she commanded. Obediently, Oscar did so. 'Too low,' Mildred said. 'Still, apart from that, does it seem like a good fit?'

'It does. How much is it?'

'For you, twenty pounds and ninety-five pence.'

Oscar handed over a twenty pound note and a fiver, all his gin money.

'We have a policy of not, as they say, making change in this shop,' Mildred said. 'Either you have the exact amount or the residue goes to the old folks. There is, you see, such a lot to be done. What with one thing and another.'

'But you said...'

'You don't have anything smaller?'

Oscar, searching his pockets, shook his head glumly.

'Then the price has gone up to twenty-five pound. Inflation, you know,' said Mildred.

As soon as Mildred had watched Oscar Todd wobbling off down the street, she picked up the telephone and dialled Tiny's number. 'Tiny,' she said, 'you'll never guess.'

'Guess what?'

'I've just shifted Tommy's bike.'

'What about the tea-cosies? That display took me yonks,' Tiny said.

'You won't worry about the tea-cosies when I tell you who bought the bike.'

'Who?'

Once Oscar Todd was on the bike, nothing could get him off it. The saddle, worn in by Tommy Wakefield, who had used it for forty years to take him to his place of employment at the coal-pit where now sinks a Barrett's housing estate, accommodated Oscar perfectly. Energy entered him through the shiny Brooks saddle as though Tommy had bequeathed him that too, and he spent whole days riding around the countryside. Only when lighting-up time came did he get off his bike, wheel it into the lovely but lonely lounge of his home and watch Newsnight while the old bike sat next to him on the sofa. He lovingly stroked it with a yellow duster.

As Oscar grew fitter, he started taking long rural rides. He kept his eyes open, wondering why the powers-that-be had allowed things to go down. Where were the bike paths? A bike was rational, built to move him and everyone else right along. He knew it made sense. He weaved through traffic-jams high on a saddle of pedagogic self-righteousness.

One such ride brought him to a ferry port and before he knew where he was he and the bike had started on a voyage of discovery to Ireland. He rode the country from end to end, staying at one of the plethora of B and Bs along his meandering route.

The B and Bs completed the change in this lonely ex-M.P.'s life started by the bike. Every evening as the sun set he would stop, take off his cycle-clips and knock at the door of a little house or bungalow with a B and B sign hanging. The man or woman of the house would answer the door, the children gather around, and in a moment he'd be taken in, given a room in the midst of the family and for the fleeting lifetime of the night enter the family's heart and soul. He'd worry about Dad's problem shifting his cattle, the slowness of the youngest with his letters… all the everyday cares and woes, highs and sighs, of everyman. Then, the next day, after the full Irish breakfast, he would head off bereft but hopeful to his next unknown manger of the night.

Round and round Ireland, South, West, and North, rode the ex-M.P. The long hours on the bike gave him all the time he needed to think about where he had been. His mind was replete with impressions, with people's joys and sorrows. He sent postcards to the B and Bs lost behind him on the road. He promised, knowing he probably wouldn't, to return one day.

It was on his bike that Oscar had his 'Great Idea'. Were not B and Bs a sign of high civilisation? You could forget your out-of-town supermarkets and seething motorways and grand projects. They all paled to nothing when compared with the concept of the B and B.

B and Bs, he decided as his legs pumped the pedals, implied something rather wonderful. A stranger taken in off the street, bedded down in the womb of the family, given keys, trusted... showed that there was such a thing as social cohesion, decency, society. Oscar began to pen his thoughts on the Great Idea that was the B and B. These soon grew into a guidebook to the friends he had made, with such entries as: 'MAIRDEC' - Two family rooms; one single room. Lovely bathroom down the hall. Ask Mairead about her youngest, Colm, and his mental arithmetic; don't forget a trip around the milking parlour from Declan. Get Maeve to play the accordion for you...' He also wrote a more scholarly tome (before becoming an M.P. Oscar had been an adviser to a Think Tank) about how B and Bs worldwide could save the planet.

These works were both published and earned themselves an admiring readership. True, many read the books because they could not believe who had written them but, just before the paperbacks came out, the academic book on the value of B and Bs in promoting world harmony came into the possession of the Commissioner for Homes and Gardens at the Secretariat of Shelter in the United Nations.

The Commissioner for Homes and Gardens, an Egyptian named Dr. Omar Al Ustad, had spent many years trying to come up with ways by which the UN Commission for Homes and Gardens could help bring peace on earth. He'd promoted domed adobe housing in the tropics; there was also his: 'Turn your garden into a shop' initiative.

But Bed and Breakfast, he decided after consuming Oscar's book, was definitely an idea whose time had come to stay. He immediately got on the phone to Oscar Todd, finally tracking him down to a B and B on Achill Island. There and then he offered the ex-MP the post of Commissioner for Bed and Breakfast, under the auspices of the Homes and Gardens Secretariat.

'You'll be a peripatetic ambassador for us,' Omar Al Ustad said. 'Worldwide.'

'Can I take my bike?'

And that was how the 'Getting To Know You' initiative got started. Oscar Todd travelled the globe on his bike, spreading the message that B and B was the way forward for humanity. He pedalled around the whole Arab World from Gaza to the Hadramaut, telling Bedouin about what guests at a B and B expected.

Then up and down Africa rode the roving Ambassador for B and Bs. He gave classes under boabab trees to women anxious to embark on a new career. He told them about the number of towels needed, the financial pros and cons accruing to en-suite versus a privy out the back; he stressed the need to provide the full African breakfast that would get the guests up and going in the morning.

On to Asia and South America pedalled Oscar Todd. In every country on every continent he left thousands of signs swinging outside huts and kraals and kampons and haciendas and wigwams and igloos - some with the highly-prized addition: APPROVED BY THE BED AND BREAKFAST SECRETARIAT OF THE UNITED NATIONS DEPARTMENT FOR HOMES AND GARDENS.

Tourists got the message. After all, what is a tourist but a shy foreign child, nose hard up against the windows of the homes of Another Country? Deep down, tourists all wanted to stay with real people, to be admitted to home and hearth as part and parcel of everything, to be intimate. The swank hotels and air-flown comestibles and fortified Club Meds had always only been second best. What tourists longed for was to meet the man and woman of the house and to find out how Abdul or Habib or Josna or Matta or Echo-Marie were managing at school. As a result of the good news of the 'Getting to Know You' initiative, the great piles of hotels around the world closed down through lack of business and were turned into hospitals and centres of academic excellence as the homes of the world were thrown open to greet foreign friends.

After many years as roving ambassador for the Bed and Breakfast Secretariat, Oscar Todd, his handle-bars loaded with honours, found himself a friendly B and B on the coast of Senegal which, he felt, would do for the duration. His cycling days were over. His bike was sent to the UN Headquarters in New York, where it can be seen in the entrance lobby, atop a plynth of black marble. It is the first thing the visitors - all staying at Manhattan B and Bs - make for.

Every evening of his declining years Oscar stands, watching the sun set over the warm Atlantic, reading his notes on all the B and Bs he has visited since getting on his bike. And every evening he thanks God that he was defeated in the election, thanks God for the bike in the window of the charity shop and, more than anything else - more than anything else at all - thanks God for the people he has found... people who would, were he standing for election, give him their vote.

ALL CHANGE AT ST BRIDGET'S

Dear Felicity:

I could not just send you the change of address card without a few lines of explanation. Are you ready? Sit yourself down on that stern chair you so favour. Are you sitting uneasily?

Piers has, after much soul-searching, decided to embrace Catholicism. And he's taking me with him. There. It's out

Naturally, I am downcast and - if you have noted our new address - you will see that the parish to which Piers has been assigned is...how should one put it?...in the very back of beyond, the very farthest polluted, overpopulated shore of the Celtic fringe.

I know when Piers received the news that we were to be sent to St Bridget's, he entertained serious second thoughts about the whole thing. I said to him, 'Darling, it's not as if priestesses will come anywhere near St Cedric's. We're only ten years from retirement, after all. Could we not grin and bear it?' But after a night of prayer and fasting in the Laura Ashley room, and an hour and a half of Tai Chi in the rose garden, Piers decided that in all conscience he could not remain an Anglican priest and was called to bite the bullet...and biting the bullet has led us straight to St Bridget's.

Giles, Nigel and Jocasta have been wonderful. They emailed to say they'd send care parcels of goodies, though whether post ever gets delivered to the dire estate of which St. Bridget's is the core, is a matter of some conjecture. Still, it is of no small comfort to me that the children have rallied round.

With the benefit of hindsight, Felicity, I rather wish that I had been more encouraging when Piers expressed an interest in renting the upper room above The Mace, and setting up on his own. With the compensation from the Church Commissioners and a bit of a top up from Piers's family, we might have survived. And we would have been able to stay in dear, leafy Gloucestershire.

We are to have a flat on the first floor of the presbytery of St. Bridget's. Piers will only be a humble curate. The parish priest is an ancient Irish personage with remembrances of dinners past down his Everton sweatshirt, called Father McNulty. Between you and me I think he strongly disapproves of married clergy but, having been ordered by his bishop to keep his trap shut, he is prepared to put up with the arrangement.

Father McNulty has been cared for by a wizened old woman called Miss Gavin. I fear that Miss Gavin is going to be a tougher nut to crack than the parish priest. On our visit to St. Bridget's - and I can't describe its hideousness to you, Felicity... Brutalist, graffiti-besmirched, rubbished further with cola cans and crisp bags - Miss Gavin over-peppered the tomato sandwiches and gave us jelly and hot custard for dessert, saying she'd laid it on as 'A Special Treat' for us. She had, she informed us, taken two buses in order to shop at Lidl which, I presume, is some sort of grocery store for the hard-pressed. She then proceeded to ask me questions - I had gone out to help her with the washing up to get out of range of Father Mc Nulty's horrid Irish cigarettes - but not only enquiries re the social niceties but such questions as 'What are the four sins that cry to heaven for vengeance?' 'In how many ways might I share in the guilt of another's sin?' and 'Why is the Holy Father the only true successor to St Peter?' Well, naturally, I told Miss Gavin that I didn't have the slightest idea what the answers to such questions might be. 'Call yourself a Catholic!' she exclaimed, and started angrily attacking the dishes, adding a dollop of Tide to the cold water, if you please.

We attended Father McNulty's evening mass. All I can say about the tone of the service is that if The Lord is pleased with such an event, he must have the taste of the types that tune into the Lottery Draw week after week. Horrid children in trainers sounding off bells and tambourines; an electric organ more fitted to the Smoke Room of The Bell than a place of worship. And painted plaster statuary everywhere! The word 'Common' came to mind, Felicity, but somehow 'common' does not do it. There are, quite simply, no words to express the banality of it all.

I left feeling very depressed, to tell you the truth. I am still depressed as I write, awaiting the removals men. What is to become of us? Heaven knows...IF heaven knows, that is. And it's rather a gigantic IF these days seeing the way heaven have all set their faces against us.

Still, I must just gird up my loins and show Piers that I'm made of the right stuff!

Think of me, Felicity! I don't expect a visit. The types who live around St Bridget's would have your Rangerover stripped down to the chassis in the time it takes to sing a verse of 'Jesus Wants Me For A Sunbeam.'...would He did.

Out of the depths.

Daphne Orpington-Gore (priest's wife)

Dear Father McNulty:

By the time you read this Father I will be far away. Don't try to find me but if you need advice on emptying the vacuum-cleaner bag I'd rather you came to me than the interloping hussy upstairs. I'm sailing away to the Emerald Isle on the Sea Cat this very day and can be found at my sister's house (14 Marian Way Abbeydorney Co. Kerry). I know the Sea Cat is a bit on the expensive side especially in the high-season but I fancy being pampered for a couple of hours for once in my poor life and I think I deserve it after a lifetime at St Bridget's Presbytery. (By the way your shirts are in the upstairs press. Who's going to find everything for you now that Miss Gavin has flown the coop I'd like to know? Not the hussy upstairs that's for sure.)

In all the years I've been your housekeeper I've never complained at all. And I'm not starting now, just doing all my complaining with my feet. I'm not the first presbytery housekeeper to be making this move and I'm pretty sure I'll not be the last. It grieves me to be laying down my heavy cross before the twelfth station but I'm hoping that The Lord will understand why I've got to do it.

I kept quiet when all those vicars in grey suits started having struggles with their consciences over the women vicars. I'd say to Aloysius the cat, 'Sure, isn't it their problem Aloysius? Not worth a decade of a Rosary between them!' I kept quiet when the Holy Father said they'd be welcome to come into the church for a warm. Having as you know a great devotion to the English Martyrs it seemed to me that maybe all the prayers for the conversion of England we'd prayed over the years were coming true. A bit on the late side but I'm used to slow service from Them Upstairs - They've got a lot on their minds what with Iraq and Mrs McTaggart's eldest's trial coming up. I even kept quiet when you divided the presbytery into flats. I suppose it didn't occur to a simple old woman what was in the wind.

But I can't keep quiet any longer. Not now the hussy upstairs has moved in with her vicar and has been busy over the last few months sowing her Protestant heresies around the parish. I thought you would step in when she barged into the Tombola and gave one and all a lecture on how 'frightfully common' we were with our pencils poised and how Bridge was more the thing... when she told the St Vincent de Paul Society that their poor families needed a series of lectures on Family Budgeting and Supply-Side Economies instead of old sideboards and a natter about Vatican Roulette. But you said not a word.

Then you started wearing out the carpet up to the hussy's flat eating her posh roasts and her gooseberry fools and her pick of Tesco wines and leaving me down here with your stew under a pan-top fit only for Aloysius and the tea stewing on the hob. And then you come back down to me saying how her's got this wonderful 'good taste' and is writing an article for The Country Rector's Wife's Monthly on how 'ghastly' it all is and wants you to let her hubby get back to Latin.

Now I know what you'd say to all this if I asked you. You'd say that I have to be more charitable and welcoming. Well why should I is what I'd like to know? I mean there you've been - your Golden Jubilee well heeled - keeping yourself pure all these years with the aid of constant vigilance and 40 Sweet Afton a day and there they are just a few joists above our God-fearing heads living the good life with their Potpourris and Petite Point and sniggering behind their sleeves at Mary Mooney on the Casio organ. To tell you the truth Father that was the first thing that really upset me. I know Mary Mooney can't hold a tune in her head but she's a good heart under her Legion of Mary medal. The will is there and sure isn't it an act of Christian Charity to sing along with the poor girl? And then there was the article in The Church Times where herself says that a flat at St Bridget's is not a patch on the country rectory in Broadway and she really misses her chums and the herb garden and the glorious performances of Stainer's 'Crucifixion' in the Saxon church and the King James Version and Heritage Walks in company with Lady Jacks and the cozy ambiance of it all - whatever an ambiance is when it's taking us for a ride. Well of course you can see her point. Now she's bang in the middle of the most depressed housing estate in Western Europe it's bound to make her a wee bit nostalgic.

So why did they come in the first place? Was it women priests that did for them? Was that it? I know I'm just an ignorant old woman but it doesn't seem fair on the rest of us. There've been times when I've yearned for all the things that women yearn for... longed to keep one of the babies that keep turning up wrapped in The Liverpool Echo looking up at me in their innocence and wanting to make a mother of Miss Gavin and be taken in. But I've put that sort of thing behind me just like you have Father. But not them upstairs! Oh no! They've had it all and now that they can't fill even the front row of all those churches they pinched from us all those centuries ago and biffed out the stained glass and toppled the saints from the niches and put up all those filthy regimental flags where a Christian puts the kids' efforts at batik they're coming across in droves with their wives and children and snobby ways.

If I was the Holy Father I'd have all the wives join the Poor Clares. 'Stay where you are or the wives'll have to go!' I'd say. I would Father and I'd be telling you a lie if I said I wouldn't. I mean to my way of thinking they knew all along that they weren't really priests in the first place. In all those Protestant places you start off with bread and wine at eight o' clock and you end up with bread and wine at a quarter to nine. They just couldn't do the business. Now you're not going to tell me that they didn't know that all along! You're not going to tell me that they didn't see that Protestantism was a wicked heresy from the day Henry did the dirty on that poor Spanish woman. But all their studying didn't bring them back did it? All the wicked armies they blessed and the terrible oppression of Holy Ireland they said nothing about...none of this brought them back to The True Church! But let a few ladies who want to climb over the altar rails come along and they're off like greasy lightning into a beautifully-decorated flat - with a King-Sized bed if you please!

Well I can't stand to think of it all going on above my head. It gets between me and the saints.

I'm not leaving you completely alone. Mary Mooney says she'll pitch in for you though I warn you her playing of the Casio is streets ahead of her cookery. Still as I say her heart is in the right place. Try to avoid the hussy upstairs for your soul's sake. Believe me the mass resignation of the altar boys is just the start of it. Getting them up like sissies in all that crimson starched stuff!

By the way, if she asks what happened to the croquet set-up on the presbytery lawn tell her I gave it to the missions.

I'm praying for you. But I can't stand the cold so I'm getting out of the kitchen.

Your loving housekeeper

Philomena Gavin (Miss - and proud of it!)

Dear Miss Gavin:

I found your letter on the kitchen table when I came back downstairs after having a magnificent dinner cooked by Fr. Orpington-Gore's good lady wife. I have to say that Daphne really surpassed herself: a starter (when did I ever get a starter from you, Miss Gavin - apart from a starter for ten?) of jumbo prawns and fresh crab-meat on a bed of avocado slithers and lettuce with frilly red ends. A main course of gammon that melted in the mouth, along with baby new potatoes, mange tout and a sauce - as Father Orpington-Gore so rightly says - to die for. All this washed down with a Tesco Graves that made our Saturday half-bottle of V.P. British sherry seem a mercifully long way in the past. Father Orpington-Gore says that you and me drinking British sherry makes us real patriots in his book. Oh, he's a real wit, my curate!

As soon as Daphne heard that my housekeeper had let me down she took me under her wing. The upstairs press is now lined with scented paper and all my shirts are beautifully washed, pressed and folded in tissue. There's a bowl of pot pourri in both lavvies and we've replaced the security bars on the downstairs with tasteful wrought-iron.

Please don't bother your head about the vacuum-cleaner bag. Daphne was into it in a second. To tell you the truth, I haven't seen sight nor sound of the vacuum-cleaner since you left. There's no banging about these days in the presbytery · nozzles biffing skirting-boards while I'm trying to get on with my sermon composing. But everything's spotless! I have a theory that an angel has come down from heaven to look after my every need. And that angel is called Daphne Orpington-Gore.

Mary Mooney and her Casio organ are, I regret to say, no more. Piers, Daphne and I agreed over a bottle of Chateaux Margaux '79 that it was really time to elevate the tone of adoration at St Bridget's. Thanks to Daphne's contacts with the Redundant Church Commission we have managed to obtain a gorgeous 18th century organ which is at present being installed. Of course the pipes take up a whole lot more space than Mary Mooney's Casio and it is with regret that I must tell you that the statues of St Maria Goretti, St. Therese and St Joseph the Worker have had to go. Daphne said they sent shivers through her and, while I know that you had developed a great affection and, indeed, devotion to them, she is, I believe, correct in asserting that they were something of a monstrous carbuncle. A few of the more traditional parishioners assert that they miss them and have taken to lighting candles outside the locked door of the garden shed, where the statues now abide under your old candlewick quilt. Still, once Piers and Daphne have the choir licked into shape and the parishioners of St Bridget's have experienced Britten's Missa Brevis and Palestrina's Greatest Hits on the new organ the statues will, as Daphne again so rightly says, be consigned to the dustbin of Celtic bygones.

The other news is that the altar rails are coming back. Daphne gasped when she found them at the back of the stage in the church hall. She said the workmanship on the oak was pure 'Arts and Crafts Movement' and got her eldest son, Giles, along to have a look. Giles is an adviser to Sotheby's, so he knows his onions. He came up last week with his best friend, Gervase. I put them up in your room - after letting Daphne give it a good turn-out, naturally. She said your St Bridget's Cross fell apart before she could get it into the bin. And she had a fit when she saw your plastic water bottle of Our Lady from Lourdes. You really let me down, Miss Gavin, by not taking it away with you when you flew the coop.

I showed Piers and Daphne your letter. We had a good old laugh, I can tell you - helped on by a bottle of Rothschild '89. It wasn't a patch on the Chateaux Margaux mentioned above, but good quaffing wine.

It took this old dog quite a while to remember the old tricks. Still, Piers has been a great help and the Latin's come back without much bother. Also, I have to confess it's a great relief to have my back to the audience again. Piers and I can have a good old natter in the Latin in a world of our own and quite forget all the crying babies and the hullabaloo behind us.

The SVP now conduct seminars in pulling yourself up by your boot-straps. We've got the sayings of John Redwood - one of Daphne's favourite people - on the walls of the church-hall in beautiful calligraphy done by her youngest son, Nigel, who is, incidentally, something big in the Min of Ag.

I've become very fond of Father and Mrs Orpington-Gore's only daughter, Jocasta. She works for Coco Chanel in Paris and is always popping over, armed with 200 Sweet Afton and a case of Vintage Merlot. Jocasta has taken me under her wing and says she's going to do out the presbytery. If you ever some back on a visit to St Bridget's, Miss Gavin, you won't recognise the place. I'm off to IKEA in the morning.

As to your mentioning - rather indelicately, Daphne thought; and Piers and I agree with her - the hanging question of my celibacy, let me assure you, Miss Gavin, that it is not, and has not been for some years, a problem. All things work out for the best in this best of all possible worlds and here I am in my declining years with a refined curate and his flavoursome lady wife a mere floor away, taking care of all my spiritual and temporal needs. Don't worry about me. And if you ever get the odd twinge...well, you remember how to offer it up for the Holy Souls, I suppose?

I fear I cannot dally longer. There's the weekend trip to Walsingham to arrange. We've turned our faces against Lourdes for the simple reason that it burns more hydro-carbons and leaves those tell-tale carbon footprints to get there - and isn't what it once was when you do get there. Also, Walsingham is English, Miss Gavin. And that's important. The Orpington-Gores see us as the Church of all right-thinking Englishmen. And who am I to disagree with that?

Also, I smell the approach of din-din, Miss Gavin. It's pasta with home-made pesto sauce tonight. Daphne cooks the most divine pasta. Daphne's pasta you boil and simmer until soft rather than open with a tin-opener and heat until glued to the bottom of the pan.

I know you will be happy to receive all my good news. Enjoy your retirement. Did you put any money aside, by the way?

Yours in the best bonds,

Father McNulty

Dear Miss Gavin:

It's Mary Mooney writing to you, Miss Gavin. I'm not much with the pen and ink - music is more my style. But I had to get out Mum's Basildon Bond and have a try at writing.

I am well. Mum is well, too. We're not happy, though. Since you left both of us have decided that it's not worth walking down the twelve flights from the flat, watching our backs past all the nasty kids, to get to mass at St. Bridget's. Our hearts aren't in it any more, Miss Gavin.

Mum says we're better off worshipping The Lord by standing on the balcony and looking out at the sky. Of course Mum, seeing as she's deaf as a post, doesn't notice the Acid House Music coming at us from upstairs, but I do, and it stops me thinking of The Lord.

I keep remembering how lovely it was at St. Bridget's in the good old days, before the new curate came. Playing my Casio and hearing everybody singing along to the hymns was the big moment of my week, Miss Gavin. But the new organ, and all those hard things the curate's wife has had the choir singing, mean that I just sit and twiddle my thumbs.

The worst thing is that Father McNulty does not seem to notice how everyone is feeling. He's put on weight since you left and is so busy rehearsing the new stuck-up services that he has no time for the likes of us.

I feel stuck, Miss Gavin - and so does Mum. Say a prayer for us.

Your friend,

Mary Mooney

PS Have you been to Knock yet? It's a very important shrine, and the only one mentioned in The Bible - 'Seek and you shall find Knock, and it shall be opened to you.' You are a lucky thing to be so near!

Dear Lady Jacks:

Thank you so much for the wonderful parcel from Fortnums and the note that accompanied it. I am so happy that you have found it in your heart to forgive your vicar's departure to the Roman Church.

There have been several obstacles to overcome since Daphne and I arrived at St. Bridget's, but after a mere six months in residence we seem to have the worst behind us. We have managed to elevate the liturgy at St. Bridget's to a point where I think - were you to venture a trip to our parish - you would find to be almost on a par with the good show we managed to put on in Broadway.

We have also been endeavouring to whittle the congregation down to a small number who can comfortably be accomodated in the front pews of St Bridget's. I never liked addressing crowds. Two or three gathered together in the name of The Lord and Seemly Ritual was always good enough for me. The single most depressing thing about St. Bridget's when Daphne and I arrived was the rabble of ill-dressed families - many in trainers and warm-up suits if you please - who insisted on turning up each Sunday. I can't tell you how dis-spiriting it was to try to concentrate on the Holy Mysteries while all about babies cried, children cackled and played with yo-yos, and the strains of Kumbaya on a frighful electric organ played by a tone-deaf spinster, wafted around like so much aural graffiti.

Now, I am happy to say, things are very different. After some initial opposition, Father McNulty has taken to my changes completely. He now says he is pleased to see that only those members of the congregation who can appreciate Byrd and Orlando Gibbons deign to darken the doors of St. Bridget's. It was he who suggested ridding the parish of the female altar-servers and readers, agreeing with me completely that they are aspiring priestesses and that it does not do to allow females within a mile of the Sacred Mysteries in case they get a taste for it.

Of course, there are many things that we shall always miss about the Anglican church. But, Lady Jacks, your parcel from Fortnums made up for the lack.

We feel at peace to have found the True Church and know that, in the fullness of time, after we have done the required clear-out, it will be a well-weeded bed fit for planting the flavoursome flowers of Albion's race.

Yours in the best bonds,

Father Piers Orpington-Gore

PS Daphne assures me that blood on the carpet can be removed with sea-salt and Cottage Cheese mixed into a cream with tepid water. I do hope that you manage to restore your paradisal Bakhtiari to its pristine condition.

ALL OVER THE PLACE

1.

A scrawl in Quink radiant-blue ink on the top right-hand corner of a
battered school desk - late of St Angela's Convent, Liverpool - now in the
cellars of Humble Jumble, Chester. It reads:

'I've got to get out of this place if

it's the last thing I ever do.

Mary Lynch, June 22 1966'

2.

Graffiti on a door in the ladies' lavatory at the Students' Union of Sheffield
University, covered by three coats of white gloss paint and then removed to
a skip when the place was converted into a second-hand bookstore.

'This isn't IT, is it? Mary Lynch on

the bloody occasion of her twenty-first

bloody birthday. I've just drunk

twenty-one halves of bitter and

it's not bloody good enough!'

3.

Notes on a Voluntary Service Overseas interview pad, now buried twenty
feet deep in landfill below a housing-estate in Basildon, Essex:

'Suggest rejection of Mary Lynch,

interviewed 12 May 1970.

Reasons: overly romantic re life overseas. When

asked whether politics was a topic open to discussion

with host-country nationals, 'Oh, yes, I think so. Don't you?

I mean, what else is there, apart from Religion and Sex?'

Candidate smoked throughout interview. Not

a fitting cultural ambassador.

Reject...unless no one can be found

for Ulan Bator.'

4.

An inscription carefully written, then angrily crossed out, on the flyleaf of a copy of Mao Tse Tung's Little Red Book which props up an unsteady table in the junior lecturers' common room at the University of Ulan Bator, Mongolia:

'It's all here. Everything we know on Earth...or need to know.   M.L.'

5.

Message on the back of a faded postcard showing an orangutang in evening-dress, which is still thumb-tacked to a wall of the nurses' room in the maternity ward at Unitarian Hospital in Bombay:

'17 April 1973. Hope and I finally made it to Shiraz

on the bus. The ride from

Kabul did us in, but everyone was

very kind. We may hang about here for a while.

People say there are jobs for teachers.

When I get the bread together, I'll kit out Hope

in pink and get her christened, I promise!

Thanks for all the TLC.

Mary and Hope'

6.

Entry for May 14 1973 from the Baptismal Register of the Christian Hospital, Isfahan, Iran. The book is now in the possession of Mullah Ali Hussainzadeh at the office of Religious Orthodoxy, Tehran:

'Name: Hope Lynch; Mother: Mary Lynch; Father: Hok Eng Lim'

7.

From the records of the Quick School of Languages - Isfahan School - dated September 17, 1975. Also in the possession of Mullah Ali Hussainzadeh at the office of Religious Orthodoxy:

'Copy of memo to Mr Neville Quick,

Quick School of Languages

Pepys Passage, London W1

Nev: Re previous memo. I have been forced to terminate Mary Lynch from our teaching staff. I did this with some reluctance because she has been an efficient teacher, rather popular with students. However, her lack of tact in matters political has forced my hand. Teaching 'A Hard Rain's A Gonna Fall' and sundry other ditties to her upper intermediate classes has not endeared her to members of SAVAK (the well-respected and ever-watchful secret police, for all you innocents back in Blighty). I have no alternative. Hands tied, if you get my drift. No vacancy for little me at the Florence school, I suppose? Love to Felicity.'

8.

Graffiti in latin script - now covered by a Koranic text - under the thirty-three arch bridge, Isfahan, Iran:

'OPIUM is the opium of the people! Down with The Shah!'

9.

Message dated December 27 1975, from the autograph book of Kamal Erol, a guide at St Sophia's, Istanbul. The book lies buried with the body of its owner:

'Thanks for a wonderful tour. I learnt

a lot. I'd recommend you to anyone. You're the best!

If you're ever in London, ring me. If I'm not there,

someone who knows where I am will

pass on the message. Love, Mary and Hope'

10.

Inscription finely carved in Persian calligraphy on a polished agate pendant, made in Isfahan, sold in the Istanbul bazaar for a fraction of its value and now in the possession of a retired American helicopter pilot residing in a mobile-home near Killeen, Texas:

'My name is Hope'

11.

Last entry in a 1976 diary, bought in Cyprus and mislaid aboard a steamer to Alexandria. The steamer is now at the bottom of the Mediterranean Sea surrounded by what remains of the Alexandria lighthouse:

'February 27th

A warm wind blows from the south.

It bears Africa on its back.

Hope's still coughing.'

12.

From an article in The Guardian newspaper of July 17th, 1977, the newspaper at present under carpeting in Clitherow, Lancashire. Below the headline, CAIRO: DANCING ON ONE LEG:

'To illustrate the point, Dr Akbar

told me of an English woman

who had brought her young

daughter to the hospital. The child had

been admitted, but there was little anyone could do.

She lingered for a week, then died. The mother took the body away.
'She seemed so poor,' Dr Akbar said. 'She shook her
head when we asked about husband and relatives.
We did not have the heart to ask her for money.
I still wonder how she
came to be here.
We have not seen her again.'

13.
Entry for October 23rd 1977, The Visitors' Book, British Club, Khartoum,
Sudan:
'Mary Lynch, guest of Washington P. Booker.'

14.
Envelope of a Christmas card postmarked 'Liverpool, 2 December 1977',
found by Hassan Ali Abdullah in some reeds by the Nile and kept to the
present, because of the Christmas stamp:
Miss Mary Lynch
C/O Washington P. Booker
US Exploration and Drilling
P.O. Box 76
Omdurman
Sudan
Africa

15.
Envelope of a greetings card postmarked 'Liverpool' 6 June 1978, picked up
from frozen tundra by an American Bald Eagle and woven into its nest -
presently unoccupied - in the Mount Kilbuck National Park, Alaska:
Mary Lynch-Booker

US Drilling and Exploration
Whittier
Alaska
USA

16.

Banker's draft for $2000, shredded after encashment and subsequently used for kindling on a bedouin's fire, made out to Dr. Akbar of the Eisha Hospital, Cairo, Egypt.

17.

Hurried note scribbled in magic-marker on a double-door refrigerator in Dallas, Texas. The words were erased with a paper-towel, which was then thrown angrily into a new stainless-steel pedal bin - now rusted through:
'Washo, it's no good.
I can't hack it here. I'm leaving.
Don't try to find me.
Mary'

18.

Message in the visitors' book at the DH Lawrence mausoleum above Taos, New Mexico, 17 July, 1982:
'Well, all I can say is that you ended
up exactly where you deserved to be, DH!
I've never seen anything as tasteless as this in
all my born days. Serves you right for the way you put down
women! Style but no substance, DH! Frieda got the last laugh!
Mary Lynch'
And below:
'I agree with Mary. You're a disgrace, DH!

All power to women!
Hilary Zeigen'

19.

Message on an answering-machine in London - a message not understood
by the recipient:
'Hello, Mary? Are you there? It's Kamal Erol, your
guide at St Sophia's. I'm here for seven days.
I wanted to stay longer because there are problems at home.
My brother has been taken away and I fear...
I am staying at The Highbury Fields Bed and Breakfast.
Please inform.'

20.

Visitors' book at the Grand Canyon National Park (North Rim) for 20
August 1985:
'Wow!
Hilary and Mary'

21.

Note on a postcard of a Grand Canyon mule, used as a mark in a library
copy of a hardback book called Habits of the Heart from the Don Scotus
Academy, Detroit, which is now in a book-shelf under 'Americana' at the
Cinema bookstore in Hay-on-Wye, Powys, Wales.
'Met a cool English chick called Mary.
She seemed hot to trot but is with girlfriend who
spits lemon-juice if I go anywhere near!
I'll tell you how I make out.
Say 'Hi' to the guys at Nancy's.
Rod'

22.

From The Grand Canyon Visitors' Bulletin of 29 August 1985:

'The tragic death of Hilary Zeigen should be a warning

to all hikers in the canyon. Always tell someone where you are going and

when you expect to come back.'

23

Fragment of a letter sent from Arizona to Liverpool, used as a spill to light

a pipe,

then discarded in the spill-holder - where it remains - though the smoker has

passed on.

'Rod's been a tower of strength. I don't know what I would have…'

24.

Words spoken on the frozen porch of a house in a rundown neighbourhood

of Detroit. The words formed smoke in the air, then fell as atoms of ice

crystals onto impacted snow:

'This could be Liverpool…'

25.

Drawn with an index finger on a bus window covered in condensation.

Mexico. The Day of the Dead, 1985:

'Mongolia…Nepal…India…HOPE…Iran…

Turkey…Egypt…NO HOPE…Sudan…Alaska…Texas…

Arizona…Detroit…Mexico…Where?'

26.

From a postcard sent from Rio, Brazil, to Isfahan, Iran - not delivered due to

the statue of Christ in the foreground - and discarded in a sack at Tehran

airport; the sack providing a pillow for Haji Ali Kardooni for the past few

years. It reads:
'Shrove Tuesday, 1986.
The Brazilians dance away the day
while the Brits toss pancakes.
I'll leave you to decide who
does it better.
Mary'

27.

Writing on bare plaster of a wall in the bedroom of an apartment which overlooks the estuary of the River Plate in Buenos Aires. Though the paper has been stripped from the wall three times between the writing and the present, the message remains:

'No se puede vivir sin amar'   Mary y Marcelino   Despues de dos anos de amar y de una casa cerca del mar! Felizidad!'
And beneath:
'Te adoro, Maria!'
'I love you, Marcelino!'

28.

From the headscarf of one of 'The Mothers of the Disappeared' which was ripped off the wearer during a peaceful protest outside the Casa Rosada, Buenos Aires in July 1990 and picked up by a gardener to secure a sapling to a stick in the Cristobal Colon public gardens:

'Mi hijo, Marcelino Jimenez, Escritor y periodista. Desaparecido 4 abril 1989.'

29.

From a study cubicle at the One World English School, Colonia, Uruguay. The graffiti remains to the present day as a sort of memorial to a teacher there who was well thought of, but disappeared without giving notice:

English Pattern Practice Drill 1

It's a book. (pen)

It's a pen. (table)

It's a table. (chair)

It's a chair (piece of chalk)

It's a piece of chalk. (bore)

It's a bore. (waste)

It's a waste. (waste of time)

It's a waste of time. (English is...)

English is a waste of time. (Teaching English)

Teaching English is a waste of time. (Life)

Life is a waste of time. (worth living)

Worth living is a waste of time. (Argh!)

30.

Internal memorandum in the archives of St Martin De Porres Free Hospital,

Catamarca, Argentina:

'Re Mary Lynch. The patient was recovering well

from a nasty attack of shingles but, when

routinely tested, was found to have

contracted HIV. We tried to locate a

counsellor who would inform the patient

but by the time this was done she had discharged herself.

Have made enquiries in the town but

have been unable to locate her.

Dr. Pablo Muñoz, 14 July 2000'

31.

Line written with Jack Daniels on a table in the Nos Pomos A Caminho bar, Recife, Brazil:

'No se puede vivir sin amar.'

32.

A burnt-down candle buried deep in a mountain-range of wax on a tray beneath a candle-holder bright with light in a Bolivian church. As it burnt, the woman who lit it stared into the flame repeating:

'Well, here we are then. Marcelino! Marcelino!'

33.

British Airways ticket-stub: Santiago, Chile, to London, Heathrow. The stub is in the side-pocket of a shoulder-bag, bought in Huancayo, Peru, in 1999:

'Mary Lynch / 26 September 2001 / Class: Economy
Status: O.K.'

34.

From the Supply Teachers' Log Book of St Angela's Media College, Liverpool (No Date Vouchsafed):

'Set work for 4B. See enclosed.

Those two at the back - the fat one and the spotty one -

drove me bonkers.

5A were difficult. They said they did not understand

the work set for them.

Neither did I.

It gave me a headache, so

I made them write an essay, entitled:

'What I want to be when I grow up.'

I have left the results for you to mark.'

Mary Lynch

THE RULE OF TWELFTHS

1.

High on the moors of Derbyshire two streams, Goyt and Etherow, chuck in their mite of an idea for a river. At Compstall they meet and run on to Stockport, where another squirt, name of Tame, joins them off the tearful moor of Saddleworth. These three meander matily across the plain of Cheshire - to Didsbury, Stretford, Urmston, Flixton, Cadishead, Hollis Green, Warburton, Rixton, Woolston, Warrington. Some confusion, local name changes, brushes with a Johnie-come-lately ship canal. Sensing something's up, they decide they're a river. What shall we call ourselves? 'Mercy! I don't know,' gurgles Memory of Goyt, still lacking iodine and capable - if left to itself - of giving you goitres.

Mersey it is then. An opening out near Runcorn. And into it, like a jittery kid in short-pants looking for the lav in a grand theatre, the wee day-tripper goes, making a spectacular entrance stage right and pissing himself at the sight of the salty world for audience.

'So, if you didn't know that, now you do,' the old man - a builder of ships where ships are no longer built - tells you. He shuts up the rutted track of his memory for the day.' There's more to me than meets the eye, mate. Socrates never charged. He called them as did 'Sophists' - with a PH, in case you're interested, pal. You can have that for nothing too. That'll be five bob.'

'I thought 'Mersey' got its name from a joining of Mercea, which means 'border', with 'zee' which means river...thus, Mer-zee, Border River,' you say. You just can't stop yourself, can you? Next, you'll be telling the poor bloke how Ptolemy called the Mersey 'Belisama', a name the Romans nicked from the Celtic 'Sequana'. And Sequana was the godess who ruled over the Seine. And while you're at it, stab his retreating back with the fact that the inhabitants of Warrington came from Northern France. Their DNA is chock-full of wine, berets and cheap fags...And, while you're at it, shout at him with your 11+ pronunciation (for he's a long way off now) that the Mersey used to come out through the Dee estuary and only changed its course when a huge earthquake in the sixth century AD demolished the isthmus on which Wallasey and Liverpool stood...and squirrels were no longer able to jump from tree to tree between Formby and Hilbre.

2

To the people who follow their daily round hard up against the shores of the Mersey estuary, its waters may be merely an obstacle; an irritation - something about which something ought to be done; flattering mirror for sunsets viewed from car-parks; final parking place for supermarket trollies, knotted condoms, dogs living and dead (their immortal remains in broken hearts, their doings in Tesco bags), dreams, a universe of plastic, shackles rust-melded to ankle-bones, late ruffians in cement overcoats, and rainbow-with-no-end petrol film.

Or maybe there's more to it. Who knows, after all, what's really going on? Who can solve the mysteries that lie snoring with the light off at the ends of the earth, or past the party wall?

The people round here suck up memories from the estuary like a thirsty child a dubious concoction through a straw. They're tattooed in queer cipher on the hearts and faces and minds of every last one. In the day-to-day care about work or no work, past glory and lost swagger, the estuary is still the focus of all memory hereabouts.

The old fellers smoking roll-ups on the New Brighton front gaze out over grey estuary on grey day or fine blue estuary on fine blue day and see their lives in those waters: shawled and uncertain immigrant ancestors; early life on the recalcitrant docks; friends sailing away to Atlantic battles and never returning, and forever returning. The present-day reality makes them want to spit. Maybe one has a go (the others can't be arsed). The froth arrows, misses, falls, joins the tumescing river, the mess that people leave -

down again to the sea, the ocean, the great world.

The estuary exhales, inhales, throws up, buries deep. Its history, like a scratchy cat we thought was a gonner, keeps coming back. Every wave that breaks purrs its presence.

3

As Brooklyn is to Manhattan; Kowloon to Hong-Kong; Oakland to San Francisco...so the Not Liverpool bank of the estuary, The Wirral Peninsula, is to Liverpool. Gertrude Stein once said, from the perspective of San Francisco, that the trouble with e-bay Oakland was there was no 'there' there. It's the contempt of the players for the sideline shiverers, metropolitan for provincial, detached for terraced, waged for unwaged, living for dead. Wirral people can see what's happening. They can sus the cut of Liverpool's jib better than the city dwellers can: it's staring them in the face. But they don't ever get a proper go at it: not the thrills, not the spills. The great estuary of Mersey becomes the great gulf.

Brawny excavators of the 1934 tunnel crossing from Liverpool to Wirral are remembered as singing, 'Dug an 'ole in the ground until we found an 'ole called Wallasey,' though if they did they were a bit off-target, the desired destination of that particular tunnel being Birkenhead. Still, truth is often blown away on the wind of a pleasing rhyme, just as the heroism of everyday folk rots, while those best forgotten grace a Pier Head plinth. The same tendency for distortion lives on round our way in such expressions as Debtors' Retreat or Liverpool's Bedroom or Fur Coat And No Knickers... aimed at Wallasey stuck up on its little sandstone outcrop as if butter wouldn't melt.

The name Wallasey is of Norse origin and means 'Strangers' Island', or maybe it means 'Church on the Island', depending on which book you read, which teacher you remember. Either name fits quite neatly the Liverpool attitude to it. 'Island' starts it; Island exclaiming the end of a peninsula finishes the job. From way back the nobs sailed away from Liverpool on ferry-boats after a hard day's ripping gold from workers' fillings to the bracing sidelines of the County Borough. There, they were able to see, but not smell, the city that kept them in clover.

And how to characterise New Brighton? Part of Wallasey but only its seaside souvenir doyley. Designed by nineteenth century gents Messrs Rowson and Atherton to provide ozone and pricy villas with sea views, and a retreat from the smoke of commerce and quivering teem across the water.

4

Stroll, Visitor, on the Wirral shore by Fort Perch Rock, built to defend the estuary at the point where it opens to western approach. Muse on change. Did New Brighton decline as a resort because it had been around long enough to become a memento mori? Does that happen to all human centres sooner or later? Can looking at the substantial achievements of the past make us, eventually, fed up? Is that the cracked rivet in the machine?

When Alexander came upon Persepolis in faraway Persia, he burnt it down, though he told his scribes to write that he had burnt it up as a sacrifice. What did the sighting of the great city of Darius the Mede say to this provincial Macedonian? From where the urge to hunt for his box of Macedonia's Glory (Made in Sweden)? Same reason, maybe, that foreigners learnt to fly planes to bash in the flashy front teeth of the New York skyline. After all, the golden towers were not their tribe's achievement and probably, deep-down, where all the weird stuff happens, did their heads in.

Ask any old feller about his summer youth in the great New Brighton swimming pool (biggest in Europe). He suspects cover-ups in its covering over. A storm did for it, undermined the Art Deco confection, stripped the dressing-rooms, allowing a tepid council to vote it down, bring in the JCBs and cover with greensward the place of rates-funded elation, of trunked, ogled, surprising, shocking, bodies... the best and worst the North-West of this surprising semi-united, semi-detached Kingdom had to offer.

Half an hour's walk past the scrappy fascination of New Brighton - you're looking out over the open sea now - view the greensward remains of the Derby Pool, another place of youthful recreation. Maybe you'll remember the picture of the pool's opening day that hung on the wall behind the permed and permanent ladies in the ticket booth (Where, Oh, where, are those ladies now? Grant them all a happy ending, O Lord of tallies and tides!). Your mother had been there - said Lord Derby had given her a smile - but you've never been able to spot her in the dotty mist of opening day snap.

Your birthday contract allowed free access to both pools. You can still hear the ratchet-steel clicks as you entered and left; the strains of Unchained Melody from the loudspeakers; the cycles parked, unlocked - and this sad memory of free-wheeling bikes fragile to theft but always in tact when, wet-haired, a damp swissroll towel under your arm, you returned to it - sparks a barrage of mental letters to the free, fit-only-for-firelighting, local press; the pattern of water streaming down aluminium slides; the explosion of bombs as, with bums pushed down and legs tucked up, the boys sprang from creaking springboards to make love to the bathing-cap-bald girls in the only way they knew ('Bet that gave you a fright!'), and were cautioned by pool lifeguards, their hands fiddling whistles as they ached to save drowning girls by method No. 3, to cup beginners' breasts in big hands, whispering, Cling to Dick!... not to be trusted, those seasonal ne'er-do-wells, near the squealing girls quaking at the wash; the bakelite tally on a string tied to your trunks containing the number of your locker. The ticket-ladies ganged up on you if you lost your tally. There was hell - and 1/6 - to pay.

All greensward. All under the hill. And that's not even mentioning The Tower - higher than Blackpool's. The Start of the Rot. Demolished after the First World War because scrap showered shareholders with more coin than entrance tickets. You can't bear to think about it. So think about it.

Meet another old man leaning on the railings of the slipway, watching low tide on the turn, who says the area is not what it was. Perhaps your life has been punctuated with such men - almost always men. A decade ago you were still impatient with them but now you've seen a bit of the world yourself, and are ready to commiserate. And add a thing or two about your own area of ruined no-call-for-it-mate expertise.

There have always been old men like this. There have always been meetings between old men on the way out and young men on their way. Old men, whether on promenades, in the dust outside mud-huts, under the branches of banyan trees, stretch back in an unbroken line to our first parents. There was an old man who, dismayed by the disgusting behaviour of Cain, remembered the recent murder of innocent Abel - nice lad who always gave up his seat, not like his stuck-up bully of a brother, and listened respectfully as the old man said how things had gone to the devil since Adam was a lad.

Old men share a number of things in common. Like Lear's contemporaries they believe they have lived through the most eventful period of the ages. Those who are young will never see so much, nor live so long. It is the duty of their listeners to realise this, their task to pass it on. Their past, be it ever so humble on the pay-packet plain, nevertheless encompassed worlds at war, imperial greatness, the construction of never-bettered architectural and engineering achievements, an Arcadia of brotherly love too and swapped bowls of sugar and over-the-garden-wall intimacies, and a few things best kept under the rug. The young will never know. The old man knows, but seldom says in so many words, that there is no such thing as progress. But on the certain side of definitely he imparts that message by the deep structure of everything he says day after day, century after century, as the tide sighs in and out.

The way in which the wisdom of the old man is received depends upon

The Age, and the age of his listener. In a more deferential jot of time than the present one, an old man might be called 'grey-beard', 'sage', 'wise man', 'he who speaks with the wisdom of the ancestors'...or some such. Respectful youth might well have gathered around him, listened with attention, sensing - because they had been brought up to the sense - that the old man could transmit to them something of value. And, receiving the respect that is his due, the message imparted by the sage would have an optimistic, half-full, gloss to it. The old man would like his listeners because they, through the respect they gave him, would show they liked him. He'd wish them God Speed towards the iffy future.

Old men round here, you may sense, do not feel that. They know they will be lucky if, like phlegm, they can get what they have to say off their chests. The younger the man the more he shuffles and shrugs off the truths the old man has to impart. But an older young man, like yourself, who has seen his hair disappearing down the plughole, policemen looking callow, women avoiding eye contact, etc., will be more attuned to what the old man has to say.

6

After five minutes of kicking your tyres, the old man feels himself safe enough. Gazing out through yellowing eyes he has pronounced himself 'Disgusted' by everything... graffiti: 'Graffiti's as old as the old earth, but the standard's never been as low as now! I wouldn't mind if they could spell...;' dog-dirt: 'These days people have no consideration. None. You know what one fellow did just the other day? He'd put his dog's shite in an Asda bag. Quite right, you say. But hold on! He comes up to me swinging the bag. Starts nattering on about stolen lifebelts. And all the time the dog dirt's swinging like some devil's thurible. What's going on there?' And you return the password most satisfactorily: 'Yes, you're right. It's disgusting' (What the fuck's a thurible, you think). You have not seen as much as the old man but have knocked about long enough to be able to connect what you know - albeit a plastic poppet of a necklace - to the antique, first, largest, best, booming, Edwardian-Georgian-National-Service golden necklace of history.

'You're probably too young to remember...' the old man continues, leaning his arms on the railing.

He has hooked you with a gaudy fly at the end of a line. The old man knows his fish; knows that you are old enough to be flattered at being perceived as too young for what is about to be cast, but anticipating that you might, maybe, just possibly, perhaps, be the age - sage - enough to share a common connection.

You listen.

'You're probably too young to remember when the big passenger liners came into the Mersey.'

'I remember them.'

The old man thinks, not like I remember them. You remember the last gasp only. But he does not say this, does not even hint that he is thinking it. He's not quite ready to cut down his listening-post. Not just yet. He knows, is completely certain, that he has lived through the last glamorous glorious gasp of history - its death-rattle haunts him - that all following him will be as nasty as a video in a Car Boot Sale, vacuous as the early-morning telly he lets partner his insomnia. Future is something that does not include him and he consoles himself with this, as some would say, pessimistic thought against the sniggering swish of crem curtains closing and an indifferent council worker (with a fag in his mouth; he always conjures up the fag-end) poking his hot ashes. He's glad that he won't be around to see his aftermath - won't have to rake up after himself - to witness the misery and mayhem, the carnage and charnel, the world whirling arse over tit, that will come when he is no longer about to mount the neighbourhood watch.

'You should have seen it. Huge bloody great liners queuing - begging -

at the bar waiting to be guided in. The pilot-boats worked flat out. Look at it now!'

The spring sun has emerged from a day of cloud. The tide is out and only damp sand signals that there was ever water here. This is Mockbeggar Wharf. Six - no eight - hours ago the sea was churning here. The old man stares, thinking of retreat in disarray.

'I remember...'

Ask, and keep asking: 'What? What do you remember?'

7

'I remember - I was about your age - and I was standing here and a feller who was probably the age I am now told me how he remembered the time when there was no promenade here. And I said to him, 'I do remember!' I didn't, though. I just thought I did.'

'We used to ship-spot from the end of New Brighton pier.'

'Which one?'

'The pleasure pier.' And you add, in order to increase your credibility, to win acceptance, be liked, 'There was a cafe on the end.' And you see it, silver dome, formica surfaces, Woolworth cruets, Belfast sink, with a view of the turn of the land from estuary to ocean, though it has hardly crossed your mind in a couple of decades. Now the pier reaches out to sea, starts the journey away from everything. The gaps in the planks show the sea breaking on rocks. And the gorgeous ghost ends in the heaven of the silver cafe, a coffee and the chocolate dome of a Munchmallow waiting to be cracked with a fist by a boy on a bench out of the wind.

'Do you remember a woman with grey hair - used to serve in the caff?'

'No.' No.

'She was there from long before The War. Wore glasses on a string. Wouldn't take no nonsense. Ran a tight ship. Famous for saying as the smallest thing would be the death of her. She died the day they started demolishing the pier.' The old man sighs. 'Just couldn't take it. How about Madame McKenzie and the blackie? you remember them, do you?'

No, you don't. Mumble quizically. That's enough.

'The blackie was dressed up to the nines. Suit and tie. Pristine black shoes on the hottest day. Nothing casual about him. Did you ever go into their place for a session on the cards?'

'No, I...'

'You missed something. Madame McKenzie was infallible. The pope himself used to go to Madame McKenzie.'

'Did he? When?'

'Way back. The one with the specs who couldn't raise a smile to save his life. Did bugger all for the Jews. Died of hiccoughs. You know...'

Shake your head. It's expected. You may be tempted to look at your watch, but don't, unless you're ready to clam up the bubbling shell.

'Used to stay at the Hotel Vic while he was here, the pope did. All very hush-hush, of course. But the regulars knew because there were those priests in dark glasses around the place. Hotel Vic ran out of brandy. St Peter and Paul's at the top of the hill had twenty-four hour masses. Me mam was made up.'

'You're having me on.'

'No, I'm not. Straight up, like.'

But you've disappointed the old man. While it is true enough that he has departed from accepted truth along a track the shape of a pulled leg, he is saddened that you will not keep pace, outdo his tale, walk away half laughing and plant the story in the propagating soil of a smoky snug. For he wants to sow seed. You know he does. He is a farmer desperate to plant out while the light holds.

'The black man and the woman. Were he and Madam McKenzie an item?'

'An Item?' The old man is silent for a moment. He watches the sun

91

inching down as a man on the beach throws a stone for his alsation to chase. When the dog gets to the stone he picks it up and runs, tossing and catching and missing it - seeking to breathe life into it each second. The man shouts, but the dog takes no notice. The old man sighs as the two figures depart further and further from the shore.

'That chap should watch himself. Should've trained that dog to retrieve. You have to get them dogs licked into shape by the time they're six months. After that, it's too late. Have you seen a nipper's face after an untrained Alsation's been left to babysit?'

Shake head ambiguously. Add merest hint of a shudder.

'The tide's well turned,' the old man says.

'It's treacherous round here. I remember that. The tide comes in at a fast lick.'

'Know about the rule of twelfths?'

Say no. It's no more than the truth.

'Not many do, but everyone should. Well, the rule of twelfths goes like this: Take the volume of water that comes in with a tide. Divide that volume into twelve parts. The tide takes around six hours to come in. Are you with me?'

'Yes.'

'OK. So in the first hour, one-twelfth of volume flows in; second hour, two-twelfths; third and fourth hour, three twelfths; fifth hour, two twelfths; and sixth hour one-twelfth. It's the third and fourth hour you've got to watch. That's when the sandbanks close and the currents pick up speed.'

'I never knew that.' You've spoken true - and well. Where are you? Where do you fit in? And you look at the old man, placing him in the last trickle of his last twelfth... and you realise something you didn't even know a moment ago.

8

'It's deceptive round here, the old man says. 'Tide sneaks up on you. Always reminds me of an alligator or a snake. Shifty.' He gestures towards the tiny-now figures. 'I'll lay you a pound to a penny that someone's rung the lifeboat about that bloke and his dog. You're never alone on a strand. We'll hear the boom any time now. See them flats? There are people in them flats with bloody great telescopes trained on the banks. They're retired mainly and there they are all comfy in their nice flats but they're bored out of their skulls and set up shop as a neighbourhood watch -'cept their neighbourhood is the sandbanks.'

'How do you know?'

'A policeman told me. Them flats are like wind-tunnels when it's blowy. Once the winds start those old people are stuck there for days on end. They once found an old woman who'd been blown down the bank in front of the blocks. Have you seen how much they go for? Peanuts in comparison to a semi, yet you'd think they'd be pricey. Know why that is? No? Well, they're prefabricated, that's why - what a bloody dead-end that was! - and the big boys in the building societies reckon they're deteriorating. Still, talking about the way the tide comes in and out. It never used to be so insinuating like. Before the promenade was built it was very straightforward. In and out like any normal tide. It's the prom that's messed it up, just like it's messed up a lot of things.'

'I don't know why the council doesn't go the whole hog and pull down the prom too.' you say. 'I mean, what's it good for?'

Why did you say that? You don't really believe it. You're as agnostic about the prom as about most things. But for a reason not quite clear to you, it feels right to say things that the old man will agree with. Then you think, you realise, you put two and two together, and it is the beginning of a kind of wisdom, I'm becoming old. You try to smirk the thought away - but you've had it mate - you've thought it now and it takes your beloved youth with it, as the retreating tide takes a beachball while you gaze after it, remembering only the sour rubbery taste it gave you blowing it up. Your breath carries it off forever. It's always been doing it, of course. Only now you realise.

9

'I can remember when the sea came in as far as...' The old man turns and points back across the generous acreage of carriageway and greensward to low sandstone rock, just below where the wind-blown old lady ended up. '..there. God, it was bloody gorgeous then. I was only a nipper, of course, but it's as clear as this morning. We'd come down here - we lived Seacombe way - and spend the whole day swimming and watching the ships. Winter or summer, it didn't make a blind bit of difference. I feel sorry for the kids today. The lamp-posts at Wallasey Village would get buried in sand-drifts. The weather was the vandal then. Wonderful to behold! Wonderful!'

Weather has been brought in to bolster the old days and set them on their plinth. When nature seems tamed, people have to look round and knock down everything themselves.

'Have you seen the people who come to ogle the storms? They'll cheer when a wave crashes over the prom and does for the miniature golf. That's how people are. Fuckin' wreckers, the lot of them.'

'All this is called Mockbeggar Wharf, isn't it? What's all that about?'

'You know about the caves, of course. They're filled in now. Health and fuckin' Safety - Council-funded cowardice, if you want my opinion, pal.' Again the old man turns, pointing back, into the peninsula. 'There's a tunnel through solid sandstone from The Red Noses to St Hilary's church. Now you can see that from St Hilary's tower there's a great view of the sea. Well, this vicar would have his verger keep a look-out and if a ship was coming in close to the Wirral shore the verger would shout down and the vicar'd tell the congregation and off they'd go down the tunnel to the sea. They'd light lamps to tempt the ships on to the rocks. Then they'd slaughter the sailors and run off back to St Hilary's with the booty in time for the morning

94

service.'

'Is that true?' Good question. But here, as on most topics in this mysterious life, that question is a waste of breath. Who knows?

'It's true,' says the old man.

10

'I remember,' you say, 'a boat went down between New Brighton and Seacombe. An ocean-going yacht, it was. Three or four people were drowned. They were stuck in the cabin. A lifeboatman told me the finger-nails on the bodies were all ripped off from the poor chaps trying to claw their way out. I don't know if it's true. That bit. It was stormy and the yacht broke up before it could be salvaged. I saw groups of people walking along the shoreline and picking up stuff from the yacht. I remember thinking of your story of the wreckers then. Times didn't seem to have changed.'

The old man reaches into his pocket. He takes out a knife and opens the blade. It gleams, golden, worn, well-used, in the light from the sunset. 'See that? I got it from that wreck. It was probably me you saw. It's been a bloody good knife. Got me out of loads of scrapes. It just goes on and on. Not like the ones you get today.'

'Can I see it?'

The old man smiles, folds the knife shut and drops it back into his pocket. What else is he holding back? 'You were asking about that blackie who worked with Madam McKenzie.'

'Did the pope consult him, too?' There's a smirk in your voice. Watch yourself, mate.

'No,' the old man replies, dead-pan. 'The pope only wanted the cards. The RCs don't mind the cards, but they draw the line at other things. And the blackie was an expert in other things.'

'What sort of things?'

The old man looks hard at you. 'Can you keep a secret?'

'How do you mean?'

"How do you mean?' isn't good enough. Can you or can't you?'

'OK. If you like.'

The old man opens his mouth to speak, but stops. He turns his face towards the sands. 'Any sign of that man and his dog?'

You look out across the sand, but can see nothing.

11

'What time is it?'

'Eight-thirty.'

'The tide's coming in. Third hour. Hope they walked back.'

'Yes.'

'I'd better be off home for me tea. What's your name?'

Tell him. What harm?

The old man nods. 'See you, mate,' he says, and he starts walking away.

'What's your name?'

'Don't get me wrong mate, but you might try to steal me identity. There's a lot of it about. Can't be too careful. Before I know where I am you could be nicking the pension, forging me bus-pass. It's Joseph, since you asked like.'

'See you, then, Joseph, '

12

As you're walking back towards New Brighton, you hear a boom. It echoes over the estuary. A flock of oyster-catchers who have been feeding on the shrinking sandbanks rise up like smoke. A fisherman looking for bait, pauses, turns, continues his digging. Another boom and you know the lifeboatmen are running to their station.

When you look over the promenade wall you spot what you take to be a lone dog walking resolutely towards the sunset. Stare harder, reach in your pocket for those spectacles you hate to be caught out in. You see the thick ginger brush on the beast, and realise it is a fox. He stops, turns and looks at you. A long straight fearless look, he gives you. Then he continues on his way out to meet the tide on its way in.

You look around for someone to confirm the evidence of your eyes, but there's no one about. You watch the expanse of short-lease sand and the dot trotting off into the submerged petrified forests between you and Formby Point. Maybe it's better you're alone. Who would believe it? Who would believe - their eyes on the serene scene in this barely-grasped present moment of a trillion, trillion, trillion possible present moments - any of it?

FAITHFUL UNTO DEATH

1.

1953 - The Queen gets crowned down in London. In Wallasey - Liverpool's bedroom - people smile extra wide at neighbours who have tell-tale television aerials on top of their chimneys. Lucky Ducks are invited in to watch the rain-spattered spectacle flicker in the corner.

Mark glugs back his third glass of Dandelion and Burdock, yawns, and goes outside to play 'May I? Thank You' with his friends. So he misses Queen Salote of Tonga working the crowd to win her place in history. Queen Salote, Mum says, is the real hero of the day. 'All the way from a hot island to a cold one, then sitting for ages in the rain! That woman is like Patience on a monument smiling at Keith.'   Dad says the crown on The Queen's head weighs a ton. Mum, Catholic and full of English martyrs and the soul's need to stay politely separate from protestant contagion, dismisses all that: 'They're born to it.' And goes out to check on the coalman. She counts his bags religiously, daring him to try and do her.

At school, a young Christian Brother with bad breath - 'You get it by not eating perfectly good food prepared by your mum with labour and love. Clear you plate,' Mum says - is Mark's hero. Brother reads the class tales of King Arthur and has started a sodality for Catholic boys called The Knights of Our Lady. Mark wears a blue sash and dedicates himself to Our Lady until death. He recites, 'Put ye on the armour of God that ye may be able to stand against the deceits of the devil.' In the road, thus spiritually attired, he pulls his protestant friends away from 'May I? Thank You' and has them kneeling on the kerb to receive Holy Communion in the shape of a wafer of Smith's crisp. He baptizes them Catholic - without their consent - in the corporation baths. He sees Mary and her Son looking down from heaven, both very impressed. His imagination soars past the stars to an eternity of hearty congratulations.

Brother gets the class to pull their desks together and gives each group a postcard. It shows a young Roman soldier standing guard at the door of a grand room. The soldier looks 'stoical', as Brother says, has them repeat, writes on the blackboard. The stoical soldier gazes out of the painting, slightly to the observer's left. 'What's he looking at, boys?'

Mark thinks he might be worrying about the approach of the rough boys from St Hugh's who will steal his helmet and intimidate his bus-fare from him. For that is what Mark worries about on a daily basis. They are commanded to look deeper into the painting; to use their powers of observation... 'The divine attibute that got Michelangelo where he is today,' Brother says.

Red glints on the soldier's breastplate. He has nice sinewy legs, like Burdeykin's, that couldn't possibly wobble. They make Mark envious, and a bit uneasy. The soldier is tall and slim and would have made the rugby team. Behind him in the room, people are panicy. Red coals fall on them. Some are lying down, maybe dead. It looks like hell in the room. Mark puts up his hand and says so. 'Good try,' Brother says, looking at his watch. 'Time to turn the postcard over.'

Mark reads 'Faithful Unto Death'. He tells Burdeykin and O' Toole that he thinks the soldier is sticking to his post in spite of invading hoards. Perhaps he is a Catholic soldier, and the heathen emperor wants to kill Catholics.

Brother tells them about the earthquake of Pompii in 66 A.D. The lava had poured out of the volcano, covering the city. In the nineteenth century archaeologists found a soldier preserved by lava in the exact position of the soldier in the painting. The artist had used his imagination to recreate the scene. He had succeeded, for the painting made it to the walls of the Walker Art Gallery in Liverpool, where it is really popular. 'Ask your mum to take you there next time you're over.'

The bell goes. They say a Hail Mary, rededicate themselves to Our Lady for life and go to drink their school milk in the clinking porch of red brick and worn chessboard tiles.

That November the fifth, Mark gets into hot water by pouring cold from a garden-hose on the bonfire of the next-door-neighbours, who are Methodists. He is discovered, and punished. 'How dare they burn St Guy Fawkes year after year!' he asserts militantly as his dad orders him upstairs to bed. Dad turns to Mum, 'Is it something you said?'

'I blame the teachers,' Mum says.

2.

1963 - Mark is still at school. He has scraped into the sixth form and wants to go to Teacher Training College - at least he thinks he does - and his Auntie Annie, who works in a school of hard knocks hard by Bootle Docks, encourages him. Burdeykin, his best friend, has gone with Liverpool's shipping to Southampton, where his dad got a job after the last series of lay-offs at Lairds. Mark gets excused games to go to confession in the Cathedral crypt. Sexual sins which he cannot jettison gobble him up. Our Lady has turned away and tells her Son in no uncertain terms, echoing his ailing mum, 'That boy is a disaster area.'

The Beatles are singing 'Twist and Shout' all over the place. A million starlings cloud Liverpool's centre, but cannot drown out the new beat. Bessie Braddock condemns the nude statue of a man - 'Liverpool Emerging From The War' by Jacob Epstein (no relation to Brian) - above the entrance to Lewis's. 'Absolutely disgusting!' People will be faithful to the phrase. Mark, shrived, wielding a Player's Weight and free for the afternoon, enters the Walker Art Gallery.

The soldier has been waiting for him. It is ten years since the postcard - the longest ten years Mark will ever live. The soldier stands guard behind glass that throws his reflection - melded with mayhem and fidelity - back at Mark. The picture makes him sad. Though still younger than the soldier, he has not learnt fidelity. He is prey to temptation. He is full of doubt. O' Leary, who reckons he's a cert for Oxford, thinks religion is rubbish. 'When you're dead, you're dead. Like God.'

Mark's grandparents are dead. They were good to him. His grandad on his mum's side cleaned windows until he fell to the ground at eighty-seven. He had come with holes in his pants from the West of Ireland and brought up five girls and sacrificed and scrimped and had fallen off a ladder dead. He had been faithful. Like the soldier. When you're dead, you're dead. Ah, but look here, Mark thinks, what about good people? Will they get the same as bad people? Is that it? Just dreamless sleep? Doesn't seem right. I'll tell O'Leary that and see what clever answers he can come up with.

He leaves the soldier faithful on his wall, guarding the doomed city. He is determined to be righteous from now on.

3.

1973 - Oil gets pricey that year. Mark is now quite the man and lights his cigarettes with a Dunhill lighter given him by a grateful student in Saudi Arabia. Teaching abroad, it has amazed him how a four-hour jet ride can make such a difference. London has one set of dogmas; Dhahran, quite another. Muslims are as certain of their rectitude as Catholics - and say so.

His favourite song is 'Who Knows Where The Time Goes?' (The Judy Collins version). A university doctor in Saudi says he knew Brother in Dublin. Brother has left The Brothers and gone to be a priest. Mark keeps in touch with the doctor after the contract is over, and returns to Liverpool to swank his travels around the place, and visit old haunts.

He goes to the new Catholic cathedral and says it is like a psychedelic beat-club. He returns to The Walker, but there is no sign of the soldier. The attendant tells him he is being rested in the cellars. He buys a dozen postcards of 'Faithful Unto Death' - money no object - and sends them to chums. 'This is me outside my classroom in Saudi.'

4.

1986 - Iran, Oman, Nigeria, Sumatra, Tanzania, Somalia. Back in Liverpool, Mark wishes he could get off the expat bandwagon. They've done up the Walker. A nice cafe in the atrium. No jobs about. Everyone seems stuck in the lava of past glories. 'Whenever I come back to England,' Mark is fond of saying, 'I feel the lack of social cohesion.' His mum died slowly through the previous year. He is there at her end. His dad had kept her at home, doggedly determined to keep her out of the hospital she dreads, tended to her lovingly. As she slipped, Dad said, 'If you're going to leave me, then I'm going with you.' Mark saw her squeeze Dad's hand and thought he saw her smile before the agony of final exit. His dad, true to his word, dies fast on Mum's heels while Mark is teaching the Present Perfect to students in Mogadishu.

Mark goes to find the soldier. He is in a different gallery, lower on the wall. Still behind glass. Mark moves from place to place to try and see him without also seeing himself reflected. But this he cannot do. Younger than I am. Still waiting for the final curtain. Stoical. Faithful Unto Death. He sits on a bench and takes in the picture. The soldier takes him in. He takes the soldier in. He says a prayer for him. For Mum. For Dad. For his Iranian students. He wants to weep. He looks back...Dhahran, Muscat, Kano, Medan, Dar, Isfahan. The university doctor from Saudi has written and told him that he is now a psychiatrist at Brixton prison. He'd formed quite a relationship with John Stonehouse. And, by the way, Brother has left the priesthood and is living with an ex Poor Clare nun on an island off Ireland. He's become an expert wood-turner. Mark sits on and decides to apply for a job in Turkey.

Outside the gallery, litter blows along the streets. 'There is no such thing as society,' some gink says. He takes off.

5.

Just The Other Day - On holiday from a London College of Further Education, Mark returns to visit Auntie Annie, his last remaining relative. He takes her to Southport and then to the Albert Dock, where they view an exhibit at The Tate called THIS SENTENCE DOES NOT CONSIST OF EIGHT WORDS, though he rather feels that it does. They go for lunch at the Walker. Auntie Annie needs guiding around or she'll wander off.

He has taken Auntie Annie around Wales in the car. She only responds to those places where trees form an arch over the road. He knows every place where this occurs between Chester and Betwys-y-Coed.

Mark thinks he knows why Auntie Annie likes trees meeting over the road. At home - before he moved her to Nazareth House - she had a painting on the wall that showed a track through a forest. The trees formed a canopy and at the end of the track shone a gorgeous light. Is that what she sees? Is there light at the end of the tunnel for her? She has been faithful to church, has been found sitting on the front step of Sacred Heart - spared by the drunks and druggies - at four in the morning, waiting befuddled for 7 o' clock mass. She sees the road she is travelling ending in brightness, in enlightenment, in what's good and proper, fair and right.

'You should've married,' she tells him.

'I wasn't made for marriage,' he tells her.

She looks at him, while making a hash of her custard slice. 'You couldn't stay still.' Then she sees Anigoni's painting of The Queen. 'Look at the neck on her!' And she starts to cry.

Mark sees to Auntie Annie and guides her through the galleries. She likes the frames but not the pictures. 'Faithful Unto Death' lies in wait in a place he had not expected it to be. Auntie Annie gives the frame a feel; bothers a dram of dust between her fingers. Frowns.

The soldier could be his son now. If things had been different. They sit in front of the painting. The soldier waits and waits for the worst to happen behind glass on the walls of the Walker. Mark still envies him. The soldier accepts the things he cannot change by doing his job. His fidelity will not change the fate of the city – Auntie Annie for all her dogged teaching at Saint Sylvester's has not stopped Liverpool going to the dogs and back – but she did what she could, year in year out. Perhaps the ashes of an inundated Liverpool will shroud her; perhaps her God will raise her up.

Auntie Annie forgets the dust and looks at him looking at his old friend on the wall.

'I couldn't live with it, Mark,' she says.

'No, neither could I,' he replies.

They leave the Walker, he thinking of other countries (perhaps he'll return to Turkey; he was happy there) and his lack of pension provision; she of canopies of kindly trees sheltering the road ahead. And that final glow at the end of the road, nearer now, that reflects on the breastplate of her brooch.

THE TESTING CENTRE

'I've seen the future and it's the twin calf to this garage,' Houston said.

His words cracked the silence in the reception room of the Car Test Centre, where Houston and three others were thinking hard thoughts on the edge of soft seats.

The man with the 1990 Mercedes dropped his vehicle details and spidered the floor to retrieve them. The woman from a wee cottage high in the Nephin Begs with the 1991 Citroen Dolly made to help him. She smiled, frowned, settled back on the seat to moither a packet of Rocket seeds. 'It's like the dentist,' she said. The young man sent along by his da in company with a 1993 Peugeot 205 that was a martyr to rust, shook his head solemnly, ''Tis like the Control Room of the Star Ship 'Enterprise.''

'Enterprise,' Houston said, smiling a private smile as he rubbed three fingers against the grain of white stubble on his chin.

The 1990 Mercedes man nodded, even though he had not been listening. 'I don't know what I'll do if...' he said. And a side of him wondered if he had really spoken, using those honest, scary words. He looked around. The group was gazing at him, waiting for the hanging sentence to reappear, complete and swinging. 'Ah, well...' He shrugged. 'There we are then. Que Sera... Sera.'

Electric shutters cackled up. The four car-owners looked through the plate-glass window between themselves and the testing area. The white Mercedes was revealed, waiting for admittance to the white surfaces, computer screens and hydraulic ramps. The bodywork gleamed. Its owner thought of sepulcres.

'Is that one yours?' Houston asked. ''Tis a fine-looking vehicle, so it is.' Mercedes tried a smile of acknowledgement that fell short; he kneaded his face with a large right hand.

Two young men in white coveralls, one holding a clipboard, set about checking the car. The engine was revved to the sort of rpm levels that the man had never heard from his car before.

'Sweet as a bird,' Houston said.

Mercedes coughed. 'I should never have bought a Merc,' he said. 'It was all I could do to put petrol in her. It used to belong to the local T.D. I thought it would go on for ever.'

'Perhaps it will,' Houston said. 'T.D.s manage it.'

'Great cars altogether,' said the young man from behind Louisberg. And Houston looked at him and could see him in twenty or thirty years' time propping up a gate and watching across the flat, wind-scarred fields whatever there was to be watched by then, and wondering where his life had got to.

Mercedes stared through the viewing-window. 'I'm doomed,' he said, already seeing himself standing at the roadside waiting for lifts, studying Bus Eireann timetables, flinching at the sight of speeding 05s, 06s, 07s passing him by with a contemptuous whoosh on their way to clinching deals, downing pints on coasters at The Breaffy House. Another sigh, and he laid his papers down on the seat beside him. He looked at the floor.

'If you're doomed with a lovely shiny car like that, then mine is...' The Citroen Dolly woman could not think of a worse fate than 'doomed'. She hunted about, said, 'Well...I'm doomed and a half.'

'Same here. On the certain side of definitely,' said 1993 Peugeot. 'The da's too ashamed to be seen out with it. He's got Ma down on her knees in front of Our Lady of Perpetual Succour. If that doesn't work - though Ma says it's never been known to fail -

it's the tractor for us. And you can't court a girl on a tractor.'

The second shutter tittered open and the Peugeot was driven in. A rust spot the exact shape of Australia minus Tasmania covered the bonnet. The dents, got in Louisberg's narrow main street from the cars of unknown assailants, vied for assessment and final judgement with a long scrape down the wing from head to tail light.

The engine of the little car was revved to the stars. The car coughed. It was a piteous and terminal sound. A whisp of smoke escaped from under the bonnet and rose into the sterile air of the testing area. It hung over the vehicle like an exclamation before a draught swerved it into a question mark.

Houston watched.

'I can't watch,' Peugeot said.

Houston said, 'This isn't like us. Here we are, Mayomen and women to a man, at a pivotal moment in our lives...well, I think we should become better acquainted. The name's Pat Houston.'

There was little reaction to Houston's statement, for all were watching the Mercedes being offered up on the altar of the hydraulic ramp.

'Will you take your eyes off what's happening and listen when I'm talking to ye?' Houston said.

The three car-owners came to order. 'My name's Pat Houston,' repeated Houston. He nodded to the Mercedes owner.

'I'm Pascal Noonan from Claremorris.'

'I'm Sarah Lyons from Bireencurrough.'

'Shane Geraghty from behind Louisberg.'

Houston frowned profoundly. 'Pascal Mercedes...candle on a car; Sarah Lyons...I know another Sarah Lyons. Shane

Geraghty...cowboy in a car. It's important to get the names. It was always one of our great things. Remembering names. Remembering. It's made all the great difference.' He thought about that. His face cleared. 'For better and worse.'

Pascal, Sarah and Shane were looking past Houston at the strange sight of the white coachwork of Pascal's car separating from the chassis.

'Never mind all that,' Houston said.

Behind the thick glass, the Mercedes of Pascal Noonan - father, widower, struggler with alcohol and religion, salesman of over-wrought wrought iron at front doors, man of few words - seemed to go into free-fall as the mechanics allowed coachwork to compact with chassis. The shriek of springs, metal on metal, competed with a groan from the owner of the car. Everyone, even Houston, looked at the shuddering Mercedes. Then he turned to Pascal.

'Doomed,' Pascal said to Houston. Quietly.

Houston spoke. 'I cannot help noticing how like the confessional this is. A perverse upside-down sacrament of penance. The sins of your cars are placed on a plinth for all to see. Your rottenness is paraded. No longer internal to be exposed by an act of courage, self-abnegation and amendment, your sin is not you but what you own. 'Bless me, Mechanic, for I have sinned. It's 20 years since I bought me car, Mechanic. I bought food and clothing for me kids when I should have been saving for a respray, Mechanic; I bought a car because the bus service stopped, because the roads became too dangerous for me bike, because in order to live I had to have one. But then I confess I did not keep it up to scratch. I confess, Mechanic, that life took up me time. I...'

Houston stopped. A door to Reception had opened.

Everyone looked towards it. A mechanic in spotless overalls stood where the door had once been. 'Pascal, will you come this way?' the mechanic said.

Pascal stood up and, forgetting the paperwork on the seat beside him, followed the mechanic through the door. It closed with a neat click. In a moment it opened again and Pascal came back, picked up the papers and disappeared again. And again the neat click.

'Will he pass do you think?' Sarah asked. She was reconciled to failure. A computer print-out would list the sins to be wiped off the slate before absolution might be granted on re-test. But that was no option.

Sarah thought herself ahead to a life in the mountain cottage without a car. She would have to tell old Pat Brown there'd be no more Friday trips to Ballina for a wander through Dunnes and a couple of jars. The organic vegetables she managed to grow at 900 feet on an acre of wind-worried stony ground would not find their way to Westport market. Friends would have to stay uninvited. She would be imprisoned in the mountains. Sarah saw herself going down-hill at breakneck speed. She would be like Maisie, unwashed, eccentric. Walkers in their bright Goretex jackets would shoot her with posh cameras while she scowled and cursed them for walking the rutted roads with their urbanity, pension plans, and smart R.V.s safe back at Flynn's car-park. Then, home in swank Dublin, she imagined them shuffling their snaps, laughing at the Kodachrome crone in their Temple Bar night-spots.

'They're going to build a grand new road from Castlebar to Westport,' Houston said. 'It's all part of The Plan. It will speed up the speed merchants. As I hear it, two of the proposed routes will pass just a few yards away from the Top of Sheean. More irony, for them as can take it. The Top of Sheean is the fairy fort where Daniel O' Connell addressed a few hundred thousand of the poor. It commands a view of The Ocean, the Partrys, The Nephins, Croagh Patrick and the Plains of Mayo.'

'What has all this to do with the test?' Shane asked.

'Connections. Connections. All of life in the fast lane is connections,' Houston said. 'The best lack all connections, while the worst are filled with passionate complexity.'

'What's that mean?'

'It means' Sarah said, 'that some revelation is at hand.' She turned to Houston. 'Isn't that so, Mr Houston?'

'So it is, Sarah,' Houston said.

'There goes Pascal,' Shane said, half rising from his seat.

Houston and Sarah turned around to look. There Pascal went. He disappeared for a few seconds round the back of the building. Then they saw him trudging down the driveway to the Clogher Road.

'He's failed,' Sarah said.

'How'll he get himself home to Claremorris?' Shane said.

Houston did not answer. He turned to look through the glass as Shane's Peugeot was stretched on the rack. A crack and a shout from one of the mechanics, and the ramp let go of the hard-pressed car. It beat back together like a warped lid on a tin. 'When you get your certificate, Shane,' Houston said, 'you'll be able to bomb up the Castlebar Road and lift Pascal to Claremorris. How does that sound?'

The engineers had gathered around the nearside front of the Peugeot. 'No way,' Shane said.

'You know what they want, don't you?' Sarah said. 'They

want us off the road, to sweep us away and make us invisible. We don't go with the Celtic Tiger, you see. We let the side down.'

The door opened and Shane was ushered through.

'He's not going to pass, is he?' Sarah said.

'You never know,' Houston said.

'Oh,' Sarah said, 'I think you do.' She watched as her car was driven in. She took in the maroon and white colour scheme, the vinyl roof to which the Nephin wind and rain had given the look of grey sycamore bark, or the hands of her gran. How many times had she driven with the top down? Not many, maybe twice or three times. But that wasn't the point really. There was always the notion that she could drive her Dolly with nothing between herself and the great world. As it was, the vinyl dispersed any heat the weak heater grabbed from the weak engine. In the rain it was like the inside of her cottage, where every drop tapped to her like the Riverdance clatter of crows. Crows! They'd called the nuns crows. The nuns had said there was no peace on this side of the grave. Don't expect it. Then it had seemed an easy thing for the nuns to say with their fine convent in the centre of Castlebar, meals made for them by humble nuns from the islands. But the convent and the attached school was for sale. For Development, the sign said, below the cream gloss statue of Our Lady over the main door. Those nuns – where were they? Those who survived in the places where old nuns went would be repeating their world-despairing mantras. For them perhaps a regret for no grandchildren at the knee, no old fella's grave to tend. For Sarah, organic vegetables rotting under plastic cloches too high in the Nephins. Sans car. Sans friends. Sans…

'But what about you?' Sarah said.

'What about me?'

'We don't know anything about you.'

'What's to know that you can't see?' Houston said.

'Where's your car?'

'Where's my car?'

'Yes, where's your car? You were here before Pascal, Shane or me. By rights you should've gone home ahead of us, with or without your car.'

'Why does it matter to you, Sarah?'

'It passes the time. And it seems to me you know an awful amount about us and we precious little about you. I don't call that fair.'

'You could've asked, you know.'

'Well, I'm asking.'

As she spoke, Sarah knew she was stepping past the norms. She hadn't told Houston or the others anything much about herself. She'd let her car say everything. A Citroen Dolly missing only the orange Summer of Love flowers while she wore a paisley ankle-length skirt that defied the nuns while copying them.

Houston didn't speak.

'What car do you drive?'

'A Volvo. 95. It passed the test this morning. I knew it would. It's never let me down,' Houston said.

'So what are you doing hanging around this place with the likes of us? You could be getting on with your life.'

'Not sure meself. I got here first thing and I've not been able to pull meself away.'

'They call it Schadenfreude,' Sarah said bitterly.

'And what's what you said when it's at home?'

' 'A malicious enjoyment of others' misfortunes',' Sarah said. 'It's German.'

'German, is it?'

'Yes,' Sarah said. 'I speak German. I'm quite fluent.'

'And have you the Irish?'

'I have.'

'No flies on you, Sarah,' Houston said.

'What's that supposed to mean?'

Before her eyes, the Citroen Dolly was being tested to the full extent of the law. She averted her gaze. She felt ashamed at being so sharp with Houston. We used to be judged by the worn state of our rosary beads, by the arthritis in our pious knees, by our regularity at Mass. But now we've grants from Europe and a free press to clarion out the Sins of the Fathers, the cruelties of Mother Superiors, all that's gone. We've become this testing centre with its comfy seats and copies of 'Mayo Life' and white jump-suits. And we're the flotsom that will be swept out at the end of the day.

''Schadenfreude'. Must remember that. Every day you learn something new.'

And every day you forget something old, Sarah thought. 'It's what you're about. Isn't that so? Making the world fit you so badly that McGrail's coffin fits just right?'

'Sarah, Sarah…' Houston said.

The door opened and her name was called. She stood up, watching Houston. His blue eyes twinkled. She picked up her bag and walked towards the door.

'Don't make off without coming back to say goodbye,' Houston said.

She looked at him. 'That depends…'

Houston did not pursue it, though he wondered what she meant. What did it depend on?

But you couldn't get an education like this anywhere else.

Not these days. Day and night Houston searched about in his Volvo for the sort of crack he'd had this day in the testing centre. Pubs were full of the blare of piped music, and the din stopped the indomitable Irishry in its tracks. Where did the plain people of Ireland dare to be plain any more? He waited, thinking such thoughts; thinking too of the new road that would turn the beacon of The Top of Sheean into an excuse for speeding up before crashing headlong into Westport's clogged streets.

The men were laughing as they reversed Sarah's Citroen off the ramp and out into the daylight. Were they happy at a day well spent? Perhaps they thought they had contributed immeasurably to the safety of Irish roads, to the elevation of the country and its citizenry? Houston wondered about that. He hoped Pascal would dust down his old bike and pedal about Claremorris and environs in the middle of the road. He hoped Shane would do his courting from the vantage-point of some old Raleigh, conduct a coleen on its crossbar to a trysting place of old stone. The Irish who failed the test, might they not put their oar in and trap the tigers, if only behind their old bikes, their ponies, and donkeys – if there were a donkey still extant in Ireland.

Houston suddenly thought of 'The Quiet Man' and wondered about renting it from Gilhooley's World Video. He'd always reckoned it a bit too Oirish by a long chalk. But now he needed it. You took what you could get.

And Sarah was there, back through the door of judgement. She was on the verge of tears, and he thought of Maureen O' Hara and the trouble over the dowry. Here's a stick to beat the lovely lady.

'How'd it go?'

'Failed,' Sarah said.

'A write off, is it?'

'Might as well be.'

Sarah handed Houston the form. As he read it, she watched the men in white hosing down the operating theatre for the day.

'I'll see to it,' Houston said.

'You'll see to it?'

'I'll give you a lift up to a garage I know. He'll collect the car, give it what it needs and bring it back for re-testing. I'll take you home. When it's ready, I'll collect you and bring you back to collect it.' He watched her face.

'I haven't the money.'

'I have.'

'I couldn't.'

'You could and you will. You came back. The others scuttled off. I'd've done the same for them.'

'I can't…'

'You can,' Houston said. 'If I'd failed and you had the necessary you'd do the same for me.'

Sarah wondered about that. Would she? Perhaps she would. What might stop her would be the embarrassment of doing what Houston was doing now, laying himself wide open as a holy joe, a crank, a soft touch, a mug, a sucker.

'No, really. I can't.'

'Sarah,' Houston said. 'Sarah, I have a pension. I have kids that are off me hands. I have a fair number of amends to make for things not done that I should have done; things done that I should not have done. Sarah, we must love one another in this world. Let me fix the old car. No strings. A favour to an old man, like.'

She opened her mouth to protest again. He frowned and

opened the door of the testing centre. 'Would ye do me another little favour?' he asked her. ' Would you tell me the opposite of Schadenfreude?'

They walked across the tarmac, past her disgraced Citroen, to Houston's Volvo. 'I don't know,' she said. 'Maybe it would be 'sorrow at another's pain'.'

'But you don't have the German for it?'

'No,' she said. 'I can't let you…'

He interrupted her as she knew he would, and she was glad of it. 'It gives me pleasure,' Houston said. 'Makes me feel like a human being. It doesn't happen every day. You can understand that, can't you?'

Sarah nodded. She got into Houston's car without another word.

Houston turned the key and the Volvo roared to life.

RUNNING ON THE WAVES

<u>Chinese Woman:</u>   They came to this country thinking they were going to have a better life. They didn't realise that the sea would take them away.

(water lapping / fog horn)

<u>Lifeboatman:</u>   Who are we after all?

Temporary immigrants

Arriving wanted or uncalled for

Through the bars of endless horizons

And the struggles of mothers

Who after many travails are sent back

Where we came from

Crammed into an airless box.

(The bleep of checkout scanners)

<u>Consumer:</u> First Biscuit Tin (99 cents). Front and back Adam's brand-new body. His left arm reaches to the right edge of the tin. Second Biscuit Tin (99 cents). The same as the first, but this shows God reaching His right arm over to the left side of the tin.

You'd need to buy the pair. Placed side by side for a dollar ninety-eight you'd have The Creation on the kitchen shelf. Adam for sugar? God for salt? It's up to you; possibilities are endless. On the side of both tins is written on a scroll within a cartouche: THE VATICAN COLLECTION – Il Tesoro de San Pietro 'Vatican Millennium Collectibles Company' Limited Edition 1998.

There are maybe a hundred Adam tins on the shelf at the 99 Cent Store, but only five or six God tins. Why the disparity? Did people only pop 'God' into their baskets, and reject 'Adam'? If so, why? It's like buying only one bookend. But I don't know whether that is why

'God' is so absent. It's a mystery.

Lancastrian Woman: For water, for the deep where the high tide
Mutters to its hurt self, mutters and ebbs.
Waves wallow in their wash, go out and out,
Leave only the death-rattle of the crabs,
The beach increasing, its enormous snout
Sucking the ocean's side. This is the end of
running on the waves;
We are poured out like water. Who will
dance
The mast-lashed master of the Leviathans
Up from the field of Quakers in their
unstoned graves?

(Robert Lowell)

(Silence)

(Checkout Scanners)

Consumer: I've bought the set of biscuit tins. It's the pairing that makes the product for me. This hasn't been the thinking of previous customers. Maybe the people who only took 'God' home felt that a naked Adam did not quite fit the bill, or might be a daily embarrassment. Adam naked as an apple. Enough to put you off your All Bran. Of course, much of the stock here at 99 Cents is 'end of line' – and end of <u>the</u> line. Maybe more Adam tins arrived, fewer God tins. Who knows? Who <u>knows</u> anything?

Like most items in the 99 Cents Store, like almost everything we buy everywhere, the tins have a gold 'Made In China' sticker on them. What were the people who made them thinking as the tins took shape and flew from their busy fingers into cardboard boxes and containers and the holds of ships?

(Silence)

Lifeboatman: The World is too much with us; late and
                    soon,
                    Getting and spending, we lay waste our
                    powers:
                    Little we see in nature that is ours;
                    We have given our hearts away, a sordid
                    boon!
                    The sea that bares her bosom to the moon;
                    The winds that will be howling at all hours,
                    And are up-gathered now like sleeping
                    flowers;
                    For this, for everything, we are out of tune;
                    It moves us not. (Wordsworth)

(Cockle-picking: scrunch of spade, scrabble of gather, click of shell
into bag)

Chinese Woman: Cockle (noun or verb intransitive) common
name applied to the heart-shaped, jumping or leaping marine
bivalve molluscs. The brittle shells are of uniform size, are obliquely
spherical, and possess distinct radiating ridges, or ribs, which aid the
animal in gripping the sand. The mantle has three distinct apertures
– inhalant, exhalant, and pedal – through which the inhalant and
exhalant siphons and the foot protrude. The cockle lives in sand and
mud in shallow water, often in brackish inlets. It burrows until only
the siphons project, pulling in water from which the animal strains
the minute planktonic organisms on which it feeds. All cockles are
hermaphroditic.

Lifeboatman: Prior to leaving check forecast and times;
Tell someone where you are going and what time you will return;
Depending on the time of year take suitable clothing, warm drinks,
snacks, etc.; If you are in a group always remain close together; if you

have any doubts about any of the above, Don't Go!

(Silence)

Lancastrian Woman: On a Thursday afternoon in February, nine days before St Valentine's Day, a gang of thirty-five Chinese immigrants went to pick cockles in Morecambe bay. As the winter light faded, they passed a sign on the shore: Danger. Beware. Fast Rising Tide. Quicksands. Hidden Channels... and headed for Red Bank.

Lifeboatman: Carry a map and compass and know how to use them. Always know the weather forecast and tide times. Be aware of how quickly the tide comes in. Have several types of communication...

(Scanner Sounds)

Consumer: Ooh! Look at this! A porcelain box, made in China, about four inches high. A globe is the centre of the piece. A rough doodle of the continents painted onto the globe, a metal ring and clasp reaches round the equator to split the world and open it up. Standing on the North Pole, though its bulky feet squash Greenland, Finland and Siberia as well, is an American eagle, wings spread, talons on guard. This is a bird you don't mess with.

I couldn't resist this box, so brought it home and put in on the piano. Only after some weeks did I try to open it. *You were distracted by other things you'd bought. Bringing the stuff home, unwrapping it. A fleeting thrill. Where does this peculiar joy of ownership come from? The hunter-gatherer with an antelope's corpse slung over his shoulder. Returning to his thin family. The children shout and turn to greet the conquering hero. Imagine the pleasure of the hunter! But it soon fades, this thrill of ownership. The bones show. If you stop to think, there's a lesson to be gleaned from the fading. But you don't stop to think. Each time is the first time. Each time is the last time. Why*

is this? New possessions warm the cockles of your flaccid heart.
(Silence)

Chinese Man: Behind the gates of the wealthy
                      Food lies rotting and wasted
                      Outside the gate it's the poor
                      Who lie freezing to death. (Tu Fu)

Consumer: Inside there is a surprise: a tiny wad of
bubble wrap tied with an inch of plastic tape. I pick it up and feel it.
There's something inside. Porcelain figure of a man in Arab dress.
He is kneeling, and his hands are up behind his head. Sun and
Moon, it's Bin Ladin!
(Silence)

Lifeboatman: Hope had grown gray hairs,
                      Hope had mourning on,
                      Trenched with tears, carved with cares,
                      Hope was twelve hours gone;
                      And frightful a nightfall folded rueful a day
                      Nor rescue, only rocket & light ship, shone,
                      And lives at last were washing away:
                      To the shrouds they took, — they shook in
the hurling & horrible airs -
                      (Hopkins)

(Wind blowing sand devils)

Consumer: I place Bin Ladin on the dun desert of the piano top in
front of the box. No hiding place. The very place! *People will pass
the piano and admire your box. Your pleasure will be in the cheapness
of the item. OK, it also shows what an odd-ball you are, but there's
pleasure there too. You and your stuff! You're a lower case Medici, aren't
you?*

                      He is so small, Bin Ladin, below the

121

threatening eagle bestriding the globe. He looks like some abject novice confessing faults. Dressed all in white, a tiny brown face, a scratch of black for beard; he is a colourless dot on the deserted piano-top before the browns, blues, and yellows of the worldbox and the imperious eagle.

(Silence)

Lancastrian Woman: From the journal of George Fox: 'From Robert Widder's I went to see Justice West. Richard Hubberborne went with me. We rid up the Sands where never no man rid before, a very dangerous place, and swimmed over the water, not knowing the way or the danger of the Sands, and came to West's house. And when we were come in, he said to us, 'Did you not see two men riding over the Sands? I shall have red clothes anon, for I am the coroner; they cannot escape drowning!' And we told him we were the men; and he was astonished at it and wondered how we escaped drowning. And then the priests and professors raised a report and a slander upon me that neither water could drown me nore could they draw blood of me, and that surely I was a witch!'

Entrepreneur: China's GDP in 2003 was estimated at $1.3 trillion. It has grown 8% per year over the last three years.

Consumer: Who made this thing? Who told the people who made this thing to make it? What was going on in the head of the person who told the people to make it? What was going on in the heads of the people who made it as they made it? Where did the clay come from? Where the paint? What did the factory look like? How much did the factory owner receive for the item? How much did the workers receive? Is Bin Ladin's presence in the 99 Cent Store an indication that something went wrong? If so, what? Chinese worker made the box, and made a wonderful job of it too. And more questions follow. More and more, thick and fast, like pottery to be worked on as it passes along an assembly-line, always a little too speedy for comfort. Did the producers earn enough to sustain their lives? Were they happy? What were their dreams?

Chinese Man (stern):   Today we produce for export globe box for America. You ten sit. Here. Now we practice with unfired model. You, Number 1: Fit metal band and clasp. You. Outline continents of world. So. You. Paint ocean with blue. You. Continents in brown and Eagle wings. You. Eagle body black. You. Little Girl. Place on tray for firing. Two hundred each tray. Fifty tray fill oven. They glaze 700 degree C. While glazing, you, you, you... take figure. Fine brush paint black. Here. Here. Here. Fire. You go home when all firing finished.

(Silence)

Consumer: I wonder if *the idea* is Chinese, as well as the work. Perhaps there is a catalogue of Chinese porcelain boxes, showing the whole range. And there is a vast range. I see only the casualties: a Leaning Tower of Pisa (good for a roll of Quarters), an eggplant, two art deco hotels on a Florida strip, A Victorian 'painted lady' house (good for pills), a fire hydrant, a lighthouse, a gazebo, an ant-eater nosing around an ant hill, a yellow taxi (good for nothing)…on and on. No, I think there was an American behind the boxes. What sort of American? Hard to say. Did the designer – ideas person – write down what s/he wanted? What then? Were the demands translated into Cantonese or Mandarin? At what stage? Perhaps in the Lower East Side the designer communicated his idea to a Chinese-American entrepreneur who translated the order and emailed it to the Chinese factory. A mock-up was made, a digital photo taken and sent to New York. 'Fine. Make five thousand! (or five million?). Pack in tissue, box and ship to Port Elizabeth.' Or Liverpool.

(Silence)

Lancastrian woman: Morecambe Bay at low tide is a vast flat area of sand, quicksand, gullies, banks and cockle beds reaching out into The Irish Sea. The tide comes in at great speed, faster than most men can run.

Consumer: In the 99 Cent Store I feel humbled, like a caveman with a weak wrist, a lower case omega male who can't do anything useful in a can-do world. I can't fix a fuse, can hardly change a light bulb. What good am I?

Chinese Man: As we walked away from the shore, I saw a huge seagull. It had a cockle in its bill. I watched, and the gull flew high into the air, then dropped the cockle on some rock. I nudged my companion to watch. The gulls in China do the same thing. They seek to break the cockle shell. They must fly high and drop the cockle many times before they can pull out the flesh, and satisfy hunger. I told the man how good it was to see that birds so far away from China shared something in common. He shrugged and walked away from me. I watched the seagull seize the cockle and rise up again. It was not going to be defeated. I thought to myself, 'I too can be like the seagull.' But that was then…

Lancastrian Woman: Everyone made mistakes that night. The Chinese who were picking cockles on a freezing night in February; the gang-masters who took the Chinese to Morecambe Bay but did not check on the tides or bother to learn the dangers; the coastguard and the lifeboatmen; the people walking their dogs by the Bay; God, taking one of His naps…

Consumer: For me, it all started years ago. I was living in Powys, that part of Wales farthest from the sea, drained by the rivers Wye and Severn. It's an area of faded towns, hard-pressed hill farmers and fit retirees on the run from London and Birmingham. Not much in the way of excitement…until, that is, Harry Tuffin opened his

Pound Shop.

(Silence)

Chinese Man: Lord, Lord! Methought, what pain it was to drown!

What dreadful roar of water in mine ears!

What ugly sights of death within mine eyes!

(Shakespeare)

(Silence)

Consumer: News spread that all sorts of things that cost a fortune at posh Prince and Pugh of Knighton could be picked up for peanuts at the Pound Shop. It was an answer to prayer. Hammers, wrenches, sets of Allen keys, screwdrivers, drill-bits, crockery, cutlery, stationery… they were all there, all a pound, and we pounced on them. But always along those affordable aisles were the things, purely decorative, that would pleasure a farmer's wife in need of a treat to perk up a window sill or a Welsh Dresser and have the farmer asking – when he got round to noticing – 'But what's it good for, Love? We don't need it.'

Lancastrian Woman: The tide was doubly treacherous that Thursday night. Heavy rainfall on North-West England caused rivers to empty into Morecambe Bay at an unprecedented rate. The water filled in gullies, closing up escape routes. The fresh water met an incoming tide whipped up by a south-westerly gale. The Chinese felt the water lapping, icy, around them. They ran. But so far from home, where do you run? Having run halfway across the world to a cold and isolated place, where a sea that was not their sea made them cry out in a language that sounded to the locals like the crying of gulls.

(Silence)

Chinese Man: And for a winding sheet a wave,

I had, and all the ocean for my grave. (Dryden)

(Silence)

Welsh Farmer's Wife: A painted bottle, I'd bought, along with dog chews and a dozen dish-scouring sponges. I just took a shine to it. No use, I suppose. But the sun was shining through them and those bottles felt like Chapel. I looked and looked without touching. I could hear Dai moaning in my head already, but I beat him back. I wanted the lot, tell you the truth. Leaves and grapes and Chinese writing and birds and clouds. All so very beautiful. I saw the one I liked best and made a grab for it. I brought it home and gave it pride of place on the dresser. Wouldn't be parted from it.

Lifeboatman: "We then found one body followed by a patch of nine. It was very distressing but we were doing the job we were trained to do. It is the worst tragedy I have come across in my time with the RNLI. They didn't have any safety gear and some of them were naked because they had taken their clothes off to help them swim. The water was not much above freezing, the wind blowing a Force 6, and the water had been moving at four or five knots. I would guess after half an hour in these conditions you would be in big trouble."

Consumer: A light-emiting diode flashlamp…can be seen a mile away (99 cents). A hand-painted mug with 'I love you, Grandpa' scrawled on it in imitation of a child's hand. Did the painter know what she was writing, or did she work from an e mailed example? (99 cents).

Entrepreneur: China is ranked Number 2 in the world in terms of purchasing power.

Lancastrian Woman: Too late for most, someone saw the lights from the drowning sands. The Lifeboat was called. Helicopters took off from Wales. A lifeboatman was to say he had never seen anything like it.

Chinese Man: Heaven took my wife. Now it
                       Has also taken my son.
                       My eyes are not allowed a
                       Dry season. It is too much
                       For my heart. I long for death.
                       When the rain falls and enters
                       The earth, when a pearl drops into
                       The depths of the sea, you can
                       Dive in the sea and find the
                       Pearl, you can dig in the earth
                       And find the water. But no one
                       Has ever come back from the
                       Underground Springs. Once gone, life
                       Is over for good. My chest
                       Tightens against me. I have
                       No one to turn to. Nothing,
                       Not even a shadow in a mirror.
                       (Mei Yao Ch'en)

Consumer: A compass immersed in spirit. It hangs from a fob
and chain like a pocket-watch ($7.99); An alarm whistle on a key
ring ($1.99); A picnic hamper in wicker with first aid kit ($9.99); A
lighthouse made of stained glass that has a nightlight inside
($12.99); pottery balls hand-painted with Chinese calligraphy (1
dollar)…

(Chinese ceremonial bells)

Consumer: Step over to The Christmas Tree Shop and browse
about. Here there is no flat price. The frisson to the pocket comes
from the fact that everything is so much cheaper than you thought.
The slogan of the store is, 'Don't you just love a bargain?' And, of
course, we do…

127

A wooden pizza board ($4.99), a canvas laundry duffel ($3.99), a painted window showing a view ($4.99), a bamboo CD rack ($19.99), windchimes ($6.99), sparkling bunny statue ($3.99), bunny emerging from eggshell ($4.99), Ship's Wheel ($19.99), talking picture frame ($6.99), stained glass lantern ($6.99), stained glass church candle-holder ($6.99), stained glass shamrock in green ($2.99), roadside emergency kit ($9.95), Poloroid lightbulbs six count ($1.69), insulated birdbox ($3.99), dog treat hamburger in two-tone brown felt, ($1.99), large canvas shopping bags ($3.99), Valentine Heart-Shaped cushion in blood-red ($2.99)…

I could make this Litany to Affordable Household Gods go on all week. I suppose only three or four of the items listed are of any use. People do not need what they buy at the Christmas Tree Shop. The people who pile their trollies high are being deeply pleasured by their purchases. They have saved hundreds of dollars by spending a hundred at this store. This may be losers' logic but, hey, losers deserve a chance to win, too. Masters of the Universe we may not be; but we can master the bargains at The Christmas Tree Shop.

Who pays, then? Ah, there's the rub. Those billions of tiny figures over the horizon (so small they make my porcelain Bin Ladin seem huge) without character traits, nerve endings or health insurance; a race – almost a species – apart. Their labour keeps us in the 'Darling' and the 'Sweet' and the 'Can't Live Without'. But it is the cheapness of their labour that keeps the product 'cheap'. Bump it up in price and it loses most of its attraction. Sell it for what it is worth and dry the tears shed for its production, or at least salve the eye-strain of the put-upon creators, and the uselessness of the item becomes apparent. An expensive impulse buy becomes hard to justify on any list of priorities to do with practicalities.

(Kathleen Ferrier: 'Blow The Wind Southerly.')

Old Merseyside Woman: I hope it was quick for the poor souls. Like I've been praying most of my life that it was quick for my Harold. He died on The Thetis in 1939. Brand new submarine fresh out of Cammell Lairds in Birkenhead, on sea trials out in the Irish sea. And off it goes and down it goes, just like it was supposed to. But it never comes back up. I hope it was quick. Me and Harold were newly-weds. I hadn't got used to the feel of the ring - or the rest - when he was taken down. Now I watch the sea from my flat. I'm stuck inside, just as Harold was stuck in The Thetis, but I have this lovely view of sea, you see. When I heard the news headlines that Thursday night, they just said, 'The North-West' and I thought it was here. I thought it was here, and I'd missed it. It could have been here. People pick cockles on the Dee and Mersey. I was relieved to hear that I hadn't missed it… There's a great long bank that pushes out to the west here. It's part of my view. I watch it. You've got to watch it. People can be so daft. Winter and summer you see them heading out and you know from the time they're doing it they haven't got a clue. I know the tides here. I know because I study. It's about six hours in and six hours out. But it's not as simple as that. Harold told me about the Rule of Twelfths, and I've not forgotten. I've saved a good few since I started mounting watch from the flat window. Not that they thank me or anything. But I get a hamper from the chaps at the Lifeboats. 'To Matron' – it's a term of endearment. I hope. I watch the banks like a hawk, like those old matrons used to watch the hospital wards. Anyway…The Rule of Twelfths…

(gulls, sea sounds, distant barrel-organ)

Harold: When the tide is coming in, Love, it doesn't come in evenly. Oh, no. Too clever for that. After low tide, the first hour of flood is one-twelfth of volume. So progress is slow. You hardly notice it. The second hour is two-twelfths. Still on the slow side. But the third and fourth hour is three-twelfths, and that's fast. That's the time when most of the sand hereabouts will be covered, when the gullies fill in. You've got to watch the third and fourth hour. Fifth Hour, it slows down to two-twelfths again. And the sixth hour, it's one-twelfth. But watch out for that third and fourth hour…

<u>(Blow the Wind Southerly)</u>

<u>Old Merseyside Woman:</u>   And that's what I do. I don't worry much about people far out on the bank for the first hour or hour and a half of flood tide. But if they're still heading out to sea after that I ring the coastguard. Don't care if they think I'm being daft. Those poor people. Those poor, poor people! I hope it was quick.

<u>(Silence)</u>

<u>Entrepreneur:</u> Ten years ago hundreds of millions of middle-class Chinese had the desire for goods. Now they have the means. By 2007 China is expected to have 500 million mobile phone users. And the rest? The 'huddled masses', you mean? At the end of the day, it's a necessary stage of development the Chinese are going through. Like the workers of Birmingham and Manchester during the Industrial Revolution, the Japanese post-war, China must do the necessary to springboard to the next stage of development. Then they will pass the torch to light the sweatshop for…where? Africa, perhaps. Or back to the West. The global village is a level playing field. At the end of the day, everyone gets their place in the sun. The what? 'The unacceptable face of capitalism'? I don't know what you mean. It is not a phrase I am familiar with.

<u>Lancastrian Woman:</u> One man stopped cockling because he had a headache. He was resting on higher ground when his wife and children were swept out to sea.

<u>Consumer:</u>   Maybe I should protest to the good folks at The

Christmas Tree Shop and the 99 Cents Store, to every owner of every shop. But if cheapness is what shifts this stuff, then increasing the costs of production might stop the trade. We might be no worse off, but what happens to the army of anons half a world away?

Pundit: I think a start to balancing value and values might be made by applauding the cunning millions of hands that produce our boxes, stained glass objects, painted bottles and glittery bunnies emerging from eggs. Applaud them for their workmanship, their industriousness and the stories the objects tell us. Bring the people to life, instead of covering them up as if there were something shameful going on. Tom of Maine, who has made a nice little earner from ethical toothpaste; he writes to me as 'Dear Friend' on his toothpaste box. Might not the talented anons borrow a leaf out of Tom's book? A couple of sentences of biography might add immeasurably to the meaning of their production. 'The box with the eagle? Yes, it was made by Fu Wat Tsu in Bo Xian. She lives with her husband, her little boy and in-laws in a small flat close to the International Economic Zone. Fu Wat Tsu enjoys her work. Her ambition is to own a fridge and visit the Grand Canyon with her family…

Lifeboatman: "At 2 a.m on Friday it was very quiet and I couldn't hear any shouting. We were being as quiet as possible in case anyone called for help."

Pundit: I wonder if Fu Wat Tsu and her billion friends find themselves musing about the tastes of the people far away who buy what their genie lets out of the bottle. The world knows us, knows our strengths and our legion little weaknesses. It really is time we got to know the people over the horizon who contribute so much to our 'Global Village'. Perhaps it's harder to diddle, even bomb, people we know.

Lancastrian Woman: George Fox, founder of The Quakers, crossed Morecambe Bay, and nearly drowned. Something spared him, but Fox shook his head at Folly that Thursday night.

(A Fan-Whir)

Fu Wat Tsu: The things fly by so fast. I add the color to one and it is gone. I wonder where it will go. Into boxes. Into ships. Across the world. The destiny of these things is so much more promising than my own. My neighbour's husband has arrived in Britain. He arrived in a box, like the figures. Now he is sending money home to his family. He picks shellfish.

(High Wind. Water lapping)

Chinese Cockler: I pick cockles. I think of Fu Wat Tsu and the others. They labour in the factory. Here the cockles I pick and put in the basket fill stomachs back home. I am cold here. I am lonely too. But I keep my mind on the family there. Dig. Bend. Scrabble. Pick. Throw. Dig. Bend. Scrabble. Pick. Throw. Cold water leaks through the gloves – from China. The water comes through the boots – from China. The wind pushes through my raincoat. Dig. Bend. Scrabble. Pick. Throw. I think of them. I think of them. I think I am the most fortunate. I think. Dig. Bend. Scrabble. Pick. Throw. I think of them as the conveyor belt passed so fast. The product disappears into boxes…dig, bend, scrabble, pick…and they say to themselves, 'Take me with you! Let me earn the money to buy these things! Give me time to play with them!' Dig. Bend. Scrabble. Pick. Throw.   I live with many others in Kensington. That's in Liverpool. I know from my England guidebook that there is Kensington in London. Museum of Natural History is in Kensington, London. But I do not think my Kensington is like the one in London. The boss says we must keep a low profile. I keep a low profile. Dig. Bend. Scrabble. Pick. Throw. I look down at my feet in Kensington. I do not look about me. I am afraid of what I shall see.

(Silence)

Lifeboatman: The Golden rules are summarised as follows:

> Always tell someone exactly where you are going and what time you will be back;
> Always know the weather forecast and tide times;
> Be aware of how quickly the tide comes in;
> Have several types of communication.

Lancastrian Woman: Father-of-two Guo Binlong used his mobile phone to say goodbye to his wife in China. He said, 'The water is up to my chest. The bosses got the time wrong. I can't get back in time.'

Chinese woman:

> Separation by death must finally be choked down,
> But separation in life is a long anguish,
> Chiang-nan is a pestilential land;
> No word from you there in exile.
> You have been in my dreams, old friend,
> As if knowing how much I love you.
> Caught in a net,
> How is it you still have wings?
> I fear you are no longer mortal;
> The distance to here is enormous.
> When your spirit came, the maples were green;
> When it went, the passes were black.
> The setting moon spills light on the rafters;

133

For a moment I think it's your face.

The waters are deep, the waves wide;

Don't let the river gods take you. (Tu Fu)

(Silence)

Consumer: You wonder about these people's dreams. Suspect they want a chicken in their pot, a Mercedes in their garage. Suspect most cannot have what they want. But you're kept going by a host of life-support systems way beyond his deservings... or wit to understand...

Lifeboatman: Let a relative or friend know where you are going and what time you will be back...

(Silence)

Chinese Man: How long can one man's lifetime last?

In the end we return to formlessness.

I think of you waiting to die.

A thousand things cause me distress –

Your kind old mother still alive.

Your only daughter only ten.

In the vast chilly wilderness

I hear the sounds of weeping men.

Clouds float into a great espanse.

Birds fly but do not sing in flight.

How lonely are the travellers.

Even the sun shines cold and white.

Alas, when you still lived, and asked

To study non-birth with me,

My exhortations were delayed –

And so the end came, fruitlessly.

All your old friends have brought you gifts

But for your life these too are late.

I've failed you in more ways than one.

Weeping, I walk back to my gate. (Wang Wei)

(Silence)

Lancastrian Woman: Twenty-three cocklers died that night. (Silence) Morecamble Bay, famous for George Fox and ferocious tides which wait for no man...

Rest In Warmth and Peace, unconsidered strangers, Drowned Darlings. Forgive us if you can our unexamined lives and the world we have made, and let encroach around us all, like a cold and indifferent tide.

(Silence.)

(Waves breaking. The lifeboatman leads his crew in the following:)

Helmsman:	Blest be the boat.
Crew:	God the Father bless her.
Helmsman:	Blest be the boat.
Crew:	God the Son bless her.
Helmsman:	Blest be the boat.
Crew:	God the Spirit bless her.
All:	God the Father,
	God the Son,
	God the Spirit,
	Bless the boat.
Helmsman:	What can befall you
	And God the Father with you?
Crew:	No harm can befall us.
Helmsman:	What can befall you
	And God the Son with you?
Crew:	No harm can befall us.
Helmsman:	What can befall you
	And God the Spirit with you?

<u>Crew</u>:	No harm can befall us.
<u>All</u>:	God the Father,
	God the Son,
	God the Spirit,
	With us eternally.
<u>Helmsman</u>:	What can cause you anxiety
	And the God of the elements over you?
<u>Crew</u>:	No anxiety can be ours.
<u>Helmsman</u>:	What can cause you anxiety
	And the Spirit of the elements over you?
<u>Crew</u>:	No anxiety can be ours.
<u>All</u>:	The God of the elements,
	The King of the elements,
	The Spirit of the elements,
	Close over us,
	Ever eternally.
	(Anonymous: From <u>Carmina Gadelica</u>)

DARKNESS AT THE END OF EVERYTHING

On a coach returning to Heartsease from a cultural day out in London organised by the Llanianto Wells Women's Institute, Hilda Widdowson had her great idea that was to revolutionise British Art.

'Beyond Sensation' at the Royal Academy had been good fun on the whole. It gave the women many opportunities for much merriment as they wandered from one exhibit to another. A configuration of fluff on a plinth inspired Mrs Pugh-George of Dolassey Farm to shout across the gallery in her high-pitched voice - as if across the bleating farmyard at home - 'I should've brought the dust out of my Dyson. That says it all really.'

Mrs Thomas from the Heartsease post office nodded and shook her head. 'How are you getting on with your Dyson? I ask because Mrs Shepherd from up Cwm-y-Gerwyn got one for her Owen's asthma and says it sucks like a lamb on the level but loses its puff on the stairs.'

'Never been bettered,' said Mrs Pugh-George.

'That's all right then,' said Mrs Thomas.

Mrs Thomas filed the consoling information away to impart to Mrs Shepherd who, due to a long-standing appointment at the organic slaughter house in Cwm Dolau, had been unable to make the trip.

Hilda looked at the mounted fluff on its posh plinth. It stated, 'Contents of an Electrolux Vacuum cleaner bag collected on the morning after my partner left me.'

Hilda pursed her lips. Not surprised he left you, letting the place get so mucky.

The women passed on, walking around a group of manikins whose parts had been put on askew.

'We had one but the wheel fell off,' said Mrs Pugh-George.

'Look at him,' said Mrs Thomas, 'I didn't know men had them there. Least they didn't last time I looked. His little head is facing the wrong way, too.'

'And people pay good money for all this, do they?' Hilda asked rhetorically.

'They do. Leastways that's what the brochure says,' said Mrs Pugh-George. 'Some tycoon who was keen on Maggie Thatcher scoffed the lot.' She surveyed the brochure with suspicion. What was she going to do with it? She couldn't take it home. Dad would have a fit. She resolved to leave it in the bin at the bus station. Well wrapped up.

They trooped out of the exhibition, crossed the road for a visit to Fortnum and Mason's, where they spent a happy, shocked hour comparing Fortnum's prices with those of the Llanianto Wells' KwikSave.

'I don't call that art even if they do,' Hilda said to Mrs Thomas as Mrs Thomas noted that a slither of game pie cost twice what she paid for a No Frills family-size steak and onion pie - enough to feed a family - at KwikSave.

'It's a swizz. That's what it is... Art, a cup of tea, a slice of pie. A big swizz. That's London for you,' said Mrs Thomas.

'What irritates me,' Hilda said, thinking of the exhibition, 'There was nothing beautiful. No colour. Nothing that cheers me up. Disgusting.'

'You never said a truer word,' Mrs Thomas said. 'Anyone could do what they did. If you want my opinion it was their teachers who was to blame. They'd come up to the teacher with some horrid daub they'd done when they should have been learning their tables and consigning the ten commandments to memory, and she'd say, 'That's really lovely, Damian.' And Damian believed it and grew up believing it and...'

'You never said a truer word,' Hilda interrupted. 'There's such a thing as spoiling.'

$

Those wise words of Mrs Thomas kept coming back to Hilda as she tried to avoid her reflection in the dark window of the coach on the way home. What, she wondered, had lifted all the rubbish she'd seen that day and made it valuable? Looking around at her snoozing friends, she thought of the produce, the cunning craft, that issued from those heads, hearts and hands each week and loaded down the W. I. table, set up out of the wind behind Somerfields. Give one of Mrs Pugh-George's jam sponges a spin and you could turn it into art. Course, it might go off, but if you mounted it in a tank of formaldehyde or marmalade and gave it a clever title like 'Even the Sweetest Get Cut Up', it qualified as artistic. Then, of course, there was all the knitting and crochet work...the blankets made of bits and bobs that warmed Ruanda and Romania, the wild designs, the cunning craft, of toilet roll and tissue box covers and tea cosies. Tea cosies! A genre all on their ownsome! Why not? Why not exhibit their craft and give it a spin to make it art?

Because nobody'd believe it, that's why! Hilda told herself.

Arriving home, she made a cup of tea and switched on the television. Some ginks were having a discussion on BBC 2, hosted by a young man everyone called Timmy. Hilda sat up.

$

She hardly slept that night. Tossing and turning, she willed eight to come when Mrs Thomas would open Heartsease's post office.

Hilda went in, mouth primed, safety-catch in her purse, only to find that Mrs Shepherd had beaten her to it.

'I talked about your Dyson to Mrs Pugh-George,' Mrs Thomas was saying. 'She said that her Dyson is a treasure. Sucks like nothing else can.'

'But she lives in a bungalow,' said Mrs Shepherd.

'What difference does that make?'

'No stairs,' said Mrs Shepherd. 'Like I say, the Dyson only lets itself down on the stairs. It's great on the flat.'

'I hear they have no bags,' Hilda said. 'But what's wrong with bags is what I'd like to know? I'm never seen out without one myself. Wouldn't feel dressed. And another thing...the other day I saw this bottle of window-cleaner and it said, 'Contains vinegar.' Then I pick up another and it says 'Guaranteed Vinegar Free.' What's all that about?'

Mrs Shepherd looked at Mrs Thomas. 'There's no such thing as progress,' said Mrs Thomas, 'when all's said and done.'

'I've had an idea,' said Hilda Widdowson.

Mrs Thomas and Mrs Shepherd looked at Hilda.

'Take the weight off your feet,' said Mrs Thomas, as she could not think of anything else to say. It was not like Hilda to have an idea. At least not one without 'shrewd' prefixing it.

'I'll stand, if you don't mind,' Hilda said. 'The best ideas are always those you have when standing up.'

Mrs Shepherd and Mrs Thomas nodded.

'Ideas,' said Hilda, 'are often the connection of two thoughts. Have you noticed?' She looked at Mrs Shepherd, who had started fiddling with her family allowance book. 'Think of an idea as the meeting of two streams. One might trickle down from London, the other from a late-night television programme of the sort that makes people worry about the future of civilisation as we thought we knew it. But when they come together a great churning takes place...'

'Yes?' said Mrs Thomas.

'Stream one in my case,' continued Hilda, 'was the London exhibition that was rotten to the core and yet packing them in. Stream two was this woman with, if I am not very much mistaken, hennaed hair, going on to a yobbo called Timmy about the importance of 'attitude' and 'in your face' and 'bad publicity is the best' - I've remembered because I wrote it down. It's always wise to write things down if you want my opinion.'

'Yes?' repeated Mrs Thomas.

'The trouble with the W.I. stall is that we're all too nice. Our cakes are just nice cakes. Our jams and preserves are nice jams and preserves.. Our crochet work is just nice crochet work. We knit nice tea cosies...'

'I don't get you,' said Mrs Shepherd, 'and I'm in a bit of a hurry.'

'This won't take long,' Hilda said. 'We've got to add value if we're going to really make some serious money. We've got to add mystery. The trouble with the WI, if you want my opinion, is that we haven't been rough enough. It's a jungle out there and if you want to make an impression you've got to...got to make an impression.'

'This doesn't sound like you,' observed Mrs Thomas, though it did a bit.

'I'm starting a movement,' said Hilda. 'It's to be called TWAWI.'

Both Mrs Thomas and Mrs Shepherd looked at Hilda

blankly.

'TWAWI?' said Mrs Thomas.

'It stands for 'The With Attitude Women's Institute',' said Hilda Widdowson.

$

Hilda enlisted the aid of her precocious niece, Lark, in order to mount TWAWI's first ground-breaking exhibition at the Methodist Hall at Howey. Lark, though only sixteen, was already in the middle of her second year at Yale College (Wrexham Campus), where she was following a degree in Media Studies and Creative Writing.

Lark pronounced Hilda's idea 'formidable' and set about helping Hilda give a suitably attention-grabbing spin to the exhibits. It was Lark who thought up the name of the exhibition and alerted the media to the event.

A reporter from the Mid-Wales Journal called Gareth entered the bible-black hall, read the luminous name, Darkness At The End of Everything and followed, with the aid of a candle and tiny light-emiting diodes set into the floor, a route that took him through it. His candle-light spangled a sponge cake set on a pile of coal. Icing sugar sparkled icily; the coal shone moorishly. The disembodied high-pitched voice of Mrs Pugh-George, wrapped around a tape-loop, repeated, 'Have another slice! Dai's down the pit! What was that! An explosion? Have another slice! Dai's down the pit! What was that...' only stopping when Gareth passed broodily on to the next exhibit. His candle caught an array of knitted tea-cosies in every colour of the rainbow. Strobe lights lit them from below. The tea cosies formed the words, 'ONE FOR THE POT. BEFORE NIGHT FALLS'. Gareth gasped. Every colour he had ever seen in his life was in those tea-cosies. Familiar objects, certainly, but... but here they spoke of domestic magic, miracles of handiwork and imagination. They were woven testimonials of life lived to the full by the soon-to-go and the gone-before. His eyes were opening for the first time to the everyday mystery of creation. He felt his own jumper. Was that not in some deep sense true art? Someone had planned the pleasing patterns, some god-like cunning had crafted the furry filaments from a lamb's back into...into...greatness.

Gareth walked on with his candle. He felt as though he was tip-toeing around a church where miracles were taking place. Tears fell down his face and he had to wipe his eyes to take in the pyramids of knitted, crocheted, chiffoned, ribboned and stitched toilet-roll covers pouring like lemmings over a dark shelf into nothingness - where Lark stood darker than the dark starting them on their journey back for another brief go on the cosmic conveyor belt of life. A single string of laser light illuminated each toilet-roll cover for a split second. He saw a Regency lady in crinoline and powdered wig. For a moment she flashed between two areas of blackness, then she fell back into the dark. He heard a high cystern toilet flush. 'The Horror! The Horror!' Gareth exclaimed.

Gareth reeled out of TWAWI's Darkness At The End of Everything exhibition. When he had composed himself he rang his friend at BBC Wales. She visited, reeled out of the Methodist chapel O-My-Goding, bought a scarlet swiss-roll with purple icing, decorated with Monopoly money (Entitled: 'Numbered Bank Account', £350.97p.)... and rang London.

$

A month later Hilda Widdowson, Hilda's Lark, Mrs Pugh-George, Mrs Shepherd and Mrs Thomas were guests of honour on the very same BBC 2 show that had given Hilda her great idea.

Timmy asked if a tea-cosy could ever be art.

'You talking to me?' Hilda asked him belligerently.

'I was, actually,' Timmy said. 'I mean, it's peculiar that people are willing to pay vast amounts for tea-cosies that a few weeks ago you could've bought for a quid in a charity shop.'

'There's art in tea-cosies,' Hilda said. 'We at TWAWI have just opened your eyes to it.'

'I can't see it myself,' said Timmy.

Hilda made a loud aside to Mrs Thomas, 'He's a rude little tyke, that Timmy, don't you think so, Mrs Thomas?'

Mrs Thomas nodded sagely. 'There's none so blind as them as will not see,'

Timmy shuffled his script, then dropped some of it.

'Untidy, too,' said Hilda.

'What he must've put his poor mother through!' said Mrs Pugh-George.

'I put it to you that you are taking the public for a ride with all this kitsch masquerading as art!' said Timmy, following the dictates of conscience whispered into his ear-piece from the control-room.

'Will you hit him, or shall I?' Hilda asked Mrs Thomas.

'You hit him first, Hilda. Then I'll hit him if he doesn't stay hit,' said Mrs Thomas.

Hilda lashed out with a green felt snake draught excluder filled with pinto beans (entitled: Death Like a Draught Under the Door; price £11,250.99 p.) and already purchased by a pension fund. She scored a direct hit on Timmy's shoulder. He beat a retreat as Hilda, Lark, Mrs Shepherd, Mrs Thomas and Mrs Pugh-George chased him... and the mesmeric, snake-eyes of cameras missed not a trick.

$

A year later came TWAWI's definitive show at the Royal Academy. Hilda followed the reverend crowds about the great halls, shouting 'Keep your grubby hands off the merchandise!' and 'If you break it, it's yours!' and, 'Don't you dare breathe on my sponge!'

The media, together with students of the history of art, all dutifully wrote down Hilda's every utterance. Fresh air had been breathed into British Art. People rummaged in drawers for long-discarded tea-cosies, crocheted toilet-roll covers, doillies... they went back to baking their own sponge cakes. They gave them pride of place in their homes, insured them against theft, suddenly seeing them as beautiful, meaningful... precious.

Which, of course - in their way, perhaps in more ways than most of us could ever have imagined before that national treasure, Hilda Widdowson, opened our eyes - they are.

GOLDEN RETRIEVER

3:17 p.m. on a Tuesday in March. Ralph wants off Interstate 95. He craves the sanity of the car-only Merritt Parkway, but has missed the exit.

He drives over the stain. It is getting on - something of an old acquaintance the stain is. In spite of time, still enough substance left to change the tone of tyre hiss for a tick - and send a shiver through him.

What have I come to? Ralph thinks. What?

He's approaching a bridge over the Interstate. A man is standing on the bridge, looking down at him. He might be about to drop a brick, a bag of nails, himself... onto the road below. Ralph holds his breath. Then he is past the bridge unharmed and the head of the watcher shrinks in his mirror, harmless as history.

Ralph has left all that back in The City and is heading for the country to lick his wounds. But this journey on I 95 - the panicy procession of vehicles, the stain, the watcher on the bridge - have set in train old thoughts of the auto-nation of which he is a part. This Is The Way We Live Now. It Depends Upon The Internal Combustion Engine And The Oil That Fuels It. Take Away Oil This Civilization Screams To A Halt. And Woe Will Be Me.

Woe. Wow. He says a prayer for Julie, which turns into a plea to Julie.

Ahead is their cabin in the woods. It will be just as he and Julie left it. Bed unmade. Stained wine glasses on the pine table. Boris the gay black bear will have played havoc with the garden furniture, demolished one more bird table, gobbled up the tulip bulbs.

And Ralph thinks of the stain on the wine glasses, the stain on I 95, the stain back in The City, with Julie embedded in everything. He knows where she is but is finally realising she is too lost to be found. He tears up; he soldiers on.

*

Mary Lyons of West Haven runs over the stain on her way home from a check-up at Norwalk hospital. A retired geography teacher, she thinks of the outline of Ireland when she sees it. She glances it in the rear-view mirror before the black blur is taken under the tyres of a Mack truck.

Mary remembers a boy she once had in her class. He could draw maps free-hand. What was his name? Christian something. 'Why, Christian, what talent you have!' she'd say. And she'd meant it too. When Christian drew North America, he'd started with Florida and without hesitation or erasure penned the whole coastline, even the Great Lakes, closing the continent back at Key West with nothing missing or out of scale. Whatever became of Christian? Would he know or care what life had in store for his geography teacher? It did not look good. 'It looks good. I can beat this.' Mary repeats the affirmation. And the stain and Christian Whatsisname fall from the nest of her brain.

*

'What was that?' the man, Jack, driving a Jeep Cherokee, says out loud to himself.

'Some goop. I remember it from last week,' the woman, his wife, Carol, says. She sits next to Jack, as England sits next to Ireland, as Greek and Turkish Cyprus are crankily joined at the hip. Only when the words are out does she remember.

'Last week? But you were in Bar Harbor all last week,' Jack says.

'Must have been week before.'

The tape is playing The First Time Ever I saw... Jack flicks the volume to zero. 'Last week is what you said.'

'Week before is what I meant.'

'OK,' Jack says, 'have it your way.' He flicks the volume back up. And the moon and the stars were the gift you gave...

Carol reads a sign. Let 'em Work. Let 'em Live. Sounds reasonable enough. Jack sounds reasonable enough. Just one more week, she thinks. Just one more, and I'm out of here.

*

Paula, 75, drives over the stain at 45 in her '69 Beetle. She has been chewing on a dream remembered from the previous night. A deputation of squirrels marched up to her kitchen window. They carried posters: 'Why should birds eat all the seed? Down with the baffle! Fair access for squirrels! Ban all discriminatory bird-feeders! Squirrels have feelings too!' They knocked on the window with their little fists. They flicked their tails and eyed her angrily. Paula had gone to the window and knocked back, but the squirrels did not bounce and scatter. They looked right back at her, hatred in their eyes.

Shall I tell someone? Paula thinks. Maybe I should inform the Adopt A Highway people about that stain. They sure as heck didn't adopt the stain. Still, I should do a lot of things. Paula sees her life stretching behind like a ribbon of road. Shoulds became should haves. And should haves were sad. Like could haves and might haves and if only I had/hadn't. Oh, my! Oh, my! Paula says.

This was the third or fourth time she'd noticed the stain. It was lessening. Every car that passed robbed it of a little bulk, took a shard on stomping treads to Milford or New Haven, The Cape or Canada. Like birds carried seeds away. Like people passed on news. She shakes herself.

Starlings arrived in The New World in 1890 as illegal immigrants. Some German yoyo wanted every breed of bird mentioned in Shakespeare to have a peck at The Big Apple. But see how they have spread countrywide! She clapped her hands to frighten them away from the seed. They looked back at her, cracking corn, spilling seed on the ground, showing no respect and cawing entitlement.

Paula's father had arrived in 1892, and been processed through Ellis Island. They'd held him back a week, citing T.B. He'd lost touch with the rest of the family, who'd been let through. If it hadn't been for Father Houston, his powers of persuasion and his little black notebook reminding him to remind the immigration men of their own pasts...

A woman Paula e-mailed in England wrote that grey squirrels were everywhere there too. One more undesirable American import, the woman had written. Paula sent her a baffle to stop the squirrels reaching the food. She had not heard back. Maybe the woman was baffled by the baffle. Paula wondered about The Marshall Plan sometimes. Was it Lear - or Nixon - who had railed against ingratitude?

That night she would dream that the squirrels carried a poster: 'You are corrupting our English brothers and sisters!' And somewhere in the mad narrative the stain crunched, as it had the first time she had driven over it.

*

Limo? Call this a limo? I don't call a dirty bus with no leg room and grimy windows a limo. Limo prices is what they charge. But what can you do, caught at Kennedy, porous with travel fever, having O.D.ed on clouds from both sides, but wait in the arrivals hall for some guy to shout your number and push you into a trashcan of a limo then charge you fifty bucks plus tip for the privilege when he throws you and your bags off the damned bus at New Haven…?

April feels a tickle in her throat. I'll get something from that recycled air on the plane. They pump it around and around. Every bug on the planet goes around and around. Even a total dumbo of a germ could infect you. That's supposing some sicko didn't open up his file of anthrax or small pox or mad cow or tetanus, and toss it into the soup. April coughs. Maybe I only think I beat the rap. Maybe, in fact, this is slow death. I've been spared the plane plummeting, the weeping passengers, the cell-phone Liebestod, only to come down with some plague. Why do I fly? On ground transportation there is a feeling that you're somehow in control. Not total control, but some. Why, if something happened now and the limo – Limo! – crashed on its side with sparks and smoke, I might make it out. When I get home I'll go straight to bed with a pack of Hall's Menthol candies and The Corrections. That silly guy! Why didn't he open himself to Opra and let her sell his damned book? No more travel for April Zeigen. No more.

*

What had Noam Chomsky said on C-Span? Terrorism is what they do to us. What we do to them the Barbie cheerleaders at Fox call a mission, an heroic enterprise, a crusade.

No, maybe miss that one. How to crash any chance of tenure in one sentence. If there's a wrong way to do it, nobody does it like me…but…Closer to the horizon things get smaller. Trees, buildings, people. Perception and camera-crews trip on the fine line. Across it people become invisible, or miraged into grotesques. Less like people. Hardly people at all with their raggy headgear and queer sanitary arrangements. Shine light and they take on life, but who can be bothered to shine that light? A turn-off. No ratings in it, Dude.

Paul Sutter, on his way to teach an Ethics class in New Haven, feels the stain pass under him. Like those people far away, it barely impinges. That first time it had waved a tail like Pampas Grass. Was it a tail or Pampas Grass? He decides to play a section of the first film of the Apu Trilogy to his group. It will be new to them. He might work it in with the last twenty minutes of Tree of Wooden Clogs in order to establish connections. Connections? Hadn't that been a lengthy series on public television? Some Brit in a white safari suit – flared trousers and disastrous taste in eye-wear – popping up week after week all over the world to tell us how one thing leads to another. Paul has connected The Grapes of Wrath with Dickens, Woody Guthrie, Dylan and, to be up-to-his-minute, Bruce Springsteen. But time is rushing past him and his students know little more of Springsteen than the name and the fame.

I am tired of this commute, Paul tells himself. The fir tree on the mirror nods. It no longer smells of backwoods pine. Time for a change.

*

Above roar of engine, jag of jetstream, the stain does not impact on the empty car-transporter. The driver does not see it either. He is thinking of Bridgeport. There is some great property in Bridgeport. Solid houses. And affordable. Trouble is, taxes are high. Like the people. He blames Giuliani. The bums he'd pushed out of Bulgari's doorway and Grand Central dragged their asses up I. 95 to Bridgeport. Bridgeport was made by P.T. Barnum. A circus. A clowns' town. He'd heard that Boston was over-run too. Boston was a building site. Bridgeport. Why not? A good alarm system and his sleeves rolled up to give an eyeful of his don't-mess-with-me tattoos.

The stars and stripes thwack in stereo against the cab-roof.

*

'So the mother says, 'Ask all the questions you want, Son! If you don't ask questions, you won't learn nothin'!"

Michael O' Donovan, hearing no laughter, glances over at his wife.

'That's where it happened. I don't get it,' she says.

'Well,' Michael says amicably. He is used to Norah's slowness, 'the mother takes her son round the zoo. The kid asks these questions...'How can a snake walk with no legs?' 'What does the camel keep in his hump?'... and the mother doesn't know the answer to any of them. The son is pissed and asks Mom if she minds being asked questions. And Mom replies, 'If you don't ask questions you won't...learn nothin'.' '

Silence from Norah. Michael sighs. 'To get a joke, you need to listen, Norah.'

'Remember I told you about this beautiful dog? Some kind of Lab?' Norah asks.

Michael doesn't remember, but nods.

'That was the place. I don't think I'll ever pass that place without thinking of the dog.'

'Sensitive as a Trojan Featherlight.'

'What's that supposed to mean?'

'I was making a joke.'

'I'm tired of your jokes. You tell me jokes and then I hear them again and again when your cronies come to dinner and then their wives tell them back to me and...I don't get it.'

'I was walking along the top corridor today. With Jack

152

Hemmings. We pass the CEO and he stops for a blow job from the foot-soldiers and asks who the new guy is. I say, straight out, 'Mr. Cabot, this is Jack Hemmings, my immediate inferior!' '

'You got that line from The New Yorker.'

'Tell me about the dog,' Michael says.

'No,' Norah says.

'Have it your way. Did I tell you the one about the parrot who wouldn't stop swearing and his owner put him in the freezer for an hour to teach the parrot a lesson and the parrot comes out shaking with cold and swears on a stack of bibles that he'll never swear again and the owner says that's fine and the parrot asks the guy if he can ask him one question. Sure, the guy says. So the parrot asks, 'What did the turkey do?'

'No,' Norah says. 'I don't get it.'

'Think about it.'

Norah looks out of the window. The traffic is building up. In an hour all this will be grid-lock. If all the people driving on I. 95 between Canada and Florida would give me their gas money for a minute - a second - of driving, I'd be one rich bitch. I could get away from here! What are men for? What are they for?

*

Jason flashes past the stain in the outside lane, cell phone clamped to his ear.

'Jason, I need help, Man…'

Help. They all need help. 'Call before you drink, Dummy!'

'I'm in the slammer, Man.'

'Call me tomorrow.'

Jason, high on tough love and his determination to avoid the stain, whacks the phone shut. Moving to the outside lane is his tribute to the golden retriever who'd run mad between the traffic.

She had seemed about to make it to the verge. Had made it. Then, like a recovering alcoholic in a moment of madness, veered back to booze, opened her throat to perdition by crossing again as cars and trucks slammed on their brakes. The dog had stopped (beautiful and golden and soft and the object of everyone's love and their longing to bury their heads in golden fleece and hug, feed and nurture and bond and share, stroke and soak bread in bacon drippings and pleasure and turn fat), looked at its death heading up, lolled its tongue and sat.

Sat! Sat, like Gandhi, like Buddha, like a pioneer on a pinnacle surveying a milk-and-honey land, like Walt Whitman at a Civil War hospital bedside… before being taken under the tyres of a trailer.

That was what Jason just couldn't get. Granted, retrievers were a serene breed. But to sit and face it like that? Such stoicism was past figuring. He'd dialled 911 and told the police what had happened at Exit 26. The next day, when he saw the mangled gold body on its side, flattened, the left front paw raised, he'd called again. They knew. Of course they knew. But they did nothing.

Somewhere in that slime was part of the answer. A collar and a dog tag. A name and an address. Molly? Biff? Countess Bridgeport? Lady Day? Footnote? Not-A-Chance? Goldie? The stain could be excavated to learn a part of the truth…and the culprit. But it wouldn't happen. Already the gold and the red had turned black and was meld-melting with the road surface.

The cell phone rings. Jason clicks and listens.

'Fine. Glad you called. Your call helps my sobriety. Just hang on in there, Buddy. This is a damned subtle disease. If a day at a time's too much, take it an hour at a time. You don't have to have a drink in the next hour, do you? The next fifteen minutes? Just talk to me, Buddy. You don't have to have one while you're talking to me. You're resting on my shoulder and talking in my ear. You don't want a drink right now.' And then, as Jason listens, he realises that despite the fifteen-year sobriety chip waving on the key fob in front of him, he himself wants a drink right now more than anything else in the whole world.

*

There it is again. He'd seen it. Seen the whole thing. Could've stood up in court and described it. Have watched, palm-sweaty, as the D.A. nodded. Recognised the nod as common ground between them. Madness. The way things were. 'An automobile – white Lexus – stops on hard shoulder. Flashing emergency lights. Man pushes dog out. Dog jumps up on slammed passenger door. Car moves forward. Dog barks, panics, chases car. Car signals left, accelerates into traffic. Dog crosses all three lanes. Makes it! Then runs back. Brakes scream. And the rest you know.'

'Did you get the registration, Officer?'

'Yes.'

'Did you make an arrest?'

'Yes.'

'What's the story?'

*

'Caroline says it was a dog, Mom. Gross.'

'That's enough, Elizabeth.'

'A brown dog, Mom.'

'Well, it's gone now. Stop pulling at your seat belt.'

The Rangerover thurrups over the stain.

'That's it,' Elizabeth says. 'It was a brown dog. That was a brown dog.'

'Oil more like. A brown dog – any dog – they'd have taken

155

away.'

'Remember the skunk outside Borders in Fairfield? They sure didn't take that away.'

'They did too. It took them a day is all.'

Elizabeth considers this. 'Is it true that oil used to be tiny plants and animals?'

'That was a long time ago. Still, I guess so.'

'So while we're driving along here, we're burning up the ghosts of little plants and animals?'

'Elizabeth, I don't know where you get these…'

'It's terrible, Mom! We could be burning up all that remains of one of our ancestors!'

'What did you do at school today, Dear?'

'I made a St Bridget's Cross from pipe-cleaners.' Elizabeth roots in her bag and produces an off-centre grey cross.

'Very pretty.'

Ms Mary May says that if I make the cross with sparkly wires it will be a cool star for Christmas.'

'I guess so.'

'But you know what, Mom?'

'What?'

By way of reply, Elizabeth bends the four ends of the cross and holds it in front of her mom's eyes.

'Not when I'm driving, Elizabeth.'

'It's a swastika, Mom. Ms Mary May says it is likely that the St Bridget Cross and the swastika are related. They come from the same root of reed-weaving. She said that the St Bridget's Cross came from India with the Celts and in India the swastika is a symbol of new life and the wheel of karma.'

'My, my…'

'She made us a 'legs of man' as well, Mom. It's the symbol of an island where they have cats with no tails. I'll make you a legs of man when we get home. We can put it on the fridge.'

'There's no room on the fridge. Come to think of it, you might make a project to have a clear-out of the front of the fridge.'

'Why did that man not bury the bodies, Mom?'

'Which man?'

'The man in The South who owned a funeral home. They found all those bodies of dead people that he didn't bury even though he'd been paid.'

'What do you want to eat tonight?'

Elizabeth says she isn't hungry. She gazes out of the window. Will she die? No, she doesn't think so. But people die all the time. She'd seen people die. She'll get Mom to write a note. 'Dear Ms Mary May: Elizabeth is excused Death due to the fact that she is a sensitive child. Do you know what she asked me just last week? We were on 95. Bridgeport exit…'

'I'd like a big salad in that blue bowl, and fresh fruit for dessert,' Elizabeth says, changing her mind, hedging her bets.

*

'It's an Altoid. Have one.' Ellen offers Susan her tin.

'Too strong. Anyway, I don't like peppermint. You know that,' Susan says.

Ellen notices that her friend is holding the steering wheel at ten of two. She must be tense. 'These aren't peppermint, Hon. They're called Citrus Sours. A new variety. Have one.'

Susan takes one. 'They're sour.'

'Sophisticated,' Ellen says. 'Made by Callard and Bowser, P.O. Box 1767, Cheltenham, GL50 3ZQ.'

'You call candies made at a post office box sophisticated? I call that tacky.'

'Don't I get one?' Jackie, slouched across the back seat of the Pinto, asks.

'No,' Ellen says, hurting Jackie twice. 'You're not allowed Altoids. They're politically incorrect.'

Jackie says nothing.

'How so?' Susan asks, shifting her hands to eight-twenty on the wheel, showing Ellen she's relaxing.

'Well,' Ellen says, 'Jackie says that she read in some book…'

'No Logo,' Jackie says. 'No Logo is not some book.'

Ellen glances back. 'Some book…that Callard and Bowser is owned by Suchard. Suchard is Swiss. And Suchard is owned by Kraft. Kraft is American. And Kraft is owned by…Who owns Kraft?'

'Paul Newman?' Susan asks.

'You're so cold…'

'Eli Lilly?'

'Try again.

Susan tries Bert's Bees, Proctor and Gamble, Bowing, Coca Cola, Monsanto, Enron, Standard Oil, Starbucks, Yankee Candle, Hershey, Hellman, Bethlehem Steel, AOL/Time Warner, The Christmas Tree Shop, on and on.

'Give up?' Ellen asks.

'Philip Morris,' Jackie calls from the back, getting back.

Susan Squeals. 'Philip Morris doesn't make Altoids! The Philip Morris I know can't even make Alison Kapolsky!'

'Hold it right there,' Jackie says. 'Alison is a good friend of mine.'

'Is she? I didn't know,' Susan says. She is steering with only her left hand. The right one she uses to caress Ellen's knee. Ellen smiles.

They continue, leaving Jackie to trail along behind them. Out of sight, but not quite out of mind.

'These candies are real good,' Susan says.

*

The police wagon passes over the stain on its way to the courthouse.

'That's it,' Sergeant Schenck tells Officer Kruk.

Kruk shakes his head, bunches his lips.

'I mean – Christ! – if you want to get rid of a dog, you take it to the pound,' Schenck says.

'Not this guy.'

'Not this guy. Jerk says he flipped. Couldn't take the barking no more.'

Kruk smirks. 'You thinkin' what I'm thinkin'? Should've kept his head below the parapet. Know what I mean? Why'd he keep a dog?'

Schenck shakes his head, bunches his lips. He has learnt this from Kruk

'Got any more on him?' Kruk asks.

'Still looking,' Schenck says.

Kruk gazes out at Bridgeport, shaking his head, bunching his lips. 'My Uncle Stan was in one of them Arab places. Says they don't have no churches. If they catch a person worshipping Jesus they cut your head off.'

Schenck shakes his head and bunches his lips. 'What they do if they catch you with one of their women?'

'Don' ask.'

*

'This is where you killed your dog,' the FBI man in the locked-off back of the police wagon, chained to the accused man, tells his

159

charge.

'You hold me for that?' the man asks. 'Only that?'

'That's what they tell me. Is there anything else?'

'The dog is…'

'Haram in Muslim countries?'

'Yes, but it is not that.'

'What is it then?'

'You love them,' the man says.

'So?'

The man is not sure himself. He wants to love them too. But he cannot love them. How can you love what you fear? But he knows well enough that the past is tricky. It trickles like the sweat through his scalp, a sluggish stream seeking a way through forest and thorn. It heads for the precipice of the present and falls at last over the forehead. And then it is all stinging and tears.

The man weeps for the sadness of it all. Villages burn behind his eyelids. The FBI man hands him a Kleenex and remembers what his aunt always said after the death of a pet: 'Brothers and Sisters, I bid you beware of giving your heart to a dog to tear.' Not that it stopped her.

'I do not like the dog. But you do not like me, I think. I think, 'If I have the dog and walk with the dog, people will like me.' Every day I see people walk the dogs. They talk to strangers. They stroke the dog. Then talk to the people with the dog. They become friendly. I think…I think…if I have the dog people will like me, and I am not…not a stranger.'

'So?'

'No good. I cannot make the dog obey. She chews my prayer rug. Makes mess in the apartment. My children fear. My wife will not go near. It steals our peace. That day the dog is very bad in the car. I get mad.'

'Ain't that a fact?' the FBI man says.

*

Kruk manoeuvres to the exit for the Bridgeport court-house. A man stands on the bridge over the exit ramp. A shiver passes through Kruk. He has time to take in the man's face. Middle-Eastern Appearance. But that facial type could take in half the world. The guy might be Mexican, Indian, Italian. He holds his breath. The car makes it under the bridge. Kruk has broken into a sweat.

What a world, Kruk thinks. What a world. He looks at the dashboard clock. 3.18 Eastern. Twelve minutes to get the bozo to court. With any luck some other schmuck will take him up-state to the pen.

By five he'll be free to head home by way of Emerson, Lafayette, Painestown and Whitmanville to connect with the Parkway. No more I. 95 for Ed Kruk today. Once home, he plans to strip off the uniform, crack open a Bud, release his fists and catch up with the rest of the story on Fox.

ROCK ME

He doesn't know the minister's name, and that's a grave sin of omission. Still, he can call him 'Your Excellency', and leave it at that. He should be more at ease. Should be used to it by now. He can't think why his hand was shaking as he handed his card to the desk officer. No, that's not true. He knows perfectly well. He's scared to death, that's why. He never learns, does he? It always goes all right. Why shake, McKenna?

He thinks that maybe his hand wouldn't have shaken if he had held the card between thumb and index finger rather than between index and middle. The way McKenna held it was arrogant, and a little effete at the same time. But McKenna was trying to look suave and in charge, to show the wretched keeper of the keys that he was in some way superior to him. But the shiver in the card spoilt it, the shiver which came straight from his heart and pulsed down his arm like Morse Code down a wire. The shake increased when the guard noticed it and postponed taking the card to show McKenna that he knew.

Yes, he knows all right. He knows McKenna is on a dirty errand.

Oh, when will he finally learn that it always goes all right! It always has.

Eventually, McKenna will be summoned to the Minister's presence. There he'll make his pitch on behalf of the firm's de-worming medicine and its undoubted benefits over all its competitors: Reasonable unit price; convenient easy-to-swallow tablet form; single application; clear instructions printed on the foil, watertight wrapper; thoroughly tested throughout the Third World and proven to have no side effects and... well, that should be enough. Then he'll exchange a few pleasantries with His Augustness on the pleasures of being an expatriate privileged to witness the enlightened progress of his country under such benign yet disciplined military rule. Finally, he'll make his Salaams, and he'll be very sure to do a convincing job of forgetting the briefcase full of Green Stuff. Quite simple. So it is worth repeating, 'Why shake, McKenna?'

Forget it. Let me help you, distract you from the unpleasant present moment. Think of something else. Better still, think of nothing. Eyes closed. Concentrate on a square inch of air in front of your nose. Steady breathing. In. Out. In…

No. You never could manage it. Come on, try again! You can't. Well, think of something happy. Glory Days? Holidays? Childhood…

Good Lord, it's Hanson from Sennett Food and Drugs. What's he want? The desk officer was about to drop everything and stand for him. Glad he thought better of it. But look! He speaks the language. And the French cologne. You can smell it from here. The card. Yes, you guessed it: a steady proffer between manicured index finger and thumb, backed by a disarming smile to ward of any impression of overconfidence or arrogance. And he used his right hand. Did you use your right hand? You should have. It's the custom. You never learn. Go on, greet Hanson. Manners maketh man. They're good business, too. No? Yes? No. He missed it. He's gone to the other end of the room to avoid you.

Think of childhood. But don't think about The Brothers. Your time with them wasn't happy. It probably brought you to where you sit now. Uneasily. The nuns had introduced you to Baby Jesus at the convent, hoping you'd strike up a friendship. But Baby

Jesus grew up oddly when explained by The Brothers. 'There is no mention in the gospels of Christ ever having laughed.' Then sending you out onto the warring rugby pitch to kill everything above a daisy. No, you mustn't think about the Brothers. Think about the convent and the Sisters.

You were never frightened there, were you? It was extra portions of mash and cuddles and gold stars for effort and Baby Jesus to turn to there at the top of the steps in his white nightie and a halo around his blond curls with bunnies and worshipping bambis, waiting for souls to join him and play.

The picture of Baby Jesus was behind your head in Sister Fidelma's class. But the picture wasn't just a picture. It served a purpose. It had a function. Sister Fidelma used to lean over you to move things on the picture. You can still remember the clean smell of her and how, though you looked high and low, you could never find a soap that smelled like her. And the voluminous robes, like a dark copse grown for your play. Their texture and the dark of them around you when she was near you...darker than the dark when the nightlight is snuffed out...

But why? Why did she reach over to get at the picture? She must have had an angle. Stands to reason. Everyone's got an angle.

O-ho! It's typical of you to think that. Ah, but she did. Her project for The Missions! Her strategy! Sister Fidelma's Little Way! McKenna, you remember now, don't you?

You had this picture of the Baby Jesus standing at the top of the steps with the door to heaven open behind Him. What else? There were cut-out black babies with different coloured shirts and drawing-pins through their middles. One for you and for each of your classmates. They were all progressing one at a time up the steps towards the open arms of Baby Jesus. And Sister Fidelma would lean over you to push them upwards. Siempre Arriba! Ever upwards. Boys and girls, we mustn't keep Jesus waiting!

Look, McKenna, Hanson's talking to the guard. Good move that. You'd talk to the guard too if they'd given you a three-month language course. What you wouldn't give to see inside his briefcase! Your dollars won't hold a candle to his Swiss Francs if that's what he's opted for. And you can bet your bottom dollar he has. Your only hope is that he's flogging some other medicament. Let us hope it won't present a predicament for His Excellency!

One thing's for sure: the minister is in for another profitable day. I bet he never thought as he sweated through his basic training that one day he'd be wooed by multi multi-nationals aching to unload Guccis full of filthy lucre all over him. Imagine!

Still, McKenna, you must close your mind and think of England; of all who labour by Mersey, Tees and Thames, willing you to dispose of their production upon a wormy world.

Where were you? Yes, you all had a baby each. You had to bring money and... no, get it right. There were thirty steps for each baby to climb before he made heaven. Thirty pennies made half a crown and each penny you brought in got the baby up one step. When you delivered a full two and sixpence you got your baby into heaven. Q.E.D. Quite Easily Done.

It seems preposterous now. Is that all there was to it, McKenna? It doesn't sound like sound economics. I'm surprised you were taken in. Must have been more to it than that. Something else to the scam.

Whatever the idea was you were certainly fired by it. You did without sweets and walked home to save the bus-fare. You pestered Auntie Phyllis out of her spare change - not that she had any going spare - with Sister Fidelma's words: 'For a good cause! For the missions!' Then you ripped out without regret all the stamps from your stamp album. They'd have been worth something today if you'd held onto them. But you sold them for five a penny in the playground. Daddy was angry but you didn't care. You wanted that baby at the top of the steps at any cost. But how did she sell it? It wasn't just the progress up the steps. What was her angle? Lord, you of all people should remember that.

Hanson's been summoned to The Presence. There goes his fat Gucci. You must hate the Swiss, McKenna. Not a crease in his jacket. As cool as Calvin. No knowing little voice whispering in his ear...

Don't scowl like that, McKenna. You'll stick like that. Anyway, you know I am speaking the truth. Trust me.

There was a strict procedure. You got your cardboard cut-out baby up the steps. Then you went and stood by Sister Fidelma's desk during the crayoning lesson.

That's it! She opened her desk and took out a large envelope. Inside there were two smaller envelopes. She opened each of these in turn and produced two identical pictures, one from each envelope. And on the pictures was your orphaned baby. Smiling.

That's the gimmick. She got you to think up a name for your baby. Christen him. Then she sent a card with the name on it to a priest she knew in Africa and the next time a new orphan came along he christened the baby using the name you had given to the baby in the picture. The idea was that it took half a crown to find the baby and to pay for the priest's time. But the beautiful thing was that you had your very own baby in Africa and you had saved him from paganism with your pennies and he would always be your baby.

That was it.

How you lapped it up! You gave your baby a place in your life. He dislodged the Guardian Angel from your right shoulder and you walked home with him and talked to him and kept back some of your dinner for him. He showed you the place where lions had their lair on British Railways property and how to avoid crocodiles in the municipal baths and you helped him up the difficult parts of trees and he warned you when the park-keeper was coming and pulled the blankets snugly up to your neck on cold nights. And you called him by the name that you had given him. It was magnificent really, McKenna. Nothing before or since has moved you like that. But what name did you give to your friend? Peter, William, George? You were given a completely free hand. You should remember the name you gave him, surely! Arthur, Patrick, Steven?

No, you can't remember. You've forgotten quite a lot all in all, haven't you? What are you doing here, for instance? The good Lord knows. What would Sister Fidelma say if she could see you now? What would Jesus say? Still, you don't believe in any of that stuff any more, do you? You don't even believe in me. You're just a blob of nervy unknowing sitting in a Third World country on a sweaty perspex seat in a compromised position. Hey ho.

Sing! Yes, sing, McKenna! Do something wild and unpredictible for once in your life! Sing Sister Fidelma's song. Just for old time's sake. Lest old acquaintance be forgot, eh? Yes, sing!
Gentle Jesus meek and mild
Rock me, Rock me, Like a child.
We shall rock you rock you rock…
That's enough. Enough is as good as a feast. Look! There goes Hanson, minus Gucci. Your turn, McKenna.

Well, that wasn't too bad, was it? You needn't have worried. Handsome fellow. Younger than expected. Bolder too.

'Mr McKenna, you have forgotten your briefcase.' If he planned to make you squirm, he succeeded. Picking it up, opening it, nodding with a smile of ebony and stars: 'For me? My thanks.' As cool as a courgette. You'll be needing a drink. Maybe several.

The sun always hits you like that. I can sympathise. Out of the Air Conditioning into reality. You'll never get used to it. Where are the car-keys? Ring the office from home and tell them it's done. Don't go back this afternoon.

Who's that? It's Hanson. He probably wants to gloat. Be polite to him, but only just.

'Lonnie...Lonnie Denka's easier to deal with than his predecessor, don't you think so?' he says.

You nod and smile. And you note with some stifled glee that, close up, Hanson looks scared and rumpled too.

And then you recall that Lonnie was the name you gave your baby. To repeat: Lonnie was the name you gave your baby.

Go home, McKenna. I'll leave you now. Go home and rock yourself to rest with a few stiff gins. You've earned it.

See you around.

Around and around...

EVEN THE MICE KNOW

Ed Welsh had thought he was going to be alone the whole way down.

The old woman entered the elevator, wheeling a walking frame. Ed Welsh pressed the door-open button for her. When the old woman was inside, he released the button, and closed his eyes as the doors shut tight.

'Only five more days!' the old woman said, startling him back.

'Oh, yes?' Ed Welsh said. He turned to her. He tried a smile.

The old woman did not return his smile. 'You don't know what I'm talking about, do you?' she said. 'I can tell from your eyes you don't know.'

The elevator was gathering speed. Ed Welsh wondered if it was a controlled descent, or a smooth but deadly plummeting. Maybe this was it? Death heading up to meet him on a day when he was ripe and it really didn't matter. Still, better to die in the company of an old woman than all alone. 'Know what?'

'What everybody knows.'

Of course he knew. Every street in San Francisco proclaimed it. The lights, bell-chimes of a thousand minimum-wage Santas, the video display in a candy store of a log fire burning with stockings hung. How would Santa make his way through such an inferno? Yes, all things proclaimed it. But Ed Welsh, hatred gobbling up the serenity of the man he had been just a week ago, looked out from his darkness at the twinkling lights everywhere – and decided to keep up the pretence. 'Why, no. Can't think of anything special.'

But the old woman wasn't playing. The elevator stopped at

the lobby. Ed Welsh held the button again to let her leave at her own pace. Then he joined her.

'Is there anything I can do for you?' he asked.

'Not one thing,' the old woman replied, hurting him, causing him to lift his hand to his face to protect it, then masquerade scratching an itch. She watched him. 'I must check my mailbox now. Goodbye.'

Ed Welch watched as she walked away from his life. Probably she was on her way to the Bon Appetite supermarket, but it would take her an age. Still, he thought, as he tried to organize his errands, it was nice to meet her. I'll think of her when the time comes. Better to think of a feisty old woman than…

He stood outside the apartment building, turning one way, then another. Now what must I do? There was much to be done, so many things to arrange, organize, buy, before he headed out, through the clouds and up over the Pacific, flying west and farther into the east. He wished the old woman well. She was the first person he had spoken to in a friendly way since the news had reached him.

On Sacramento Street, he turned right, but could not remember why he had come out.

'Spare a quarter to go some small way toward the cost of a cup of coffee, Sir?'

Ed Welsh was on top of the beggar before he knew it. He stopped dead in his tracks, searched through his pockets and handed the man all the change he could find. He walked on.

'Thank you, Sir. May the holiday season bestow all kinds of good things on you and your family.'

He did not turn to make an acknowledgement. He walked resolutely up Sacramento, lost in his own dark thoughts. It was only when he reached the top of the street that he realised he'd have been better heading for Market Street. What was there on Sacramento that had anything to do with anything that had anything to do with him?

He turned and saw the pinnacles of the Bay Bridge emerging above the fog. No sign of Oakland. Gertrude Stein had said that the trouble with Oakland was that there was no 'there' there. Whatever that meant. What does it mean? What does any of it mean? Damn it all to hell!

'Spare a quarter to go some small way toward the cost of a bagel, Sir?'

'You've already done me,' Ed Welsh said. He repeated the statement, straining his head back and addressing the grey light and the swirling fog that blocked the ears of the God he now addressed. You've already done me.

He had walked on past the beggar, but stopped on an impulse, searching for any remaining change in his pockets. Finding none, only his fingers caught in a cat's cradle of pocket litter, he miewed. He heard himself doing it. Was that me? Is that where I've come to? Who's that? He disengaged his hands from the pockets of his jacket and fixed them to his side. He took a couple of deep breaths. Then slowly he reached with his left hand into the right inside pocket of the jacket, pulled out his wallet and removed two bills, a five and a single. He retraced his steps and gave them to the beggar.

'Thank you, Sir. May the holiday season bestow all manner of good things on you and your family.'

'I haven't got a family,' Ed Welsh said, 'but thank you for your good wishes.' He walked on.

Arriving at Market Street he could still not recall the errands that had brought him out. Maybe all those wants, needs and whims were just so much nonsense. What did he really need anyway? Apart from a wife, and two grown daughters he had been about 'to get off his hands'? Well, they were off his hands now, weren't they? Were they? He sniffed his fingers.

You could get paper tissues in Singapore, couldn't you? Probably some enterprising salesman would be selling them outside the mortuary. Mort. You. Are. Eeee! He stood on the corner, slowly shuffling around and around. Was it sudden? Had the plane disintegrate like a struck match? Or had devils shouted their cause around the cabin, paraded their killing paunches, and told the passengers to prepare for their deaths? Was there a saying in Arabic for Live and Let Live? Was there? If not, why not? I think we should be told. On second thoughts, he decided, I do need something. He went into a drug store and bought a packet of double-sided razor blades. His mouth would not work to ask the girl for what he wanted. His palate and tongue were stuck, as if clogged with powdered bone.

Half an hour later Ed Welsh was passing Bon Appetite on his way back to the apartment building. He came upon the old woman, her walking frame weighed down with stretched-to-screaming-point plastic bags.

'Remember me?' Ed Welsh asked.

'A guy with total amnesia is not so easy to forget,' the old woman said.

'Those bags must be slowing you down. Let me carry them for you.'

He made to unhook the bags from the frame, but the old woman slapped his hand. 'No!'

'I only wanted to…'

'Do you know yet?'

'Know?' he asked, shrugging, thinking to continue the game begun in the elevator. 'Know what?'

'What everyone knows. You must know! Why, even the mice know!'

She seemed on the verge of tears. He decided the game had gone far enough. He knew well enough. The trouble was that he had no feeling for it.

'Yes,' he said flatly. 'Christmas is coming.'

'Good,' she said. 'I'll let you carry my things for me now. But I warn you, you're in for a long walk home.'

'I've got all the time in the world,' he said. 'If I'm quick about it.'

Ed Welch took the bags from the old woman and began walking home with her. She started talking to him. He had to lean over to catch what she was telling him. And as he listened and carried and bent his stiff back towards her, the weight of his fifty-five years lifted off him, the pain and rage and wild plans for vengeance that had murdered the last days and trashed his life, dissolved, as he took tiny baby-steps beside the old woman back along the sidewalk he had come.

At last he wished her Happy Christmas, left her at her floor and continued up to the twenty-third.

Back in the empty apartment he took his revolver, wrapped it in several plastic bags and dropped it down the refuse-shute. He sent the razor blades the same way. Then he stood in the middle of the room and smelled the air. There was family there still. There they were. Cologne and moisturiser, vanilla and coconut and

173

scorched ironing. He breathed them in over and over again. He went over to the window and opened the door to the balcony, leaving it open behind him. He stepped outside.

Below him to his left, the clock on top of the Ferry Building chimed six, and then launched into a Christmas Carol to which he could not put a name.

'I shall go to Singapore and identify the bodies. Then I shall return to…' The head and tail lights from the lines of traffic on the bridge were like the pattern on Christmas candy canes. The waters of the bay turned deepest blue as the mist dissolved to release a moonless sky. '…to help the old woman with her shopping.' He laughed at the foolishness of the thought, but then caught himself. For that thought was a long ways less foolish than most thoughts he'd had in the last week.

Then out of nowhere, as he looked out over Ferry Building and Bay Bridge and dark bay waters and lapis sky and lights of Oakland, Ed Welch was weeping. The carol continued and he was bawling like an infant as tears and snot dropped from his face and fell - fell past all the apartments below his and onto the sidewalk, where old women struggle and beggars ask for aid and people lose their way and their minds and their hope and where, perhaps, when everyone is tucked up in their beds, the mice come out. And tell one another what they know.

DUET FOR FLUTE AND WHISTLE

For Angela Scott

I'm running out of puff, but Dr. Azimzadeh won't have it. He reckons I'm on the up and up. I nod and smile, like you do. Haven't the heart to embarrass him by insisting my number's up. But up it is. The brass, string, wind, reed and percussion sections have done all they can. It's up to The Conductor now. The last bars of my life - ewig…ewig… are fading into infinity, and it only remains for him to nod and let the real silence in. So Fiat and that.

Those who are about to die juggle heavy burdens. Apart from worrying about what lies behind the blank wall, we have to help the poor buggers who still have it all to face at some lonely place just a few stops past the bus-pass. In spite of pain, lack of a prompter and poor acoustic, we salute you with an impression that this dying business is as easy as falling off a log.

I think I've been doing rather well in this regard, even if I do say so myself. When Dr Azimzadeh perches on the side of my bed - a high contraption with a motor the carers from North-West Home's Best wheeled in for the duration - he coils his stethoscope around his young hands as he prepares to lie in a good cause. I reach across and stroke those hands, vain enough to note the difference: mine grey and liver-spotted, his the shade of a cherished Strad. Vain enough too to think I can still charm a young man, and make him remember me. Remember me, but forget my fate. Remember me, but forget you're running late.

That first time, I caught him outside Gracie's house and said,

'Er…, Doctor. I'm sort of a friend of Gracie's, Doctor. From her orchestra days. How's she doin' like?' He looked at me like he'd seen a ghost and said Gracie was as well as could be expected, and I said that's what I'd expected he'd say. But friends from the orchestra are all sure it's bad. He nodded. Hadn't looked me in the eye even the once. Then he fled. He must've seen my sort before. Every day of his working life, shouldn't wonder.

Why don't I go up, pay respects and that? I practise doing it. And it does me head in. What's going on? Embarrassment is what - Fear's snotty little brother. I'd go up the steps to Gracie's place. She'd talk for a few minutes, wondering who in hell this stranger was, and I'd tell her she'll be better in no time and make clumsy goodbyes and wallop down the stairs. Weeping. And I wouldn't have said anything. I wouldn't have said what I mean. I mean, I wouldn't help. A dumb brawn-box ghost from the past mumbling at a bedside. Why would she remember me, anyway? What's in me to remember? How could I tell her that she's made all the great difference to my life? All sorts of big shots have been telling her that for years, shouldn't wonder. I'd stand there fidgeting, not able to get a word out.

It's weird, all this. There's poor Gracie on her last legs. We all have to do it, don't we? You'd think we'd have something useful to contribute. It ought to be in our genes, giving comfort to the dying. It ought to be part of the National Curriculum.

Dr Azimzadeh was telling me about his childhood in Nairobi. The family fled there from Iran after the Shah was shifted. His dad owned a restaurant called The Curry Pot. Had six kids. All doctors. All funded from that curry pot. Both parents still alive - living with the eldest on Vancouver Island now - and nicely placed for terminal care with oodles of expertise and TLC for when their time comes.

'They must be proud. You do them credit.'

He smiles. Perfect teeth. Lovely lips. Cavern of a palate behind them, shouldn't wonder. Born to blow.

I hear Dr. Azimzadeh go, the beat of his footsteps on the stairs. My head slots back into the pillow, like a flute in a case. And I am left, waiting for the whistler.

Back-breaking loads of instruments pulled into the lorry, strapped down, shrouded and padded. But you couldn't stop the bloody things making a racket. 'Can I come with you?' she says. In Barnsley it was. Barnsley! Was it Barnsley? Taking culture to the cotton-towns. 'I've missed the coach.' And what have we here? I'm thinking, remembering how Alf had copped off with a harpist. But Alf was Alf and I was me and married to Her At Home and all I wanted was a sup of coffee and a kip. But I let her in. I wasn't going to make her go to Glasgow on the puff-puff.

Sorry to go on about my hands. Mighty fallen. Veins like choked streams meandering towards the ox-bow of my broke heart. I look at them out of the corner of my eye as I did when playing the flute. I squint, trying to recall how they used to mesmerise me as they flashed along the instrument. 'Oh, yes! You are clever!' people said. I'd say it myself sometimes. But there was no cleverness. Not really. Gifted is better. My hands were gifted. They played on their own. I don't even remember learning to read music. It was just there, like a stocking of gifts at Christmas. Are these the hands that never put a foot wrong?

There is a river in Iran called Zayandeh Rud. It flows from

the Zagros mountains through the city of Isfahan, where it is crossed by three ancient bridges. Zayandeh means 'Giver of Life'. It's an apt name, for the river showers abundance on every inch of ground she passes; she sired and nourishes great Isfahan, whose name means 'Half The World'... Nesf-e-jahan.

But Zayandeh ends in a marsh surrounded by desert a scant seventy miles from its source. Not all rivers are fortunate enough to reach the ocean, you see.

What made me think of all that? Only that I was telling the doc I was once in Isfahan with a small orchestra financed by the British Council. The secretary there - a sad-eyed Baha'i called Ruhullah - told me all about the Zayandeh Rud, and my Bartholomew map backed him up. A sad end for the giver of life...

Where's the whistler?

I learnt everything that night. The burdens I carried day in day out from lorry to concert-hall, from concert-hall to lorry, from place to place, were no longer burdens, but my key to peace. If you'd asked me the day before it happened, I'd have told you not to be so daft. Ask me any day since then, I'd shake my head at a past of stony deafness. And all that wasted time. But stop all that. One foot in the past, one in the future, and you're pissing on the present. No more. No more of that.

Life is...life has been... one long surprise. Had I been a more introspective girl, I suppose I would find...would have found... life to be terribly strange and depressing. But praise the Lord who gave us wind to blow with, I've never been one to mull. We flautists, like our instruments, can soar above life's cares and woes. We're a merry, light-travelling, bunch. 'There you are! That's life! Keep it simple! There's another octave above that just waiting for you... so pucker those lips and fly right!' It took no effort on my part to make a noise that people found delightful and were willing to pay to hear. Though I'd have given it away for free. They'd only've had to ask.

My mother told me to be a teacher. I'd have something to fall back on if the music let me down. But how could my music let me down? If orchestras fall apart, record companies break faith, there are streets and subways and shop-doorways where I could earn a crust and pleasure the people. It never came to that. In some ways, I wish it had. I wish I'd gone into the town to share my music with people passing by. It would have been so easy. The flute is so easy.

In my experience it's double-bass players you've got to watch. How they suffer! 'Why me? What's it all about? How am I going to get this incredible hulk to the next gig?' But the flautist can pack away her magic wand in a neat little box with a handle and hightail it around town. You can flag down a taxi with a flute, skip through life lightly. Thank you, God, for making me a flute-player.

Where is that damned whistler? Hope he's not sick as well.

I come each night to this house. I mooch outside, and do not go in. I do what I can do.

Not a day has passed since I first saw you when I haven't thought of you with love. And thinking of you has made me better. Better. Day by day. What was I before? Not much, and I don't look like much now, I'd say. But I know. I realise. Does she remember me? You've been through this before. Silly bugger. A life full of event. Applause as a night-cap. Gets to be routine, like feeling hopeless.

What was I to her? A common bloke, a bit of rough, who shifted instruments.

I would like to be able to say that I'd been as successful at love. But I can't. If into every life some rain must fall, my puddle on the parade route was love. What can I tell you? My men were either sharp or flat. They were forever begging me to tune them and I was too busy making music and whoopee to have spare energy for that sort of nonsense. Of course, that's probably why I'm left all alone and forlorn as I prepare for my ferry across the Rubicon. It's too late to worry my head about that now. 'Dear God, grant Ruhullah a happy ending!' It doesn't look likely. After the Revolution they rounded up Baha'is. Thousands were killed. Ruhullah wore a badge with the Shah on it. Can't have gone down well. Dear God...

Don't worry your head, Gracie. Thanks to you, my life became harmonious. They're everywhere, those tunes. I live for them. My music is filed alphabetically in the cages where I used to keep the pigeons. As I collected all those magic halos I freed the birds one by one to make room. I've left the whole collection to Didsbury Library. And each one will have a label: Listen and remember Gracie Grace, Flautist and Teacher.

Love. No, what I said is not quite true. Nothing one says ever quite is, is it? I once - just once - fell madly in love...with an instrument removals man from the Halle. Being a dainty flautist I didn't have much call for his services. But one time I found myself left behind by the charabanc in Huddersfield - I think it was Huddersfield - and went up to Glasgow with him in the back of a lorry.

Not only did I fall in love in that lorry, I also discovered something wonderful: that the instruments of the orchestra produce beautiful music while on the road. The piano and the harp vibrated throughout their range, while draught and slipstream activated the wind instruments to breathy sighs; the strings, never a group to be outdone, laid down their pennyworth of sound on the moving counter. And the percussion banged, walloped and tinkled with every run-over cat's eye.

I sat with him. He had a flask of very sweet, milky coffee which we shared from the one beaker. We lay back and listened to the music. I told him I thought it was beautiful music, and he said, 'Pull the other one!'

I told her not to be daft. The instruments in the back of the lorry made a racket. A racket is what they made. Call that music! If you'd had to listen as often as me! And then…and then… as Alf drove North, she played, and I suddenly felt it. Like the flapping wings of a pigeon who doesn't have to come back to a cage ever again: who has the whole kingdom of clouds for playground. Marvellous. Bloody marvellous!

I pulled out my flute, clicked it together, and started playing whatever came into my head. We flautists are always on the look out for additions to the repetoire, so I wasn't going to let the chance pass. I watched him as he relaxed into the music, closed his eyes.

Felt it. And the feeling has never left me.

I kept on playing until there came a moment when it was

more important for me to find out what he was thinking than to see where the music would lead. I stopped, but the instruments of the orchestra continued and I did not know where my music ended and theirs began. It was seamless sound in the back of a lorry.

It was like being asleep – those cat-naps just below the surface. Not dark deep-sea sleep, but breasting through mackeral-sun-sparkle waters. Never been more awake. I suddenly understood what all my life of heavy lifting and shifting was about. Gracie had used her flute like a surgeon's scalpal to cut open my cloth ears and end a lifetime's deafness.

He did not open his eyes. Just said, 'That's really lovely...' I felt like Orpheus charming the creatures of the forest. I had given him my best. He had loved it and I had planted that love and so I loved him.

I had loved it and she had planted that love and so I loved her.

Of course, nothing came of it. He had a wife and I had my flute. But for a couple of years I travelled about in that lorry from gig to gig just to be with him and to accompany the random music of the magic orchestra.

Bach, Vivaldi, Gluck, Britten, Beethoven, Teleman, Percy French, Palestrina, Mozart, Monteverdi, Louis Armstrong, Mahler... she gave me my baptism and I sought about for confirmation. I sneaked in to the concerts, stopped the booze because a round cost a record...every beer mat in every bar that I covered with a pint, whined, 'You'll never know me now!'

Gracie gave me new life. From then on I started lifting the instruments of the orchestra like a rabbi his Torah, like a priest His God. My brain opened and my heart opened to receive and to transmit and music became my passion. I cannot think of Gracie without thinking of music. I cannot think of music without thinking of Gracie.

The sound haunts me still. It was as unplanned as birdsong. As beautiful as birth, as… The lady doth prattle on too much, methinks. Who wants to know about the sordid life and loves of a fast-fading flautist? Not me for one.

My piano teacher years ago told me that Kathleen Ferrier had a palate you could have fitted an orange into. I don't know how he knew. I don't know why I think of it now. Perhaps it's because Kath recorded 'Das Lied Von Der Erde' when she knew she was not long for this world. In the same leaky boat in which I roll now. The last long song, Der Abschied, Kath and Bruno Walter recorded in one take. The story goes that they were listening to the play-back. When the piece faded away, with Kathleen repeating 'Ewig…Ewig…' – forever and forever – they looked at one another. Both were weeping. Both considering their own farewells. 'Let it stand! Let it stand!' Walter said after listening, though close to the end there is a bang, as if someone in the orchestra has dropped something. And so it is. Funny, I can't listen to the recording without hearing the flaw, without looking forward to it, and my heart lifts that the artists forgave it, let it stand, let it roll.

Enough of this! Let's get to the hard part! I want to know where the whistler has got to.

I can't say much about the whistler, I'm afraid. I wish I could. Every day around this time someone passes my window whistling. The window is too high off the ground for me to see who it is. But it is peculiar that he passes the house. This house, you see, is at the end of a Victorian terrace, the side wall of which is joined to a high wall that stretches right across the street, making mine the last house in a very determined cul-de-sac. Atop the wall are thousands of pieces of jagged green glass which protect the derelict warehouse on the far side. There is no way over, through, or, as far as I know, under. Yet every day somebody passes my window whistling. I can hear the sound approaching. It reaches full throttle as it passes the window, and, this is the peculiar bit which, were I a double-bass player, would surely send me off to the pub or the shrink: the sound slowly fades stage left, where common sense tells me is the depressing brick wall and the padlocked warehouse.

It's a peculiar thing to happen to Gracie Grace in her last agony. But there's more. The whistler is wonderful. He or she has perfect pitch and a splendid tone. The sound belongs in a symphony hall rather than hard up against the blank wall of Rhondda Terrace. And this gorgeous sound is not used to puff out any old stuff. No 'I Did It My Way'. Only the best, the most taxing pieces, for the whistler.

One day last week, for instance, the whistler was doing, 'Erbarme dich, mein Gott' from the Bach St Matthew Passion. And not only did he whistle the mezzo role but also the sorrowing dance of the violin. 'Encore!' I croaked from my bed of pain, but too soon the sound had faded, and everything was once more as silent as a wall.

Then only yesterday he whistled the opening Sea Interlude from 'Peter Grimes' and I lay here weeping, for the high clear notes made me see a little boat, empty, blue-and-white, on an empty ocean. I longed then to board that little boat and be on my way. Oh, he really knows how to compile a programme!

Other pieces have included snatches from Orpheo Ed Euridice – we hear a lot from Orpheus and Euridice, but nothing from Ed - Vivaldi, and pieces to which I cannot put a name. And it is these other pieces that I do so love to hear.

Where is he? Hurry up, there's a good fellow.

I am growing impatient. I am taking on the weight of a double-bass player. Dr Azimzadeh told me to look forward with positive attitudes, but looking down at myself beneath the covers tells me that I am a husk. And that is why I look forward to the whistler. You see, I feel he is whistling for me. Maybe this is an old woman's foolishness too. There must be thousands of whistlers in this city. Nevertheless - I can't help myself - I believe it.

Yes. No. Yes. There he is now. The song...I know it. I know. What a coincidence! No, there's no such thing. What's it all about? Magnum mysterium! The world in the back of a lorry. Mystery - Mist. Story - where all the good stuff hides: heaven's gate opening to limitless sunrise expanses behind a blank brick wall! Dr. Ruhullah Zayandeh Rud! End in a marsh! You? I'll not believe it. I'll not…

Thank you, Tommy Wakefield. I thought you were dead. Thank you. *Ewig…Ewig…*

Thank you, Gracie Grace. Not dead. Not me. Can scarcely remember the last time I was dead... ...*Ewig…Ewig…*

VERY MUCH REALITY

'We were put on this earth to see visions and dream dreams, Love!'
I said, exasperated like. I mean, I'd had enough. You get nicely
settled behind the Virtual Reality specs with your fingers on the
touch controls of the console, and you're all comfy and calm and
that, and people can't stand to see you having a good time. They start
making comments to pull you back.

Heather loves doing it. She's got it down to a fine art.
Doesn't chirp up straight away, mind. No, she waits until I'm really
involved, really carried away, like you get... and then she puts her oar
in.

'We were put on this earth to see visions and dream dreams,
Love!' I said again. This time there was iron in my tone.

'Not those visions; not those dreams,' Heather said, all tart.
'What you do makes our Justin's audio implants look really social.
And what's the milk bottle doing on the coffee table? Standards are
slipping all round round here, if you want my opinion.'

I gave the Virtual Reality spectacles a wipe on my shirt tail
and tuned Heather out.

Vogumska is pounding towards me on her white charger
across the Siberian steppe. She carries a spear. The setting sun behind
her tosses rubies and amber over her blond hair. The horse is so close
I can smell its steedy breath.

'Come, Ron!' Vogumska calls out in that deep feminine
voice of hers. And with one muscled arm she reaches for me, picks
me up and I am sitting in front of her on the horse, cradled by her
thighs, feeling the wind on my cheeks, the horse's every movement.
'At last, my love!' croons Vogumska.

'You took your time, Vogumska!' I say, with a manly pout.

'I'd started to give up hope.'

'Here we go again!' Heather said, 'It's that floozie on the geegee, is it? I'd have thought you'd have worn her out by now, Ron. And you've gone and knocked the antimacasser off the back of the settee. You know what it means to me after it being left me by Uncle Peter's mum, and all you can do is crinkle it under your fat bum.'

But I was not listening. There is another in my life. Vogumska's scent of pine and steppe and sweat is intoxicating me as she bends low over me to speak:

'Ron, my little lost hero, I fear your head is full of demons. Be not afraid! Soon we shall arrive at the city of the Great Khan. There, all will be well. I, Vogumska, will bathe you in the holy pool of the dragon's cave, pour precious unguents over the length and breadth of your sore body. I will sooth away the voices that so distress you with wines pressed by the feet of virgins and brought from Shiraz by Tartar runners.'

Vogumska leans forward and kisses me. 'Will these delights pleasure you, Ron? Vogumska's heart and soul pants to give her young and glorious lover numberless embraces. Our coupling shall in number be like unto the sands of the desert, the drops of crystal water in the great Oxus River.'

I feel the peach-fur of her cheeks pass over my five o' clock shadow. We lock like Velcro. 'Would you like that, Ron?'

'Yes, please, Vogumska,' I say. 'Sounds really lovely.'

We kiss. Her tongue is like that first swallow of Old Reliable mild after a summer day on the shore searching for sea-coal.

'Just the job,' I say.

'Oh, it's just the job, is it? It's funny you mentioning jobs. Ha-bloody-ha, like. I've got a good mind to take that console of yours and chuck it in the bin like they told me on the helpline.'

'Don't you dare!' I shouted, all militant like.

'If anybody'd told me when I married you that I was marrying a bleeding Virtualrealaholic, I'd have told them not to be so daft. Back then it was EuroTrash that kept me awake at nights. I should've married Kevin Earnshaw.'

Across the endless steppe we race. I marvel at the strength of Vogumska's steed; the way it seems to fly. At last, on the far horizon, a great city comes into view. At first a dot, it slowly grows until I can see domes and minarettes and pleasure palaces and gardens where beautiful maidens are waving and great bazaars with rainbows of carpets and golden bridges across a blue river.

'Where are we?' I ask.

'Where do you think you are?' Heather said. 'You're at 17 Jubilee Terrace in case you've forgotten like. Have you seen Justin's P.E. Kit on your travels, by the way?'

'Khonsarobad! The great city of the Khans!' Vogumska says, 'The city is yours, O Ron!'

From the battlements of one of the palaces thirty-three buglers play a fanfare that knocks spots off the Opening of Parliament. As Vogumska's steed trots through the streets the whole population of the city comes out to greet us, throwing rose-petals and offering sherbets.

At last we come to a really lovely white palace. The steed climbs the steps. At the top Vogumska lifts me down. I stand beside her, facing the cheering people.

'People of Khonsarobad!' calls out Vogumska in her voice of anvil and cracked ice, 'I present to you your prince and saviour, Ron, from beyond the far seas! After many travails he has come to save your Khan from the encroachment of the infidel hoards.'

Then she whispers in my ear, 'Speak to the people, Ron!'

'I don't know what to say,' I say.

'Funny,' Heather said, 'I was just thinking that myself. 'Dear Mr Fowler: I would be ever so grateful if you could excuse Justin from games today owing to the fact that we cannot find his P.E. kit, and even if we could it would not be presentable as he left it somewhere in an unclean condition. If I had been able to find it - which I haven't, like I said - I would have washed it and made sure he would be all ship-shape for games. I am a mum who believes in men's sana in corpore sanitary – women's too for that matter. Believe me, Mr Fowler, I know what happens when men's sanas get ignored.' Will that do, d'you reckon?'

'People of Khonsarobad!' I say. I do not have any idea how I will go on. I just hope that words will be given me. 'People of Khonsarobad, I have come to relieve you with my mighty sword and my stout heart! My paramount and conkerbin, the glorious Vogumska, has told me of your plight. The infidels are massing across the steppe. Truly they are a terrifying army and we know their works. Your city, Knonsarobad, is a bright beacon of civilisation and achievement. Vogumska has told me of your library, your great codes of law, your kindness to strangers. And I am here to see that the light is not put out!'

'Put out the light before you come up,' Heather said. 'And see if you can get that floozie to do the necessary. I've got a shocking headache.'

'All around the beacon of your city,' I say, 'are malevolent influences. They shall not win! They must not win! Vogumska and I are here to console your sorrowing Khan, to win the great war to end all wars!'

'But first,' Vogumska says, 'I must prepare with love my lord for battle!'

The people cheer, and Vogumska leads me away into the Great Palace. We prostrate ourselves before the throne of the sorrowing khan. He does not speak to us. The tears he is shedding have filled many large golden bowls held by stern slaves. When each bowl of sorrow is full it is placed around a bejewelled map of Khonsarobad.

'He has vowed to drink only his tears until the city is saved,' Vogumska tells me as she leads me towards the Hall of the Warriors' Rest.

'Poor bloke!' I say.

'Where's Mum?' Justin asked.

'Bed,' I said.

'You are so eager, Ron!' Vogumska purrs.

'You're not into that Vogumska again, are you, Dad?' Justin said, 'She's ten million pixels short of reality, that one.'

'Mind your own business!' I said. 'Anyway, where've you been? You've got school in the morning. Your mother and me were worried sick.'

'Give the old girl my love,' Justin said.

'Don't talk about your mother like that!'

Cloth of gold sheets, stained glass windows, caged birds singing, pitchers of fermented yogurt where Heather keeps her Teasmade.

'I wasn't,' Justin said. 'I was remembering Vogumska. I thought she was pretty cool at the time; but she's yesterday's Virtual Reality, Dad.'

'Don't weep, Vogumska!' I say. 'It's only Justin. You probably don't remember him. He got you for Christmas in '08. He was tired of you by Boxing Day. That's kids for you.'

Vogumska is pouring fragrant oil through her hair,

preparing to lash my paunch with her tresses. She is weeping the while. 'I remember Justin,' she says 'He was like a lion in the Hall of Warriors' Rest, but at the first sight of the infidel hoards he capitulated and joined the forces of evil produced by Nintandy Inc. You'll never do that, will you, Ron?'

I vow that I will not. Vogumska dries her eyes and sets about turning the couch-potato that Heather sees into the warrior fit for Vogumska.

In the midst of cloves and ambergris and attar of roses I smelled a burning Poptart. 'Justin, get to bed!'

She dresses me in silk and golden chain-mail. At the steps of the palace a horse the twin of Vogumska's stands, panting and kicking the marble of the street with its hooves. We ride out of the city at the head of a vast army and on the horizon I see the great infidel hoards massed. Samurai Sayarama, G.I. George, The Sewer Rats, The Nippie Pushers, The Dianetic Pinstripes, bear down on us. I unsheath my sword and let out a great cry.

'Dad,' Justin said, 'have you seen my P.E. kit?'

'No prisoners!' I call, and sever the head of three of Samurai Sayarama's men with a flick of my mighty sword. Ten take their place and once again I flick their heads off. Then, with a mighty blow, I cut the Jinn From The Great Marsh in half.

'Ah!' Vogumska calls, 'you are a real man, Ron! In the late years the people will sing sagas about the Great Ron! The king of all kings! The man above all other men!'

I can see a pincer movement of Sewer Rats and Nippie Pushers surrounding my beloved Vogumska. I ride into the middle of the fray and strike them down.

'Yo! Ron!' Vogumska calls, striking my palm with hers. 'Go for it, Ron!'

'I am your slave, Vogumska!' I cry.

'I've got to find that P.E. kit, Dad.' Justin said. 'Mr Fowler'll make me pick up litter if I don't, Dad.'

'Watch out behind you, Ron!' Vogumska cries. 'It's the Sewer Rats! They're the ones who threaten civilisation as we know it! Destroy them, Ron, so that the city of Khonsarobad will live in peace and keep its great library!'

'I will!' I shout. 'I will scatter them!'

A pincer movement of Denghi Mermaids and Dianetic Pinstripes are bearing down on Vogumska.

'Help me, Ron!' Vogumska cries.

'Look out, Vogumska! Behind you!'

But I am too late. A Pinstripe plunges his laser dagger into Vogumska. I wade through them, careless to my fate, dispatching the rest. I cradle Vogumska close.

'Remember me, Ron. Only remember,' Vogumska says.

'I will, my love!'

'Tell Justin I was faithful, even though he was not. His P.E. kit is in the cupboard under the stairs. It's hidden behind his…his Goretex,' Vogumska whispers. Then she dies, and my world goes blank.

I passed on Vogumska's last message to Justin.

'Phew, saved by the bell. Thanks Vogumska!' Justin said.

'Vogumska's dead, Son,' I said.

'Justin, get to bed!' Heather called down.

'Night, Dad! Sweet dreams!' Justin said, all chuffed and deaf as a post.

'Night, Son,' I said, still staring through my V.R. specs, trying like buggery to recapture something wonderful where there is now only dots, lines, grey, and the sad - so sad - sound of static.

CONSOLATION

The New Brighton piers aren't there anymore. This is not to say they do not exist still. They do. They're as solid and amazing as anything in the heads and hearts of people. After all, you come to a certain age and where do the set-aside people live but in a ghost landscape?

One of New Brighton's piers served as floating landing-stage for the ferry to Liverpool. This pier brought in trippers and sent them home of a night drunk and incapable - and capable of anything. When the sun rose over Liverpool, sick washed off the decks, the same ferry became sober transportation for the nobs who worked in the city, but lived in the posh villas of New Brighton.

Like a floozie with theft in mind nuzzling a straying magistrate, lay the pleasure pier. This was loaded with rides and attractions and caffs and bars and weighing machines that trumpetted out your sins in stones or silently printed out the bleak facts on a discrete card. The boardwalk was made of hardwood planks slung over an iron frame. The gaps between were wide enough to give folk a view past their boots, of rock, sand or sea (depending on the state of the tide) and to allow all manner of coins of the realm to slip through.

Some of those coins may still be there if they have managed to dodge the hoovers of time, tide and metal detectors. But, before you start treasure-hunting, be warned that the pick of them was pocketed by Manny Mann before a single tide could wash them, or wash them away.

Manny would greet the rising sun on a summer's day with a hymn whistled to the evening. A sunny day in summer - especially a weekend summer day, and, best of all, a Bank Holiday sunny day - brought out the trippers as sure as a syrup tart on a table brings out flies....and trippers had purses and pockets and, likely as not, a balled hanky or two. And there was nothing like a pocket hanky for nicking coins from people. It left the pocket like an ice-cream scoop pulling, on snot-stiff edges, loose change.

Manny would spend a busy day on the pier, where he operated a Prize Every Time stall. While sirening trippers to his stall, Manny whistled, and dreamed of his evening tryst with Lady Luck on the shore below.

A row of six bakelite geese was the basis of Manny's living. These geese rotated through one hundred and twenty-five degrees, their mouths agape, intriguing the passing populace as they made their way along the boardwalk. Manny stood rolling-them-up, and prize-every-timing them, offering smiles to the girls, and those mums whom he judged might feel flattered by the attention. He didn't as a rule try to get the kids directly. Wouldn't do to overdo it. They'd get enough stimulation from the odd behaviour of the geese and, if that didn't do the trick, from the glittery prizes on the shelves of Manny's stall.

Soft toys filled with rags of old clothes - dogs, babies, lions, innocent girls with big eyes; hard toys that you wound up being really careful not to overwind, for that would be the end of it: tin clowns and trains and dogs (can't have too many dogs) and buses and planes...'Does it fly?' 'No, Mate, but with a bit of luck and a following wind it'll taxi across a few feet of lino.' Objects that were a bugger to dust: Tureens from American-occupied Japan, from Macau, from Hong-Kong; silvery toasters and fruit bowls so elaborate that'd fit right in on the high altar of St Peter's and Paul's R.C., kettles, electric and manual, radio sets, model ships. More dogs, some with jewelly glass eyes.

And so on.

Hidden out of sight in a large box were the 'every time' prizes:

rubbish on cards...watches with elastic bracelets and no time to give that the loser did not set for himself; compasses on a pin in a cardboard circle; paper flowers that sometimes swelled when put in water; tiny ships that took a piece of camphor - if you had the good luck to find any - and sailed around washing-up-bowl millponds (if you were extra lucky); colouring books and crayons (Don't for God's sake let the little tyke put one in his mouth!); sewing kits from Yugoslavia; tiny rubber balls that bounced as unpredictibly as people, badges; little tin soldiers... anything really, that would take the edge off the punters' disappointment that God had not smiled and given her the huge dog filled with rags she deserved; anything, in short, that would roughly comply with the law and provide consolation.

Consolation. Roll it around your mouth. Give it a good sucking: it's too sweet a word to just chew and swallow. After all, what was a holiday resort like New Brighton but a bit of consolation for the toiling masses, a place where Reg - fresh-out but rusted and livid from a Jap POW camp - might get the feel for life back in the temperate winds, and stop crying in the night? Where Bill might forget for an hour that he'd had his scrotum shot off by a Jerry sniper? The whole place was a Consolation Prize for lives passed by, wounded in action; for the walking wounded soldiering on; old industries on the Mersey dying on their knees and being replaced by nothing but dole; for the tsunami of war and the new flaccid-wave traumas of peace in the fifties.

But back to Manny sirening up the punters, while dreaming of an evening's productive mooch below the walkway of the pier. Manny did not hold with people winning his big prizes (they became 'Star' prizes in the sixties as a result of the baleful influence of television). Indeed, winning them was something highly unlikely, nudging total impossibility. Why? Well, you had three balls. These you popped in the goose's mouth. The balls would pass through the simple innards of the goose, roll down a slide into one of the waiting cubicles with numbers on. To win a star prize you had to get fifteen or more. But as there were only two fives and nothing higher, you'd have to be a very lucky duck to manage three balls in the fives - especially as Manny operated a subtle tilting device with his foot that caused the balls to veer safely out of Star Prize privies. No one seemed to care. 'Oh, dear! Sorry! Have another go!' he'd say. But they were there for consolation - and consolation prizes - though they might think them a swizz and say so. They'd turn away sad, Sod 'im under their breath, on the look-out for a different kind of consoling. It was all part of the fun. It was, like the popular shows run up the road at the Floral Pavilion, Variety. And that was the scarce spice of life. At least they'd be able to have a good moan on the boat back. And a good moan, then as now, meant the whole world to them.

Manny was up against a lot of competition on the pier. The wages he gleaned from it - after he'd paid rent to blood-sucking Mr Watson who owned everything - barely paid for his bachelor rooms in Victoria Road over Benson's Tasteful Souvenirs Ltd. It was his walks under the pier that allowed him to charge the greedy gas meter with coins, to live in a modicum of comfort.

Manny got on well enough with the other toilers on the pier. He was best mates with Harry, who ran the Pull A String store - and had got Harry out of many a tangle. Harry had come back from service on convoys completely stripped of skin on face and neck. After some shocking ops at Clatterbridge Hospital - they'd taken the skin off his behind to put on his face, though his family was sworn to secrecy - the pain had gone, unless he looked at himself in a mirror or shop window, or woke up in the night convinced that the candlewick bedspread was a flaming oil fire and the churning Slumberland the swell on the Malacca Straits. He looked a sight, but the punters pushed their yowling kids towards Harry out of a sense of patriotism. He made a good living - better than Manny, who had been in Bicycle First Aid, and had only got roped in for that a year after the Blitz blew over.

Harry's strings were all connected to consolation prizes. There were some quite spectacular prizes on show, mind - a Goblin Teasmade being top of the bill. But none of the strings from the Star Prizes reached the thick skein that Harry held in his hand and offered to punters for a pull. The star-prize strings came to a dead-end on a little hook in the invisible ceiling. No one had ever been known to moan when something cheap and cheerless rose from the other end of the string. It would not have been seemly. After all, they were looking at someone who had pulled out the worst Booby Prize anyone could get, and was well and truly stuck with it. In spite of herself, Harry's wife closed her eyes tight in the oil-black bedroom when he got in the mood.

But, apart from Harry, Manny was distant from the others. He greeted them, mind, would even pass the time of a dull day with them, but he didn't get close. And he kept a great distance between himself and the fortune teller, a black man with no right hand called Professor Briscoe Chadwick, who wore a turban and a black suit and tie, and was in 'partnership' with Madam McKenzie, a bubbly blond woman of some girth with many more miles on the clock than she would admit to.

'That woman's been turning the clock back again,' Manny would say to Harry when Madame McKenzie and Professor Briscoe Chadwick passed along the pier in a stately manner on route to the well-placed fortune-telling booth, set up in the centre of the boardwalk at the very end. 'Hasn't she heard about growing old gracefully? And,' he'd add, more often than was seemly, 'it really turns me stomach to see them together, Harry.'

'Live and Let Live,' Harry would respond. Live and Let Live was Harry's favourite phrase. He didn't mean any offence by it. And Manny didn't take any offence. After all, Harry was only stating a point of view that chimed very well with his own. What was the point of defeating Mr Hitler if you couldn't come home from foreign parts (or wheel your bike home from the Birkenhead bombsites) and say what you meant without fear of being gassed? It wasn't as if Manny was going to break into Professor Chadwick's villa on Victoria Road, find him and Madame McKenzie entwined like some Tableau Vivant liquorice allsort, and empty the barrel of his Enfield into them, was it?

No. It was just that Manny did not approve of the mixing of the races (he rather disapproved of the mixing of Catholic with Prod, Anglo with Saxon, man with woman, dog with bitch, for that matter). But Manny was icy with Professor Chadwick and his Jezebel. It only made him harden further when Professor Chadwick gave him one of his dignified waves. And each day Manny, when he was the unwilling recipient of such unwanted attention, responded with a nod whose coldness would make an Orange Maid lolly-ice seem too hot to risk a lick.

Professor Chadwick had not fought in the war. According to Harry and others who had time for him, Professor Chadwick was too old for all that. Manny did not think the black man was too old, though it was hard to tell with them. Manny thought Professor Chadwick had used his lack of a right hand as an excuse. Surely he could have done something dangerous, more dangerous than, so rumour had it, what he had done...banging the drum at that daft church he'd set up on Hope Street, where he told stories that went on forever.

'A Belgian did that to him when he was a nipper,' Harry said, referring to Briscoe's absent hand.

'Caught it in a cashbox more like,' Manny said.

'What's he ever done to you? Live and Let Live and that.'

Manny would think about that as his geese went through their never-ending 'Nevermore' mime day in and day out.

Consolation. When people left Manny's geese or Harry's strings all disappointed and God-Has-Turned-His-Back,   likely as not they'd arrive at the fortune-telling booth of Professor Chadwick and Madame McKenzie. It was hard not to. The plank road led to the booth, just as all roads once led to Rome. There they had the choice of colour and gender. If they arrived on a slack day they'd see their fortune tellers sitting companionably on a bench-for-two like sea salt and black pepper in a cruet. Which one would provide what they wanted?

Many who came had heard of the marvellous things their friends had heard: how one or the other of them had made such a great difference in their lives. And the fortune tellers for their part felt they knew a little of the expectations of their customers by the choice they made. Observers, partial and impartial, were caught on the hop, though. Sometimes a big bruise of a scouser would insist on seeing Professor Chadwick, a little slip of a girl ditto, and where was the logic there? Well, there was no logic. On the surface. Each saw things in either Briscoe of Madam McKenzie which shall forever be a connundrum. Why choose pink candy-floss over treacle toffee? Why suck rather than crunch a stick of rock? What's going on? As well try to tell Stork from butter. And, sure, isn't 99.999 per-cent of human doings and those of the great world and what's above it and below it a mystery (as Father Mullin, who conjured St Peter and Paul's Church out of a battered collection plate in the dark days of the Depression, was fond of saying)? A Joyful, Sorrowful and Glorious set of miriad mystery... was that not the rosary of life?

But it was consolation all were after. Briscoe specialised in throwing the bones, while Madam McKenzie used cards and crystal ball. But Professor Chadwick had a strange custom which has a bearing on this account. At the end of a day's work he would drop a tithe portion of his takings through the slats of his booth and into the sea, or onto the shore, below.

These morsels from Briscoe's cornucopia might have been dropped through the slats in order to propitiate some faraway god from Briscoe's childhood, or maybe to make Manny Mann feel better...or worse. Or perhaps he thought of the bones of slaves down there in the black ooze at the bottom of the swirling river that currented past what by all accounts was the harshest of slave cities, the one that fought emancipation to the bitter end, whose slave captains would have thought nothing of dropping a sickly piece of unacknowledged humanity - already trussed and weighted with chains - into the cold and filthy stream.

One thing was for certain: the rain of manna money in no way improved Manny's attitude to Briscoe Chadwick. While Manny came to assume there would generally be something for him lying in the area directly below the fortune-tellers' booth, he would often scour every inch before searching for the certain stash and sometimes, if he had done very well, he would let a day pass without bowing to pick up The Briscoe Shilling.

And sixpences, half crowns, and, once, even a Festival of Britain crown. He would pick up the money and look up and hate

Professor Briscoe Chadwick for daring to know his need and give him charity. Then he'd pocket the bounty, along with anything else he had found, and take it home. Once there he'd wash the lot in a basin of hot water and Tide.

Time passed; enough for people to seek consolation in sunshiny places with duty-free and winking waiters and freshly-milled black pepper, but not enough for Manny Mann, Harry, Professor Briscoe Chadwick and Madame McKenzie to get the deep structure of the sunny postcard of a donkey in a sombrero, and the message on the back: Having A Wonderful Time. New Brighton Seems Like A Bad Dream To Me Now. They struggled on. The geese necks swayed from side to side, but they were desperate in their search for punters. Their bakelite feathers had become chipped and cheap-looking. Manny's takings under the pier fell off alarmingly, and he came to depend on Briscoe's contribution which, despite falling attendance at the fortune telling booth, never failed.

> The geese looked better than Manny felt, though. He put it down to the leather saddle on the bike he'd been lent for his wartime service in the Bicycle First Aid. Some years after the cessation of hostilities he had felt an intermittent pain 'down there', right in the spot the unyielding leather saddle had caught him. The pain brought his war back (any excuse) and he wondered if the saddle had pushed something out of place.

> Back then, Aloysius, his boss at the Bicycle First Aid, a Kerryman who seemed, despite heroic exploits during the Birkenhead blitz, to want the Germans to win, had said that the saddle would adapt to fit the shape of Manny's physiognomy. That was the beauty of leather. Well, it hadn't. But maybe it had left its mark. Either that or there was something seriously wrong. Most nights he felt a pain that

he could not quite put his finger on, let alone scratch or prod. It was becoming unbearable, and it paniced him and made him miew into his pillow.

Manny confided his ailment to young Maureen, who kept the candy floss stall at the entrance to the pleasure pier. Maureen said he should visit Dr Faulkener in Zigzag Road. But Manny knew that his symptoms would give Dr Faulkener carte blanche to delve into his private regions. He'd die of embarrassment, so shook his head.

'O.K., Manny,' Maureen said, 'there's nothing else for it. You'd better just go and see Professor Briscoe.'

Manny looked hard at Maureen. 'What do you take me for?'

'Briscoe's been the making of me,'

Yes, Manny thought. And we know how. In this he might have been correct. Maureen had taken to allowing Briscoe into her booth to fix the faulty door. And the door had more faults than Adolf Hitler so far as Manny could see. Up the shutters would go - though there was nothing wrong with the shutters - and click would go the lock that was in such constant need of attention. Something disgraceful was occurring in the shut-up candy floss booth. Mind you, whatever it was - and the image of fit black key breaking fragile silver lock kept invading with pain the pain-free parts of his body - it seemed to be doing Maureen no end of good. Her candy flosses were more generous than they had ever been. She doted on her work, was never known to complain about the segs on her stick-swirling hand - before Briscoe she had never been known not to complain - and was as sweet and light in temperament as the product she tumesced and sold on a stick.

Manny felt a sharp twinge somewhere between his Jimmy Riddle and his sit-down, but a few inches up the Great North Road. The pain made the question that wild horses wouldn't under normal circumstances have come up to his gob come up. 'How can the blackie help?'

'Well,' Maureen said, 'I can only tell you that it worked for me.'

That was no answer.

'Professor Briscoe knows you're not well, Manny,' Maureen added, whisking a white floss to build up her stock against a sudden rush off the boat.

Manny watched the sugar whisps gather around the stick. There was dosh in candy floss. A scant egg-cup-full of sugar, a dash of synthetic cochineal and a farthing became sixpence. But the pain was back, together with knowledge that Maureen had the concession. And who would come under his cloud when there was sweet and sunny Maureen around?

'How does he know?'

Maureen shook her head, tidied up the candy floss and popped it into a holder. 'What's his job?'

'They're all charlatons,' Manny said - forgetting for a moment his own vocation and the pedal that nudged hope-against-hope balls away from a winning destiny.

'You know,' Maureen said, 'I'm not surprised you never married. You're a real Bag of Nails.'

'What's that supposed to mean?' Manny asked, though he knew perfectly well.

'You're always thinking the worst. What's that ahead? A bag of gold? No, a bag of nails.'

'No more than the truth.'

'But why must the truth always be so gloomy? It's not as if you know what the truth is. Maybe it'll all turn out to be really nice.'

'You can go off people, you know.'

Maureen poured a portion of sugar into the bottom of the candy-floss bowl. She switched on and started twirling. 'La, La, La,' she sang to the tune of Que Sera. The stick travelled around the bowl, seeking out angel hair in pink. But none was rising. The stick remained bald as a baby. 'Bugger!' Maureen said. 'The air hose is clogged again. That's what I get from talking to you.'

'Sorry,' Manny said.

'Not to worry. I'll say this once and then I'll shut up. Go and see Professor Briscoe. You won't regret it.'

Manny let the sun set on his pain. It stopped him sleeping. Ahead lay the morning, a dark ship, with Briscoe Chadwick standing at the bow and Dr. Faulkener at the stern. And both were pointing to the West, where lay Ireland, the great world and, perhaps, the destiny of Manny's soul after its endless bleak and solitary journey.

It won't hurt, he told himself again and again, as the pain pulsed. I'll go to the doctor. I'll go to see the blackie. I'll...

In the morning he woke, having dreamed of terrible procedures being inflicted on him at the Zigzag Road surgery. He was sweating. He was in pain and, most of all, he was frightened. Manny decided to follow Maureen's advice.

That morning, on a rain-drenched pier empty of punters, Manny and his geese watched out for the arrival of Briscoe and Madame McKenzie. They did not come until well into the afternoon, both sheltering under an umbrella. Briscoe greeted Manny, and Manny nodded back. The pair walked on, but Manny saw Briscoe turn and look him in the eye.

A tear formed in each of Manny's eyes. He blinked them away. But the tears were replaced by others. Over and over he blinked. Over and over the blinked tears, finding the watershed of his eyes saturated, were deflected down his face, like pills along a conveyor, like a river's first spit, like balls through a goose.

This was odd, Manny thought as he blinked. This was all very odd. It was not like him. Not at all. Never in the annals had he wept. Well, a couple of snuffles during The Quiet Man at the Trocadero, but that was about it. Something was up and no mistake. Manny wiped his face, shut up the stall, leaving the geese turning in the dark - regardless of expense - and followed Briscoe through the curtain of rain to the end of the pier.

'You are most welcome,' Briscoe said.

'I just thought...'

'Yes,' Briscoe said.

The pain kicked in. 'I have this pain.'

'I know. That's why you're here. It's pain that pulls people to me.'

'Can you help?'

Briscoe smiled. He placed the red turban on his head, then held his left hand out. 'Cross my palms with silver.'

The mean side of Manny hesitated. The critic in him winced at the cliche. He delved into his pocket, past his hanky, to his meagre stash. Grabbing a handful of threepenny bits and sixpences (he knew each coin as a blind man knows his braille), he let a little fall craftily back, and brought out the rest. With these coins he crossed Briscoe's palm.

Briscoe inverted his hand, and the coins dropped on the table with a tiny crash. He picked out some of the coins and dropped them on the floor to his right. 'My offering to the River Gods,' Briscoe said.

'Er...' Manny said.

'Put your hands together on the table,' Briscoe said.

Manny did so.

Briscoe covered Manny's hands with his one black hand,

forcing them hard down onto the top of the table. He gave Manny no further instructions. Time passed, enough for Manny to wonder why he was in the booth with Briscoe, what a strain it was to feel his hands burning and sweating and together below the black hand of a stranger he neither approved of nor liked, to a slow-dawning realisation that a strange thing was happening.

For the decades remaining to him, Manny Mann would often wonder what that strange thing was. To his dying day he never quite got a handle on it. But every day between the dying of his pain and his painless death, Manny would consider the hands that Briscoe had forced together and, for what seemed like a lifetime in the booth with raindrops cracking on the tin roof and a lazy neep tide sloshing around the barnacled columns at the end of the gaps below him, wonder what had happened, where the stillness and the warmth had taken him.

For it seemed to him that he had travelled many thousands of miles that day in Briscoe's booth. Sometimes he wondered whether just being 'touched with intent' had done the trick. Looking back at himself from a future when he was no longer his old self, it kept occurring to him that he had never in his life been touched like that. He was no stranger to loveless gropes up jiggers with women as pissed and pissed off as he was. He occasionally shook hands; it was the thing to do. But he could not recall much in the way of sweet and serene intimacy. Not one occasion, in fact. But there had to be more to it than that. The tears had recommenced as he sat there. He knew through the blur that Briscoe was seeing him. But he did not mind. When he died, he died weeping enjoyably. Weeping was something Manny Mann became known for in the years between Briscoe's hand upon his, and his own death.

Anyway, the pain went that day. Dr Faulkener had been denied his invasive procedures. And Briscoe Chadwick became the object of the one loving obsession of Manny Mann's long otherwise loveless life. He became a devout attender at the Church of the Happy Ending in the corrugated iron chapel on Hope Street. There Briscoe told stories which the old Manny would not have believed for a minute. He spoke of the wretched of the earth and the consolations of paradise that awaited them. But he did not stop there. Sad, bad people who everyone had heard about...the Bad Thief, Judas, Genghis Khan, Hitler... Off to hell he took them, but then...then...something happened and Briscoe's Strong Brown God - being Good - could not bear to see their sufferings and, eventually, opened His arms to offer them a place of consolation in His Bosom. Bygones would be bygones. In the end, all would be well. You just had to carry the story - past breaking point - to its ending at the very farthest edge of eternity.

For reasons that might strike a chord, it did not occur to Manny to doubt the consoling truth of Briscoe's happy endings for even a second. And it made all the great difference.

And explains - in so far as any of us can penetrate the deep mist of story, the queer consolation of memory - why the demolished piers are still holding their own above even the wildest of wasteful tides.

CONSTANT REPETITION

People in the ward keep telling me that I keep saying the same old thing again and again...and I keep telling them that if I do it's only because I want them to get it into their heads. You've got to keep telling them. You've got to keep telling them. Constant repetition. It never fails...and if it does it's not going to be my fault. Not my fault at all.

It's like I keep saying to my son. 'William,' I say, 'get yourself a nice girl who'll take care of you. A nice girl, William. Your old mum isn't going to last forever, you know.'

'Mu-u-um,' William says, 'don't say that! Please!'

'Have you found one yet?'

'No.'

'There you are then,' I say. 'There you are.'

His chin quivers. 'Don't start, lovey,' I say. 'Tell me about the good old days.'

' O.K., Mum. On Friday, January the thirteenth 1989, Daniel Barenboim was sacked as artistic director of the new Opera de la Bastille in Paris.' he says.

'Fancy.' I knew I was going to have to gird up my loins. It's my own fault in a way. Ages ago I'd complained about William having no conversation and no idea about history. We can learn lessons from history, I said. World War Two taught your poor dad a lesson he never forgot, I said. And William straight off emptied his money-box, ploughed up our road like a great big ox - and bought this huge book of dates. And now all he can talk about is dates, dates, dates.

'On Friday the thirteenth of September 1907 The Lusitania arrived in New York after a record-breaking transatlantic voyage of 5 days and 54 minutes.' William says, made up with himself.

'What's this bee in your bonnet about Friday the thirteenth?'

'I like to keep topical, Mum...Friday, September the thirteenth 1918 fourteen million Americans register for conscription.'

'Trust them! Those Yanks will be late for their own funerals.'

'Friday the thirteenth of November 1981: a bomb exploded at the home of the Attorney-General, Sir Michael Havers, while he was away.'

'It was lucky,' I say, 'that Sir Michael was away. Very lucky for Sir Michael. Nevertheless, not very nice to come home to...not at all nice.'

'Friday...'

'Let's have a little rest,' I say.

'O.K., Mum.'

We sit on in one of our two-minute silences for a couple of minutes - there's been quite a lot of them over the years, too, I can tell you - and I use the time to think about escape.

I've got my easy chair nicely positioned so's I have a good view of the door to the ward. As they're dead scared we'll wander off they've got this contraption on the door which takes some working out even for the visitors. And that's what I've been studying. There're these two levers, top and bottom. To open the door you have to pull the top one up while you push the bottom one down. Then you push the door if you're on the outside; pull if you're on the inside. Anyway I think that's right. Don't quote me, though. I could be wrong. Still, one thing's for sure, once I've mastered it - I said, once I've mastered it - I'll be through that door! Then the whole world will quake at the sight of my wheely-walker with brakes.

'William,' I say, at the end of the silence. 'William, you ought to find yourself a nice young lady. There're plenty about. I keep seeing them, William.'

'Mu-u-um...'

'You're a big boy now, William. You're fifty-two next birthday.

Find yourself a nice girl while you're fresh. While your sap is high, William!'

But just then I see Old John heading for the door. Everything else goes flying as the whole ward - those who are half with-it anyway - turn their attention to John in his rude pyjamas with no buttons, making a bolt for freedom. But I know he's doomed. I know they'll drag him back. He can't even crack open a chucky-egg and I reckon if you can't crack open a chucky-egg then you're not going to be able to solve the mystery of the door. And sure enough Old John pushes when he should be pulling and pulls when he should be pushing and before long the light and the heavy brigade in the shape of Sister Mary and Nurse Oleander have heard the racket and the shouts of that snitch who gets her hair done every day in return for shopping her kith and kin. We'll get her one day. Trouble is she's well protected what with a private room next to Sister's office.

'Now, John, love,' says Sister Mary to Old John, 'there's nothing out there for you.'

'How's that jigsaw I gave you to do?' asks Nurse Oleander.

'It's a puzzle,' Old John says. Going quietly.

All the drama sends everything flying, of course. William and me have another silence. I offer it up for the boys who died on Flanders Field, where the poppies grow row on row. On row. On and on. And I keep wondering if there is a field somewhere, a field, a field anywhere, that has not seen blood, a date in the calendar from the year dot without some wickedness or other - one pure date - from the very start of things. It doesn't seem like much to ask. That's why I'm here, I suppose. Original sin over and over again, though I know I'm not very original to say so. It's written all over me. Written all over me it is.

Then Florrie's over. Florrie has adopted me. I know what she's going to say. She'll pinch my cheek and say as how I'm a poppet and a lovely girl and no trouble. No trouble. She's like a stuck record. I keep telling her that she says the same old thing again and again, but it does no good. No good at all. Absolutely no good.

'You're lovely,' Florrie says. 'A real poppet.' She turns to William, who's biting his nails, 'She's no trouble. Everyone loves her.'

'Sit down, Florrie,' I say, but I'm not taking the least notice of her. You see, there's a youngish bloke behind the door with a great big bunch of flowers - a great big huge beautiful bunch of gorgeous flowers - and he's trying to get in. But he's pushing down when he should be pulling up and pushing the door when he should be pulling. And all the delay alerts Frank who wants to go home to number 17 Talbot Close where, he says, there are two spanking new Sunbeam Rapiers on the drive. He is walking slowly down the corridor, watching the hopeless visitor's battle with the OAP-baffling door. I wouldn't be surprised if some gink got a prize for thinking that trick up... disgusting. Frank pauses to study a painting of Mrs Horse minding Baby Horse on a windy moor but I know what he's about. He's no culture-vulture. I've seen him snoring through Sister Wendy Beckett. And him a Catholic! Suddenly the door yields to the youngish visitor with the flowers. He's through and Frank is striding towards him...up to him...'Ta, mate,' as the youngish visitor holds the door open for him. Not knowing.

We hold our breaths. He's gone. We wait on tender-looks for Sister and Nurse. We wait to hear their tights rubbing, their starched skirts crashing creases, as they run to get Frank back. Nothing. A puzzle.

'She's a little love...' says Florrie.

'Shut up, Florrie,' I say. 'I can't hear myself listen.'

'No trouble! No trouble at all!'

'On Friday, the thirteenth of July 1923, Lady Astor's bill banning the sale of alcohol to persons under eighteen was passed,' William says.

Florrie smiles and William, seeing smiles as a green light, continues.

Now, if Frank had an ounce of common sense - which he hasn't and that's the problem - he'll have gone into the Interdenominational Chapel by the lift, hidden under one of the pews and waited until the heat's off. But I bet you a pound to a pound he'll get distracted by the sweets in the Volunteers' Shop and the good ladies down there will rat on him.

The electric clock with a chime you know isn't real because it make you think of Dr. Who, strikes four. Which means it's quarter past five. Now I thought that was odd from day one. I kept telling the nurses, thinking the daft clock might be a daft test of my sanity, but they looked at me as if I'm daft. I kept at it of course and then I was 'Mrs At-The-Third-Stroke', which is not very funny because that's one more than I've had.

'What's that clock ever done to you?' Nurse Oleander asked.

'Don't start me off, Nurse.' I said. Cold, cold as community. 'Nurse,' I said, 'Nurse, many of the senior citizens you have here are a touch confused. A clock which strikes the hour at the wrong hour is not going to help matters, now, is it? Is it, now?'

I got this blank look back and she took my blood pressure really rough as if she wanted to wind me up. And I thought, You don't get it, do you? You just don't get it!

Florrie's fallen asleep under the barrage of dates. William is twiddling his thumbs. Well, he needs the exercise.

'Talking of exercise,' I say, 'go and get your mum a big slab of

Dairy Milk from the shop.'

He shakes his head. 'You've got sugar.'

'Isn't it about time you got yourself a bit of sugar yourself?' I ask.

'Mu-u-um!'

'Mu-u-um!' I mimic, just like he hates it. 'The main thing is, William, that you're looking after the house. I don't want the place smelling of burnt toast, William. I don't. I didn't buy that smoke-alarm just to remind you that the toast was done, William.'

'Mu-u-um,' he says, 'Mu-u-um, you know I'm not at home. You know they won't let me stay by myself, Mum. I'm in a..another place.'

'Well I never! I didn't know that!' I fib. 'That's all right then. You're in a home and I'm in a home so we're both in a home and two homes are better than one.'

'No, Mum, it's not all right, Mum, it's not all right.'

'Hold on! Hold on!' I say, so's he won't see me blubber. 'They've caught Frank.' They have, too. Of course, I knew they would. An escape takes careful planning. The complicated door's the least of it.

'Don't you worry, William,' I say. 'Don't you worry. I'll be home and when I'm home I'll bring you home.'

'Will you, mu-u-um?'

'Will I? 'Course I will. Blood is thicker than mortar. Tell me some dates. You don't believe in Friday the thirteenth, do you, William? You don't believe it, do you?'

'Do you?'

'No, I do not, William. I do not. Not while I'm alive and ticking! You won't forget that, will you?'

He nods his head. He shakes his head.

Top lever up. Bottom lever down. Push. Walk...don't run...walk to Interdenominational Chapel, carrying clothes under arm. Lie under pew until the heat's off. Out the door. Number eleven bus.

'Do you want some more conversation?'

'Go on. Go on.'

'On Friday the thirteenth of March 1987, Liberal Matthew Taylor won the Truro bi-election.'

'Did he?' What the hell am I doing in here with him out there without me?

'On Friday the thirteenth of May 1904 the Anglo-Chinese labour convention was signed, permitting the exportation of coolies to the colonies.'

'Tut-tut.' Top lever up. Bottom lever down. Push. Constant repetition. Constant repetition. That's the ticket. Just the job.

Sister tells William it's time to go. There's a man waiting.

William tells Sister that on Friday the thirteenth of May 1988, Kim Philby was buried with full military honours. He's got it bad today.

He comes over to kiss me, blubbering. 'Don't worry,' I whisper. 'Don't worry, I have a plan. I'll be out in a jiff. '

William nods, shakes, believing me. At the door he pulls when he should push and a chap outside has to help him. A chap outside has to help him! A chap. Outside.

It should be me. It ought to be me. I'm his mum. I'm his old mum. Push up. Pull down. Push the door. Pull up. Push down. Pull the door. Constant repetition. Constant repetition. That's it. That's the ticket. 'Friday, the thirteenth of January, Mum comes home to William and everything in the garden's lovely. Everything in the garden's a treat.

Mum comes home!

UNDERTOW

A fat Alsatian bitch lumbered up and squatted on the pile of wet sand Stanley knew was hoping against hope he would chisel into a romantic castle.

'Go away, Sheba! Bad dog!' Stanley said. But he was not so much worried about Sheba's antics. It was more what Sheba's presence implied. Today Mum had forgotten to remind Stanley not to speak to anyone strange. But if she could see who was coming now she'd tell him straight.

'Hello, Stanley! Digging to Australia, are we?'

'No,' Stanley told Disgusting Derek. 'That bully from 67 our road emmigrated there. Don't want to go to Australia.'

Disgusting Derek stood at the edge of Stanley's hole, rocking from foot to foot. He was sixteen - three ground, window, mother's-heart... breaking years ahead of Stanley - but looked older. Tall and fat, but fat in a solid sort of way as if beneath the surface there was a really muscular Derek plotting to make a spectacular entrance through a layer of flab. He had a severe Number One haircut on top of a fleshy face, and big ears that stuck out and didn't match at all - and a very small mouth. Derek always seemed to have something foreign round his mouth, which did nothing for him in the glamour department. Today the menu was chocolate. This Stanley reckoned was probably caused by forcing something large like a maxi Mars Bar into a mouth that was not built to take it. He was wearing a white training suit much too big for even him. His ensemble said 'Tommy Hilfiger' on the front in embroidered red letters. This on anyone else would have screamed cool, but on Derek did Tommy Hilfiger no favours at all. If he was Tommy Hilfiger, Stanley decided, he'd have sleepless nights worrying about people like Derek letting down his line of training suits.

Derek had to step back sharpish when the bit of sand he was standing on started caving in. He stepped back, and it caved in. 'Sorry,' Derek said.

Stanley just nodded magnanimously, and kept digging, hoping Derek would move on.

'It's disgusting,' said Derek.

'What's disgusting?'

'The way New Brighton's been allowed to deteriorate. Disgusting.'

Derek often went on about the deterioration of New Brighton. In this he echoed Stanley's mum... Derek's mum... pretty much everyone.

Stanley's mum loved the remote past: 'If only you could have seen it, Love!' she'd say. 'Hundreds of charabancs! Trippers off the train in their thousands! Souvenir shops! Donkeys on the beach! Bathing beauties at the baths! Motor boats on the marine lake! It was great for a kid. Great!'

Great. And here he was on an a beach that the Queen couldn't be bothered to clean up, even though, according to Grandad, she said she owned it.

Still, odd that Mum and Derek's mum did not form a Nostalgia Society, sit on a bench together and share reminiscences. 'Nostalgia' – according to Stanley's favourite teacher, Mr Sutch – was 'seeing the past through rose-tinted spectacles'. Mr Sutch was nostalgic about a big heavy dark-green Raleigh bike which had been miles better than his present old Raleigh. It'd had a Dynohub, a chain-guard, a battery pack, a reliable bell...it was the Rolls-Royce of bicycles. But, though securely locked, it had been stolen from outside Woolworths, never to be seen again.

'And you know what else is disgusting?' Derek said.

'No. What?'

'The milkman didn't come this morning.'

'I know. You know what I had to put on my cereal?'

'No. What?'

'CoffeeMate.'

'No.'

'Old CoffeeMate.'

'No!'

'Old CoffeeMate that had stopped being a powder and had gone through a chemical change - well, an extreme physical change – into becoming a solid.'

'Disgusting. And you had to get it down you?'

'I did. Mum added water.'

'And have you kept it down?'

'So far, but it's early days.'

'Disgusting.'

'I paid him yesterday, too,' Stanley said.

'Paid who?'

'The milkman. Jim.'

'And then he goes and lets us down.' Derek shook his head. 'Typical.'

'He can't manage a smile. Mum says he's like a wet weekend.'

'It's lucky he comes so early,' Derek said. 'Seeing him would do me day in.'

'Mind you,' Stanley said, 'he's not shifting milk like he used to. You've got to remember that. Mum says he's being done in by Tesco.'

Derek nodded. 'There's a lot of it about,' he observed, and looked about. He took out his trademark Altoids tin, opening it to reveal a row of lolly-stick-thick roll-ups. He reached for one, lit it with one of those lighters a chap outside the Liverpool Playhouse sold 8 for a pound, inhaled and coughed.

'You shouldn't smoke those,' Stanley said. 'My mum says they lead straight to hell in a hang-glider. You should smoke low tar.'

'I know,' Derek said. 'I'm a slave to me passions, me.'

'Mum gets them imported from France,' Stanley said. 'Well, from that chap at number 17 with the purple Lexus.'

'Your mum should give him a wide girth,' Derek said.

'What's a wide girth?'

Derek considered. 'These pants are Extra XL. They're a wide girth.'

'Cool,' Stanley said.

'I got them in Blackpool. Me and me mam went there on a day-trip with North of Warrington Expeditions.'

'What's Blackpool like?'

Derek thought how best he could put it. 'Have you been to Las Vegas?'

Stanley noticed that he had sunk to his knees in the suspended solution of water and sand. He wondered if he'd ever get out. Perhaps this was his death. 'BOY KILLED IN QUICKSAND HORROR' the Wallasey News would thunder. People would tut, fidget, and forget him as they turned to the pages of houses for sale and used cars and 'lovely lampshade hardly used' ads. And it would be as if he'd never been. Mum would have all the expense of a funeral and he'd be put in a hole in Wallasey cemetery where nasty vandals barged the crosses down and cut off the heads of marble angels and smoked spliffs on the steps of the mauseleum to FLOYD – Captain of Industry. Plucked Away in His Prime. In The Bosom of Jesus'.

There were a lot of graves claiming that the poor man or woman was in the bosom of Jesus. Jesus beat Abraham, the second most popular according to Stanley's research, but both had lots of dead souls in his bosom. It must be crowded, though. What happened when all the desirable bosoms got filled? What then? Maybe he should opt to lie in a deserted bosom. But why would he want to lie in a bosom when he could be picking chocolate off the trees in paradise, and refreshing himself on cool ginger beer from the gushing streams that Miss Magee kept advertising as one of the rewards of a righteous life?

'I said,' Derek said, 'have you been to Las Vegas?'

'Sorry. I was thinking. No.'

'You know what thinking did,' Derek said. 'Well, if you went to Blackpool you wouldn't need to go to Las Vegas. Mind you, there are disgusting things in Blackpool. It's not all tasteful by a long chalk. It's like me mam said. She said, 'In my day, Derek, they used to have 'Kiss Me Quick' hats. That was a bit disgusting, but now…'

'What do they have on their hats now?'

'I don't like to say,' Derek said, looking to right and left.

'Tell me.'

'It's what else they have on their hats – after Kiss Me Quick.'

'What else do they have on their hats after Kiss Me Quick?'

Derek stepped back a pace. He buried both his hands in the pockets of his pants and jiggled them about. 'No,' he said. 'I can't tell you. I've got to exercise restraint in pen and tongue. Me mam told me.' He clapped his hands, and the Tommy Hilfiger letters on his sweatshirt jiggled where Derek's fleshy chest was. Then, hands back in his pockets, he ran on the spot for a second or two. This made the chest-jiggling worse. Stanley thought that if his own chest was that fleshy, he'd not move a muscle.

'Have you heard this one?' Derek asked. 'Adam and Eve and Pinchmetight went down to the sea to bathe. Adam and Eve got drowned. Who do you think was saved?'

Stanley said nothing.

'Who do you think was saved?'

'I know the answer. You've done me already. You gave me a bruise.'

'Oksorry.'

'What else do they have on their caps in Blackpool?'

Derek looked nervous. Right to left. Left to right, along the deserted beach. 'Sheba's having a swim,' he said.

That was daft. Sheba never swam. Sheba hated water. Sheba just liked to bark at waves.

'There are germs in the water,' Derek said.

'In this day and age,' Stanley agreed, sounding like Grandad, and knowing he sounded like Grandad. Who else did he sound like? Mum said Stanley sounded like Jeremy Paxman when he ventured his opinion on the state of the NHS. Mum said she wouldn't mind a sleepover with Jeremy Paxman. Stanley hadn't taken much notice of that. She'd had one of her wine boxes from Bargain Booze on the floor next to the settee. Whenever that happened Mum's good taste went out of the window. She always came home coarse from the Women Only Night at the Hotel Vic as well. But they'd knocked the Hotel Vic down, so Mum came home coarse from some dive in Seacombe these days.

'And we pay the water people an arm and a leg to keep everything spic-and-span,' Derek continued.

'It's nothing but the truth you're telling,' Stanley said.

Now he was sounding like Phyllis, who visited Gran at the Seaview Home, knitting endless lengths of grey scarf as she nattered. Mum said Phyllis couldn't stop talking and never listened when she did. But she was Irish - more Irish even than Gran - and genes will out.

'OK,' Disgusting Derek said. 'But don't tell your mum I told you, will you?'

'Told me what?'

'About Blackpool hats.'

'OK.'

'Promise?'

Stanley promised.

'Kiss me quick but shag me slowly. That's what they have on the hats in Blackpool. Me mam said that says it all. Disgusting, she said. And do you know what I said to Mam?'

'What?'

'I said, 'Mam, you never said a truer word. Disgusting."

'Did you go on the Pepsi Max?'

'What's that?'

'It's this ride in Blackpool. Costs an arm and a leg to go on apparently. Uncle George – that's my mum's brother - not the one who died, the other one – says it jiggles you about. He blames the Pepsi Max for his hiatus hernia.'

'No. Does he? Disgusting.'

'He says the Pepsi Max put him on the sick.'

Derek tutted.

'What does 'shag' mean?' Stanley asked. 'I mean, I think I know but I'm not sure and that.'

Disgusting Derek looked about. He jiggled himself through the pockets of his pants again. Stanley looked down at himself. He had sunk up to his thighs in the hole. The solution of water and sand had only a couple of inches to go before it reached his shorts. He tried to prise his left leg out, but couldn't. 'Sexual intercourse,' Derek said.

'Don't be daft,' Stanley said. 'You don't say, 'I'm just going to run the Hoover over the sexual intercourse rug in front of the electric fire', do you? Course you don't. Pull the other one.'

'Take it or leave it,' Derek said.

'Have you ever had sexual intercourse?'

Derek thought about that. 'In a manner of speaking,' he said.

'How do you mean, 'in a manner of speaking'?'

By way of reply, Derek jiggled, removed his right hand from his pants and made a gesture with it, as if pumping up a bike tyre.

'That's not sexual intercourse! Mr Sutch says that sexual intercourse involves a wife or partner.'

'A man's gotta do what a man's gotta do,' Derek said.

'You're disgusting, Derek.'

Derek looked around the deserted shore to see who might have overheard Stanley's ejaculation. 'I've got feelings, you know,' he said.

It had not occurred to Stanley that Derek had feelings – at least not feelings like Miss Magee had: feelings that were easily hurt, that made her bow over her piano and weep buckets if he massacred The Jolly Farmer on his viola that had 'Property of The County Borough of Wallasey Education Committee' printed on it just above a crack you could – and someone had - insert a penny through. 'Sorry,' he said.

'You're stuck, aren't you?'

Stanley looked down. 'Yes.'

'And the tide's coming in.'

'Yes.'

'It's disgusting you calling me 'disgusting'. In a couple of years I'll be able to vote. Me mam AND me therapist say I'm sensitive. I'm going to vote Liberal Democrat. I wrote to Angela Eagle about the disgusting state of the motorway signs.'

'What's disgusting about them?'

'They've peeled off. There was just white where there should be

'WALLASEY'. Now to my way of thinking Angela Eagle should do something about it. It's like dog-dirt on the doorstep, me mam says. I wrote Angela Eagle a letter and she didn't reply. Called her 'Right Hon' on the envelope too. That's why I'm going to vote Liberal Democrat, even though Mam says that Dad'll turn in his grave.'

'Can you help me out?' Stanley said, tugging at his stuck legs.

'Well, seeing as you said you were sorry,' Derek said, 'I suppose I can.' He came to the brink of the hole and reached for Stanley. 'You see, sensitive people like me are not only sensitive about ourselves, we know how the other fellow feels. We can step into their shoes in no time and feel their pain.'

'Thanks, Derek.'

Derek regarded Stanley in the hole. 'Mind you,' he said, 'there are some who might think of taking advantage of you.'

'Are there?'

'There are. It's disgusting the things you hear about – people taking advantage of people who are stuck and that. Me mam says I'm not to talk to strange men, seeing as they might take advantage of me.'

'My mum says that too.'

'Me mam says she'd be absolutely devastated if anyone took advantage of me,' Derek said proudly.

'Has anyone tried?'

Derek shook his head. Then he produced a stumpy grey tongue and started licking around his mouth. This, Stanley noted with approval, was clearing away the chocolate stain.

'Pull me out, Derek. Please.'

Derek hesitated. He looked to right and left. He ground his teeth. They were false; he'd taken them out and showed them to Stanley about a year ago in Harrison Park. That had been both disgusting and funny, the best sort of feeling Stanley knew. Derek smiled. 'O.K,' he said. 'Seeing it's you.'

Derek took hold of Stanley under his armpits. He pulled. For a moment there was a mighty battle between the wet sand and the tugging arms until, with a farting sound, Stanley found himself sitting on the edge of the hole.

'Thanks, Derek,' Stanley said.

'What are friends for?'

Derek rewarded himself with another roll-up from his Altoids tin. 'Ever had an Altoid?'

'No. They're a bit pricey.'

'You can only get them from the chemist,' Derek said. 'Too strong for sweet shops.'

'Better safe than sorry.'

'There's a story behind Altoids.'

'Is there?'

'I've got this friend who works in New York. He shouldn't be working there. Hasn't got permission. But he got the sack from Birkenhead Belgian Chocolates for weeing in the chocolate vats. Anyway, he sells Altoids there in a kiosk and he says the Yanks can't get enough of them. They love having fresh breath. You know what they're like, the Yanks. Me mam says that when you see a Yank on the telly and that, you don't know how much is Yank and how much is paint and plastic and stuffing and that. Anyway, Altoids used to be owned by Callard and Bowsers and if you look at the box you can see… 'Callard and Bowsers'…but me friend says that Callard and Bowsers were bought out by Suchard…look at the small print on the back… 'Suchard' – whoever they are when they're at home. Now you'd think that would be it, but Suchard are owned by Kraft who make cheese and things. And you know who owns Kraft?'

'No. Who?'

'Philip Morris,' Derek said.

'That's rubbish!' Stanley said. 'Philip Morris is in my class and he doesn't even own a PE kit.'

Derek thought about that. He looked around for inspiration. Then he pointed to the approaching tide. 'What's Sheba got?' he asked.

Stanley looked. From where he was standing, he couldn't see that Sheba had got anything. That didn't mean that she didn't want to get something. Trouble was she was not enthusiastic about getting her paws wet. Barking at waves was what Sheba liked. She was barking at them now.

He followed Derek as he trotted off in pursuit of Sheba. The sand was hard and corrugated. Mr Sutch had told him that the corrugations were like fingerprints. Never the same, and everything changed after each tide. Together they were God's handprint, as was everything else... 'Even you, Grogan!'

They arrived at the brim of the sea. Bubbles percolated through the shiny sand as waves retreated before Sheba's barks. But there was something at the back of them. Something white. Just that. The white was lifted high by the next breaking wave, and Stanley saw a body in clinging and ballooning white undulating to the contours of the swell. The wave broke. The body disappeared from view for a moment. Derek and Stanley ran backwards to escape the surf.

'What are we going to do?' Stanley shouted.

'Dunno.'

Stanley watched as the wave turned the body over. Now it was floating on its front and the head was under the water and it didn't seem to be doing anything to right itself.

'Hold me clothes,' Derek said. And a Tommy Hilfiger sweat-shirt struck Stanley in the face. He caught a whiff of school dinners on the turn. Off came the ancient trainers, while Derek danced about, his jiggling chests on view in all their glory. He hesitated then, pulled the elastic on the pants and looked down. 'Bugger it,' he said, and took off his pants and threw them at Stanley. 'Don't let any bugger nick 'em.' And he made off, nude and lardy, into the surf. Sheba made to follow him, but didn't. She looked at Stanley. She looked at Derek. Her jaw dropped, her tongue fell out of it. Stanley took Derek's clothes and threw them a few yards above the tide-mark. He heard Derek shout, 'Fuckin' 'ell! Disgusting!' above the roar of the waves.

Stanley stripped off his clothes down to his underpants and thinking of nothing ran into the cold. A wave biffed him like a playground bully, but he shouldered it back. He could see Derek up to his chest, pulling at the body. But the undertow was pulling Derek back. He lost his depth and was being sucked farther out. Stanley got as close as he could, paniced himself at seeing Derek's panic, hoping that the monster wave behind Derek would bring him back. But it failed to break, merely lifting Derek and the lilo body high before hiding them behind its bulk for a second, and crashing down on Stanley. His body spun and for a moment he didn't feel like Stanley. Thought stopped. Everything changed. He came back - where had he been?- and crunched into the sandy bottom. He stood up, pulled his underpants from the tangle at his ankles. They were heavy with sand. The wave retreated between his legs. He turned to see Derek, holding on to the figure, far out, and out of his depth. Stanley ran back, breasted another wave, and swam his inelegant crawl, that at the best of times looked panicy, towards the impossible goal. Another wave was building behind Derek. Stanley crawled, his head jerking through one hundred and eighty degrees, seeing the wave and praying for a break that would bring Derek back and make things better. The wave obliged. The next time Stanley caught sight of Derek he was behind him in the shallows and Stanley, recovering from another spin, coughed up water and germs. He had a taste of salty CoffeeMate in his mouth.

Derek was lying next to a man on the shore.

'Is he…?' Stanley felt like a stupid character from some stupid telly programme. He started again. 'Is he dead?'

'Think so,' Derek said, still spluttering on the sand next to the man. 'I feel disgusting.'

'We'd better make sure?'

'You make sure if you want. He's dead.'

'I'm going to turn him over,' Stanley said, thinking of the lessons in resuscitation they'd had from a visiting lifeguard. It had cut into the PE class, saved him from running endlessly round the playground with Mr Polletto shouting unflattering things. Mr Polletto had stood dumbly against a radiator in the hall while the lifeguard had them practising on a model rubber casualty he said had cost the earth.

Derek, still prone and panting, turned his head to watch. Stanley with difficulty got the man over. The man's face, the open eyes - blue and clear - the slack jaw, stared at him. Stanley, shaking with something more than cold, checked the man's airwaves, cocked the head and pinched the nostrils between two fingers. He opened his mouth to screaming point, slotted it around the cave of the man's mouth, and blew mightily five times. Then he felt for the meeting of the rib cage, put both hands, one on top of the other, and compressed the man's chest (100 a minute) for fifteen repetitions, felt about for signs of life, returned to the man's mouth and repeated the procedure. Mr Polletto would be proud of him now. 'That's it, Lad. On! On! On! It's not over till the fat lady sings!' Miss Magee was playing 'How Beautiful are the Feet' on her Bechstein, that had survived The Blitz in circumstances little short of miraculous, and Mr Sutch, for once in his life, was lost for words.

He kept on and on, but there were no signs that his efforts were producing any results. He placed his eye close to the man's mouth and tried to detect breathing. He felt all the pulse points he could remember. 'I think he's dead,' Stanley said.

'Told you,' Derek said.

Stanley looked up and saw a group of people watching the tableau from a vantage point above the high water mark. Stanley and Derek were no longer above it. The waves were breaking over them. How had that happened so fast? How peculiar Time was! Not as though thou hadst thousands of years to live. Death hangs over thee: whilst yet thou livest, whilst thou mayest, be good. Mr Sutch was back - he never went away for long - quoting his friend Marcus Aurelius. A wave crashed over them. The crowd shrank back, then farther back when Derek stood up and addressed them: 'Has anyone rung The Filth?'

The people looked at one another. Stanley looked at Derek, and saw somebody else. Somebody Amazing, as different from the fellow he had been talking to in his hopeless hole as the man with the suit and the parting was different from Superman.

'Disgusting!' Derek said. 'Fuckin' go and fuckin' do it!' And he was like Sir Bob Geldof in those tapes Mum never tired of, where he's telling the world to give him their money so that he can help the starving people. Mum always put a sharp emphasis on 'Sir Bob Geldof'. 'The only bugger who deserves his gong,' was what she said.. Sheba tried to nose at the body. Derek aimed a kick at her. He pulled the body further up the beach. A deep trail mark formed behind it. A wave erased it. Stanley wanted to cry.

Then he saw that Derek was looking around. He knew what for. He knew where the Tommy Hilfiger gear was. It was…he looked back to where the waves followed hard on one another, sure now of their conquest of the beach. No sign of Derek's clothes, nor of his for that matter. Not that it mattered. What mattered was lying there between them.

Derek got a man to lend him his golfing umbrella. He opened it and used it to hide himself from the watchers. 'They've had enough excitement for one day,' he said, loud enough, Stanley thought, for the people to hear.

Stanley joined Derek behind the umbrella, waiting for something to happen. The people, he knew, were as fascinated by the dead man as he was. But now, knowing he was dead, he felt a need to show some respect. In films people covered the faces of dead people. But they had nothing to cover him with. Stanley was standing in his unflattering y-fronts, brought out for their third consecutive day, despite Mum's insistence that two days was the maximum. Derek had even less.

But Derek solved the problem. Holding the umbrella out, he ushered Stanley closer and, like policemen in a riot moving behind their shields, the two shuffled closer and closer to the body until the three of them were safe from the eyes of the watchers.

'You know who he is, don't you?' Derek said. It felt like they were at camp together, talking in a private place about a friend sleeping nearby.

'Yes,' Stanley said. 'He's our milkman. He's Jim.'

GRATITUDE LIST

Wherlys, Turnbulls, Scotts, Lyons, Foys, La Tourettes, Haigs, Burts, Houstons, Newmans, Evans, Coles, Goldsworthys, Oxlands, Blackstocks, Witts, Nicholsons, Tayabas, Maitlands Morts, Ntangares, Clarkes, Mlalazis, Ranges, Murfins. Waterhouses, Pepps, Butts

Browns, Dinges, Lamberts, Newtons, Clees, Van Wensweens, Houstons, Schencks, Kruks, Neilsons, Andersons, Flannerys

Phil the Fish, BMW Pete and all friends of Bill and Bob

Bliss, Rileys, Ruddells, Ferns, Polettos, Scharfs, Smarts, Martins, McGregors, MacArthurs, Harkess, Boyces, both Jasons, Latos

LeFanus, Crowthers, Kishkas, Niknafs, Ghoseimis, Stauntons, Goldsworthys, Oxlands, Arnolds

Aguirres, Drurys, Edgars, Tencers, Sherrys, Murphys, Tuccis, Smiths, Lightfoots, Thomas, Cuppers, Henchers, Grouts, Donners, Cohens, Selwyns,

All the Wirral Beach Lifeguards

And all who stare out to sea from New Brighton prom

And the people who have managed to trudge across sand, mud, bank, bog, tide, slippery steps, red rock and eccentric spelling or sentence... to reach this place.